Vicious Circles

JL Paul

Copyright © 2011 JL Paul

D1254201

Chapter 1

I have never been in love in my life – nor have I ever fancied myself in love. That just wasn't me. I wasn't built to be a one man kind of girl. I was more of a – well, for lack of a better term – love 'em and leave 'em type.

I hadn't always been this way. There was a time in my life when I actually did care for a boy. He was sweet and I was smitten and we were both young. If things would have continued, I'm sure I probably would have fallen in love with him.

But, that was ruined by a spiteful little witch and that's an entirely different story for another time.

So, I was pretty shocked when I realized that I was in love. And I was even more shocked that it hit me out of the blue while I was lounging at the pool with one of my best friends.

"Oh," I said, as I bolted upright in my chaise, my arms extended behind me to prop my body. "Hm."

"What?" Morgan asked as she eased her sunglasses down her nose and peered over the top.

I bit my lip, my eyes blurring as they gazed abstractedly at the high school kids splashing in the pool. I couldn't see anything, really, just his face and it made my stomach lurch a little. My heart fluttered quicker than normal and my pulse hammered in my veins. At first I couldn't figure out was wrong with me – I'd only been thinking about the last conversation I'd had with him. Then I realized that I'd had similar symptoms all week whenever I was in his presence or thinking vaguely about him. Not only was it bad timing and totally inappropriate but it also sucked big time.

"Bailey?" Morgan said, prying into my insight.

"Yeah?" I said as I eased back into the chaise, adjusting the top of my simple, black string bikini.

"Is something the matter?"

"Nope," I said with a little smirk. "Nothing." Well, nothing I could discuss with her at that moment. I needed to sort this out by myself.

"Are you sure?" Morgan persisted as she removed her glasses to gaze anxiously at me.

Some people couldn't figure out why Morgan and I were such good friends and to be honest, it was sometimes a mystery to me, too. She was a little more moral – take the high road kind of person – while I preferred to live and let live. Her parents were well off, like my father, and I suppose that was pretty much the only similarity.

But Morgan was fun, too. And a good listener. She knew how to have a good time even if her good time wasn't quite as 'good' as mine. I truly adored her.

"Yeah, Morg, thanks," I said. I snuggled into the chair and lifted my face to the sun. "So, do you work this afternoon?"

"Yes," she pouted. "It's too nice out to work."

"I don't see why your parents insist you take a job," I said. It was a statement I'd been making ever since we'd decided to rent a condo near school instead of spending the summer in our respective home towns.

"I told you," she said with a touch of impatience. "My parents are more than happy to help me with my share of the rent but they think that I need to earn some of my own money. They think it will help me to appreciate things."

I snorted and rolled my concealed eyes. "All you need to do is look at Irelyn and it will make you appreciate what you have."

"There's nothing wrong with Irelyn. Now," she frowned. "Lucas keeps telling her that she doesn't even need to work – he makes enough to support them."

"Yeah but she won't let him help her with school," I pointed out. "She's getting financial aid and loans. She doesn't need to pay the loans back until she finishes school. I think she likes it. Makes her feel all domestic."

"I think they're cute," she giggled and I rolled my eyes again.

I did have to agree that Irelyn and Lucas were a great couple – and they'd been through hell to get together. Although I hadn't seen a problem with her seeing Lucas while she was still dating Dustin, I did see how it was tearing her apart. And Dustin really was a bore. But she ended up with Lucas who she loved more than anything. I was happy for her.

"So, you're working until when?" I asked, as I opened the datebook in my head. If Morgan was going to be stuck inside a bookstore all afternoon, I'd have to figure out some way to entertain myself.

"I'm working until eight," she said as she glanced at her watch. I chuckled. Only Morgan would wear a watch while sunbathing. "What are you going to do?"

"I don't know. Maybe I'll go bug Irelyn"

"Why don't you call Spencer? Or is he working?" she asked.

My heart plunged as I remembered Spencer. Sweet Spencer who was doting and kind and fun. Spencer who was enjoyable – especially when we spent the night together. Spencer who'd been my on-again-off-again fling since last winter. Spencer, who'd promised me that we'd not take things too seriously. Spencer, who was starting to get a little too clingy…

"It's Thursday – they're rehearsing tonight," I reminded her.

"You need more friends," she said then collapsed in a fit of giggles.

I had to laugh, too. "Yeah, maybe. But no one understands me like you, Morg."

She actually snorted. "No one can tolerate you but me. And Irelyn."

"True," I said as I groped the concrete next to my chair in search of my water bottle. I found it and took a long drink. "I'll probably hang with Irelyn or with the guys. I'm not particularly picky."

"I'll call you when I get off work," she said as she sat up and collected her belongings. "Maybe I'll come by and hang out with you guys."

"Sure thing, Morg," I said as I waved. "Have fun at work."

She glowered at me before scurrying to the pool house to change.

Once she left, I closed my eyes and pondered my earlier revelation. I wasn't sure what to do with it at that moment – it wasn't exactly a wonderful thing like one might think. Matter of fact, it was kind of crappy.

Oh, I didn't think I'd have a problem attracting him – not in the least. Confidence had never been much of an issue for me. But whether or not I could make him love me back – I wasn't so sure.

I laughed aloud and drew a little attention from the high school boys horsing around in the deep end. I fluttered a couple fingers at them and they smiled. Let them think I was flirting – what did I care? I had other things to worry about – especially how to deal with this problem.

I sighed, not able to resolve the problem lounging by the pool. It was something that I'd just have to get over and that would take time.

I grabbed my towel and my water bottle and sashayed out of the pool area, pulling a sheer bathing suit cover over my head. I rode the elevator back to the condo I shared with Morgan and showered once I let myself in. Morgan had left already though the scent of her body lotion lingered in the hall.

I dried my hair, letting it hang in a dark curtain down my back, and chose my clothes carefully. I pulled on a pair of navy blue capris topped with a white tank and slipped my feet into a comfortable pair of flip flops. Not too sexy and not too conservative. Forgoing makeup, I grabbed my bag and headed out the door.

***

"You've been at the pool all morning, huh?" Irelyn said as she handed me a soda.

"Gee, how'd you guess?" I asked as I raised a brow.

She pointed at the touch of red on my shoulders. I shrugged. I often burned slightly but it usually faded to a tan in a matter of days. That was the beauty of inheriting my father's dark complexion. "What else am I going to do while all my friends slave away?"

"You could get a job," Irelyn suggested, her eyes twinkling like Santa's.

I frowned thoughtfully. "Sure – for shits and giggles."

"You have a wonderful way with words," she laughed.

"Why beat around the bush," I said, smiling. Irelyn was always great to hang around – even when she was stressed. She wasn't whiney or preachy. She took my moods for whatever they were and never faulted me. And damn, was she fun.

"The guys are rehearsing," she sighed, leaning on the counter in the kitchen of the apartment she shared with Lucas. "And I'm bored. Want to go over there and drink their beer?"

See what I mean about fun? "You are a brilliant woman."

***

We arrived at Collin Newton's place and could hear the muted screams of the guitars as soon as she parked her car in the drive. My heart twittered again and I mentally chastised it – forcing it to calm down.

I followed Irelyn into the garage and glanced at each of the boys in turn. Lucas was sitting on an upturned barrel, guitar strapped around his neck. Spencer was standing as usual – he was always full of energy. And Collin was perched on a stool behind a set of drums.

I watched – a little jealously if I were to be honest – as Irelyn's face lit up when her eyes fell on Lucas. She hurried over to stand behind him, waiting for him to finish the song so she could kiss him.

I turned my attention to Spencer and earned a smile. I returned it though it was forced. He didn't seem to notice so I snagged a couple bottles of beer out of their cooler and handed one to Irelyn. As I opened mine, I found a lawn chair that wasn't too dirty and looked like it wouldn't split with the application of any weight and shook it open. I sat, crossed my legs, and listened to the music.

When they finished, Spencer and Lucas set their guitars aside while Collin jogged around the drum kit. Lucas wrapped Irelyn in his arms while the other two raided the cooler.

"Hey, Bailey," Spencer greeted as he kissed my cheek and draped an arm around my shoulders. We were currently in the on-again stage.

I patted his stomach and mustered another smile. I could already tell my jaws would be aching by the time I got home. "Hey, Spence."

"Nice tan, Bailey," Collin smirked as he nodded at my shoulder.

That little flutter in my stomach woke. "Thanks," I said, flustered. I concentrated on the bottle label, peeling it away from the glass. "You guys sound great. Are you playing at Rusty's tomorrow?"

"Yeah," Spencer said as he opened a bottle and tipped it to his lips. "For the rest of the summer and probably the fall."

I filled my mouth with beer and bobbed my head before swallowing. Spencer's nearness was a bit unnerving and I was rethinking my decision to accompany Irelyn. I should have stayed at the pool.

"Where's Morgan?" Collin asked and my bottle slipped out of my fingers. I caught it before it could crash to the floor but I managed to splash beer all over my shirt.

"Damn," I swore as I slammed the bottle on top of the cooler. I wiped futilely at the wet spot. "Wonderful."

"Come on, Bailey," Collin chuckled as he squeezed my arm. "I'll give you a dry shirt."

I followed him into the house and to his bedroom, still blotting my shirt, and ignored the rapid beat of my heart. I had to stop it before it got out of hand.

He opened a drawer and dug out a clean t-shirt with some sort of beer slogan printed across the front. He handed it to me with a smile curling his lips and I nearly gasped. I'd always thought Lucas was the hot twin and even though they were fraternal, there were still several similarities. Their eyes were the same deep brown with flecks of green and they had the same, slow, sexy smile.

But now, standing in his bedroom with my shirt covered in beer, I realized that Collin's sexiness came not only from his looks but also from his charm.

I raised a brow. "Trying to tell me something?"

"Yeah," he teased, his smile slipping into a smirk. "Spilling beer is alcohol abuse."

I snatched the t-shirt from his outstretched hand and snorted at him. "So suck it off my shirt if you're so concerned about waste."

His eyes narrowed as his smirk widened. "Is that an offer, Bailey?"

My heart jumped to my throat as I started to lift my shirt. I gave him a pointed look. "Depends, you taking me up on it?"

He laughed and chucked me under the chin. "You are something else. I'll leave you to change. If you want, just toss your shirt in the basket over there and I'll wash it."

"Hey, a clean shirt and laundry service – I'll bring my entire wardrobe over and spill the contents of your fridge on it."

"Just the undergarments and you have a deal," he winked as he walked out of the room. Once the door shut behind him, I sank to the bed and pressed a hand to my chest. My heart was beating a mile a minute and I was afraid it would jump right through my skin.

"What is wrong with you?" I whispered. "He's just a guy. And he's Spencer's cousin. This ain't cool."

I drew in a few breaths, hoping it would calm my heart, and quickly changed shirts. His was long and I tied it in the back to keep it from falling down to my thighs. As I dropped my tank top in his laundry basket, a little thrill shot up my spine. Something about my clothes mixing with his did weird things to my body.

As I rejoined the others, Spencer snagged my hand and pulled me next to him. He wrapped his arms around my waist and I tried to just lean into him, but the usual affection wasn't there. I was far too aware of Collin to relax.

I knew I couldn't have Collin, but I couldn't string Spencer on any longer - especially if he was getting as close to me as I thought he was. Although he'd been the one to suggest a break the last time we'd split, he'd also been the one to suggest we give it another try a month later. He was such a sweet, fun guy that I hadn't been able to say no. Plus, I really enjoyed spending time with him. But, the romance was no longer there. So, when they decided to break for the night, I asked Spencer to take me to Irelyn's to fetch my car. He agreed, chattering happily all the way, talking about their gig the next night. I soaked it all up – biding time until I would tell him it was over.

When he parked in front of Irelyn's building and turned to me, I hoped he wasn't expecting an invitation to follow me home. But he didn't - he just took my hand and stroked it softly. "What's up tonight, Bailey?"

I cringed – he was going to be nice and understanding and it would only make things worse. I sucked it up and laced my hand with his. "Listen, Spencer, I think we need to cool it. I mean, we agreed at the beginning that we weren't going to take things serious, remember?"

"Sure," he said as a flash of pain flickered in his eyes. "I know. Are you seeing someone else?"

"No," I answered quickly, praying he could read the truth on my face. I'd always been straight with him. "Nah – I just want us to be friends. I'm not into the dating thing right now."

"That's cool, darling. Don't sweat it. As long as we still hang out. I'd hate to lose you as a friend," he said with a sad smile. It nearly broke my heart – a feat that was not easily achieved.

"Oh, sure. I'll be at Rusty's tomorrow night."

"I'll see you then," he said. He leaned over the console and pecked me on the cheek. "Good night, Bailey."

"Night, Spence," I said as I hopped out of his car and ran to mine.

***

Morgan was camped out on the sofa, a pile of books next to her. She smiled as I breezed inside. "Hey, how was your night?"

"Eh," I said as I raided the fridge and dug a beer out from the back. Returning to the living room, I sat on the floor. I picked up a book and glanced at the cover. "It was fun."

"Is that... Collin's shirt you're wearing?" Morgan asked, her eyes wide and her brows nearly in her hairline.

"Oh," I said as I set the book down and glanced at the shirt. "Yeah. Me and Irelyn went to Collin's to watch the guys rehearse. I spilled beer all over my shirt so Collin gave me a dry one to wear."

"I see," Morgan said. She dropped her gaze and rifled through the pile of books. "Where's Spencer?"

She kept her eyes on the books but I noted a hint of speculation in her voice.

"What's going on, Morg?" I asked. "Out with it."

She looked up, startled. "Nothing," she said with false innocence. "I just wondered if he was coming over tonight."

She was lying, I could tell, but she wasn't ready to spill and I wasn't going to force her. "Nah. We decided to cool it for awhile."

"Why?" she gasped as she dropped her book. "What happened this time?"

I shrugged as I picked at the label on the bottle. "It's just not there anymore, I guess. I don't know."

"Are you interested in someone else?"

I snorted. "Nah. Not really. Just want to chill out and see what's out there."

She rose and began piling the books in neat stacks. "Well, I don't blame you. You're a beautiful girl and if things aren't there with Spencer, then you want to find someone else. It's not like you haven't tried with him several times already."

"Yeah," I murmured. "Maybe."

She paused in the mouth of the hall, her arms heaping with books. "Bailey, if you don't love Spencer and you're not comfortable with him anymore, then you did the right thing. Don't make the same mistake Irelyn made. Yes, it did work out for her in the end, but a lot of people got hurt."

"I know." I jumped up and handed her the book I'd been perusing. "I'm going to bed. Good night."

"Good night," she said as I brushed past her on the way to my bedroom.

I climbed between the sheets and rewound my day. Okay, so I was a little in love with Collin. He was very good looking and talented and charming. But it was wrong – way wrong. Nothing would ever come of it because he would never date me– it would probably be very awkward for Spencer. And I didn't want to hurt Spencer, either. He was a good guy.

Yeah, I'd have to get over this little crush. Maybe I'd meet a new guy at Rusty's or at the pool or something. The new school year was just around the corner – I could meet someone there. It didn't matter where I met the guy – I just had to meet him. Then I'd banish these silly feelings.

As I drifted off, I knew I was only fooling myself.

Chapter 2

Rusty's was pretty packed Friday night, which wasn't surprising. It was stifling hot outside and the beer was ice cold.

We took our usual table, where Irelyn already sat, and I immediately ordered a drink – coke and whiskey. Marissa, the waitress, raised a brow – I was usually just a beer girl – but I thought I'd need something a little stronger to get me through the night.

Irelyn smiled her thanks when Marissa returned with our drinks then pointed her eyes at me. She lifted a brow in an effort to be coy but I knew her all too well.

"Just spit it out, chick," I said, smirking. "You have something on your mind."

"I heard you and Spencer called it quits," she said and caught her bottom lip between her teeth. "Why?"

I lifted a nonchalant shoulder and sipped my drink. It was strong – just the way I liked it- and I welcomed the burn of whiskey on my throat. "I just don't really like him that way anymore," I explained. "We agreed from the start that we were just fooling around – we were both able to see other people."

"I see," she said, her brow furrowed. I rolled my eyes and watched as the guys took the stage. They usually wore jeans and t-shirts but Collin had on a pair of khaki shorts and I couldn't help but admire his well-toned legs.

"Take a chill, Irelyn," I said, trying hard not to snap. "We weren't serious, all right? I didn't love him, he didn't love me. And when I realized that it just wasn't there for me anymore, I told him. End of discussion, case closed."

She blinked at me, a little stunned. "Bailey, I wasn't accusing you of anything. I just wondered if something was wrong, that's all."

I nodded, a little ashamed at my tone. But I always struck first when I felt threatened – it was safer that way. "So, I think I'll go see the folks next weekend. Anyone interested in tagging along?"

"Can't," Irelyn frowned. "I have to work that Saturday and I can't request it off because I have to be off the following Saturday to go with Luke to his parents' place."

"I might be able to go," Morgan offered. "I need to check my work schedule."

"Cool," I said as the guys ended their first song. "They're playing at that party that weekend, right?" I asked as I gestured toward the stage. "That girl who graduated high school or something?"

"Yeah," Irelyn said, her eyes on Lucas. "Friends of Luke's parents – their daughter graduated high school and asked Out Back to play at her grad party. They volunteered to do it free of charge."

"Hm," I said, deliberating. "Maybe I'll tag along," I mused. "It's been awhile since I've been to the Chicago area."

"Sure," Irelyn said, dragging her gaze from Lucas to meet mine. "Luke's parents won't mind and I'd be happy for the company. I don't think I could handle sitting through their entire set alone or listening to Mrs. Newton subtly tell me that Luke and I should just go ahead and marry since we're already living together."

I laughed as an evil smile took possession of my face. "Did you tell her what happened the last time someone proposed to you?"

She narrowed her eyes at me but I could see that she wanted to giggle. "No, I don't think I've shared that heartwarming story with her yet."

I shrugged a shoulder. "Maybe I will."

"Maybe I'll tell her about you and her nephew making out in the pool house while the over sixty group did their water aerobics just a mere fifty feet away…"

I laughed and nearly choked on my drink. "Yeah, I'd love to see her face. Who knows, maybe that will give her ideas and Mr. Newton will be smiling the same way Spencer was that day."

"You're terrible," Irelyn laughed.

I leaned closer to her. "That's not what Spencer said."

She actually blushed and I straightened victoriously in my chair. I finished my drink and motioned for Marissa to bring us a round. That's when I noticed Morgan and her full glass.

"What's up, Morg?"

She jumped and turned her lovely eyes on me. "Huh?" she asked.

I smiled. "What's the matter? You've hardly said a word and you haven't touched your drink. Something wrong?"

She shook her head and forced a smile. "No, not at all. Thanks." She picked up her glass and started taking frequent, tiny sips as if to appease me and assure me nothing really was wrong. I raised a brow at Irelyn who just shook her head discreetly.

When the guys finished, Collin invited everyone to his place to chill out for awhile. It took both me and Irelyn to convince Morgan not to go home but to come with us, but she finally agreed.

At Collin's place, we gathered in the kitchen around the table and enjoyed a pizza and plenty of alcohol. Tori, Collin's upstairs neighbor and daughter of his landlord, came down to join us. She was a pretty girl and I knew Irelyn liked her, but something about her always struck me as odd. She helped herself to a beer and sat in the only available seat next to Spencer.

I thought things would be tense and a little weird with me and Spencer but he acted as if everything was normal. I knew how people liked to hide unpleasant feelings from others – I myself was a master at it – so I kept a close eye on him. I didn't want him anymore but I still genuinely cared about him and hated to see him hurt.

Morgan continued her zombie-like behavior and I managed to corner Irelyn in the bathroom about it.

"I'll talk to you about it later," she insisted before I could delve any further. "Just let her be tonight."

"Do you know what's bothering her?" I asked, astounded. How could I not know when she lived with me?

"I think so," Irelyn said. "We'll talk about it tomorrow, okay?"

"Yeah, sure," I mumbled as I left her alone and made my way back to the table.

My drink had been refreshed and I smiled my thanks at Spencer. He took it as an invitation and dropped into the empty seat next to me.

"How you doing?" I asked.

"Bailey, I'm fine," he insisted. "Geez, it's not like we were engaged."

I fake pouted. "Maybe I was expecting you to pine for me." I sighed overdramatically. "Did you even shed a single tear?"

His eyes grew as he snatched a slice out of the box. "Did you want me to? Because honestly, I'd rather eat pizza." I laughed and patted his stomach. He draped an arm over the back of my chair and leaned his head in close. "Bailey, I'm fine, honest. We're cool – we'll always be cool."

I nodded and wished that I could have fallen in love with him. He wasn't quite my type – and neither was Collin, actually. They were both such good guys; nice, sweet, charming. Spencer was more of a goofball while Collin was the quiet one of the bunch.

I pecked Spencer's cheek and ruffled his hair. I was hoping he was telling the truth and maybe it was my overconfidence that was making me worry. Perhaps he wasn't all that into me. I'd have to ask Irelyn – maybe she knew.

The party started to break up around one-thirty when Morgan announced she was tired. I offered to follow her home but she would have none of it- assuring me she was fine.

Irelyn followed suit – claiming she had to work the next day. Lucas kissed my cheek and whispered in my ear that they would make sure Morgan made it home all right.

As if on cue, Spencer stood and yanked me into a hug. "I'm out of here, too. I'm supposed to head over to Owen's club. He thinks he can talk me into convincing you guys to play over there."

Collin shook his head as he chanced a quick glance at Tori. "Tell him hell no."

"Aw, mate, come on," Spencer whined, his accent more pronounced.

"He expects us to do it for free," Collin continued.

"No he doesn't," Spencer argued.

Collin held up a hand. "Okay – go talk to him. Find out what he has to say and we'll discuss it."

Spencer grinned, shot me a wink, and bolted out the front door. Tori got to her feet, yawned and headed to the back door.

"I'm out of here, too," she said. "See you later, Bailey. Good night, Collin."

"You don't have to leave," Collin said, his eyes lingering on Tori's face.

"I'm tired," she said with a sad smile. She waved and disappeared before Collin could argue further.

"Well," I said as I drained my glass, contemplating whether or not I should leave, too. "We know how to clear a room."

He snorted a laugh and finished his beer. He scrutinized me briefly from across the table. "Are you abandoning me, too, or shall we partake of the good liquor?"

"Bring on the liquor," I said, smiling at him. He winked and my pulse kicked into higher gear.

"I have some stuff my uncle gave me for Christmas," he explained as he slammed a bottle of mescal on the table. "Straight from Mexico." He picked it up and shook it. "See the worm?"

"Yes, he's lovely," I said dryly as I watched the limp worm sink slowly back to the bottom of the bottle. "You sure you want to open this?"

He grabbed two shot glasses from a cabinet above the stove. "Absolutely."

He cracked the seal and poured the amber liquid into both glasses. He nudged one across the table to me and lifted his. "To friends."

"Here, here," I said and tossed the shot back. The mescal was harsh – scalding my throat. My eyes watered and I really wanted to cough but I sucked it in, not wanting Collin to think I was a wuss. "Smooth," I choked. A tiny cough escaped my lips and I felt heat in my cheeks. I wasn't sure if I was blushing or if the liquor was making me warm.

"I can tell you thoroughly enjoyed that," he said with a laugh, his glassy eyes shining. "Ready for another or are you a chicken?"

I leaned over the table and slammed my glass down in front of him. I leered in his face. "I could out drink you any day."

"Ha!" he said as he filled the glasses again. "I think not. Cheers," he said as he lifted his glass. He downed it before I could pick mine up. He set his glass down with a flourish and lifted an expectant brow at me. "Scared?"

I slammed the shot, relieved it went down easier, and slid my glass across the table at him. I smacked my lips and grinned. "Tasty. Please sir, may I have another?"

He tipped the bottle over my glass but paused halfway. "Um, you're not driving home, are you? You'll crash here?"

My heart leapt but I was able to keep my excitement masked. "Sure. You're making breakfast right? Because I'm rather particular about how my eggs are prepared."

He filled my glass and scooted it to me. "Sorry, but it's cereal and milk in the morning."

"Geez," I groaned, making him smile. I drained my glass and my head went into motion, spinning slightly. "Wow. It does have some kick. Think we'll finish the bottle? I'm a little eager to see you eat the worm."

"Not happening, sweetheart," he slurred. "I think you should eat it."

A sexual remark was on the very tip of my tongue just dying to jump out but I was just sober enough to keep it tucked inside. Mostly. "I could make a really crude remark about the eating of worms but I think I'll just shut up this time."

"Think you can handle that?" he challenged as he dropped his arm and knocked the bottle over, splashing mescal on the table. The liquor ran off the edge and into his lap before his mescal-fogged brain could function properly enough to pick up the bottle and jump out of his chair. "Damn."

I laughed, tilting my chair dangerously back. "Now that's alcohol abuse!"

"Funny," he said as he pulled at his shorts. "What was it you said about sucking the alcohol out of the clothes?"

My heart stopped dead in my chest and desire ripped through my body. I knew it was wrong – terribly wrong – to even suggest anything with him sober let alone drunk, but I couldn't help myself. I got up and yanked a wad of paper towel off the holder and proceeded to wipe up the mess on the front of his shorts very slowly and deliberately. He stilled – his body tense.

"Will this do?" I asked as I peeked at his face.

His eyelids were heavy and his breath coming in quick gasps as he took the paper towel from my hand and dropped it on the floor. He gripped my hips and eased me closer. I toyed with the collar of his t-shirt, my heart hammering. I fought to stay coy and nonchalant but my insides were cheering and egging me on.

"I was going to suggest that you stay in Lucas's old room tonight but I have a feeling you'd rather not," he said, his voice husky – his lips inches from mine.

I realized in that moment that he was really tall and it sparked my desire. My groin was on fire and I trailed my fingers up his shoulders to wind in the back of his hair. "You're right. I know what your brother and my best friend got up to in there. I don't think I want to sleep on that mattress. Any other suggestions?"

He drew me flush with his body and inched his lips closer. "Well, I could be a gentleman and offer you my bed while I take the sofa, but, I'd prefer not to sleep on that lumpy thing."

I raised a brow in an attempt to maintain my cool while my insides melted into a big puddle of mush. "So, I take it you'd rather share your bed with me?"

He brushed his lips softly over mine and I could taste the mescal. "Very much so."

I crushed my mouth to his and his grip tightened. I ran my tongue over his bottom lip and he parted his with a soft groan. I pressed my body into him and my desire shot out of control as I could feel the effect I was having on him against my leg.

His hands worked under my shirt and up my sides, producing embarrassing goose bumps. He dragged me toward his bedroom, his tongue probing my mouth. Once we crashed through the door, I broke the kiss to yank his shirt over his head while he did the same to me. His eyes feasted hungrily on the black lace bra barely concealing my breasts.

"Take the damn thing off," I whispered hoarsely as I tussled with his shorts.

He did, moaning ecstatically as he dropped my bra so he could massage my breasts. He lowered his head to them, his breath warm on my skin. "I always said you had the best ones out of all the girls we hang out with," he mumbled.

I grinned in satisfaction as I finally worked the button on his shorts and let them fall to the ground.

"Just, finish getting undressed, Bailey," he said, his breath raspy. "I can't wait much longer – I'm liable to shoot off in my pants."

I chuckled and shed my shorts and panties while he kicked off his boxers. I crawled on the bed and he was over me in a second. I watched him fumble with a condom and offered to help but he wouldn't let me. Once it was on, I pulled him back to me and planted a wet kiss on his lips. When he pushed inside me, we groaned in unison, the release very much welcome.

I arched into him with every thrust as he continued to kiss my face, my neck, my lips. I rode wave after wave of pleasure until the waves grew more intense and larger and I finally succumbed, shuddering massively on the mattress.

"Damn," he huffed as he rested his forehead on mine. His breath was uneven and smelled of liquor and beer but I barely noticed. I was still clutching his shoulders, not ready to let him loose.

When his lungs finally settled, he collapsed next to me. I closed my eyes as my entire body tingled – satiated for the moment. But it didn't take long until I was aching for more.

Rolling to my side, I wiped the beads of sweat off his brow. He cracked open an eye and grinned at me. "Wow, Bailey."

I kissed him hesitantly but he was more than willing to return my kiss. Smiling against his lips, I shifted until I was almost totally on top of him. His arm rose off the bed as he planted a hand on the small of my back.

"What are you up to?" he mumbled, both eyes closed again.

I kissed the soft spot under his jaw and he shivered. With a smile, I placed my lips near his ear. "Just relax," I said in what I hoped was an alluring voice.

I kissed all along his jaw and jumped to his throat, blazing a trail down to his stomach. He sucked in a breath as I removed the condom and tossed it to the floor, hoping no one stepped on it in the morning. I stroked him as his hands fisted and he made little sounds of pleasure. Kissing his stomach, I ventured lower, teasing him with my tongue until he reached for me, pulling me on top of him. His lips were all over me and I prepared for another session but he flipped me over instead.

"My turn," he whispered against my throat as he mimicked my movements. But he couldn't stand it for long, his desire too intense, and before I knew it, he was reaching for another condom.

"My turn," I stressed as I sat up and pushed him to the mattress. He smiled eagerly and grabbed my hips, hoisting me in position. His eyes fluttered shut as I lowered myself on him. I started out slowly but my body would have none of that. My blood was scorching and only he could quench the flame.

"You're going to kill me, Bailey," he said in a strained voice, but his hands held my hips tighter and increased my pace.

All too soon, I was consumed by pleasure and it was my turn to fall on him. His arms wrapped around me and he kissed my hair. We stayed in that position, our heartbeats slowing and our breath catching up to us. I toyed with his hair, very much satisfied to stay in my current position for a long, long time.

Then I heard his light snore and I drew back to shake my head in amusement. His eyes were closed and his lips parted slightly to allow quiet snores to escape. I kissed his forehead and cheeks before dropping beside him and falling into a liquor-induced sleep.

***

"Damn."

I winced, the soft oath penetrating the protective sleep that was keeping me from experiencing a full-blown headache. I rolled to my back, my eyes pressed tightly together.

"Bailey, wake up," Collin said, his voice horribly hoarse. "What the hell did we do last night?"

"If you don't know, then you have serious problems," I mumbled.

I felt the bed give as he rose and stumbled around to the other side. "Don't step on the condom I tossed over there."

"Fuck!"

I grinned. "Now you're on the right track. Unless you just stepped on the condom."

He sank next to me as he pulled his shorts up his legs. "Bailey, I'm sorry."

My heart paused, preparing to shatter. I swallowed a huge helping of bitch and urged my heart to suck it up. "For what?"

He shifted and I opened my eyes to see his concerned face. Sighing, I sat up, taking the sheet with me. "Don't sweat it. It's fine. We had a good time but no one needs to know - if that's what you want."

"I'm sorry," he repeated. "I shouldn't have let this happen."

I grabbed his chin and held it firmly. "You didn't start it, Collin. I did. Don't beat yourself up over it. It was one night and we can keep it to ourselves."

It hurt – I actually felt pain when I uttered those words. And the relief in his eyes was even worse. He was ashamed and I couldn't really blame him. I was Bailey, after all – the girl who'll give just about anyone a turn.

He pressed a chaste kiss to my lips. "I'll leave the room and let you get dressed."

"Kinda late for that," I whispered, sucking back stupid tears. He smiled and got up, crossing the room to the door. He hesitated briefly then left. I let my head fall back to the pillow as I closed my eyes and mentally went through every swear word I knew in every language I knew them in. What an idiot. How stupid could I be?

I hurriedly dressed and rushed to his bathroom. I washed my face and did what I could with my hair. I needed to get out of there quickly before my face brought more guilt and shame to Collin's.

When I slipped into the kitchen, my heart fell. He stood near the coffee maker, his back to me. His hands were planted on the counter and his shoulders were slumped. I longed to go to him and comfort him but I didn't think it would be well received. I took a deep breath and cleared my throat.

He spun around, his eyes bloodshot and his face pale. He attempted a feeble smile. "I'm making coffee. Would you like something to eat?"

I shook my aching head and tried to avoid his eyes. The mess on the kitchen table was a reminder of our evening. I couldn't leave it for him to clean by himself.

"I'll just start on this mess then I'll head out of here," I said.

"I got it, Bailey. Don't worry about it."

"You're not doing this by yourself, Collin," I insisted as I tightened the lid on the mescal bottle and shoved it in a cabinet. I scooped up the empty glasses and rinsed them in the sink while he gathered the empty pizza boxes and tossed them in the trash.

Once we finished and he was sipping on his coffee, I turned back to him. "Okay, I'll see you around."

"Bailey," he said as he approached me, taking my hand. "I really am sorry."

I pressed a finger to his lips. "If you say that again, Collin, I'll kick your ass. I swear."

He smiled against my finger and I dropped it. Pulling me closer, he kissed me softly. "Okay. We'll keep this between us, all right? I'll make sure Spencer doesn't find out."

"I'm not seeing Spencer," I reminded him.

"Yeah," he said with a wince. "But I still think it would bother him if he found out."

He was exactly right. I set my lips in a line and nodded. "Yeah. Okay."

"And," he added as he rubbed the back of his neck. "I'd prefer if Tori didn't find out about this."

That threw me. Why would he care if Tori found out? Unless he had something going on with her. I'd have to ask Irelyn.

"Sure, no problem," I said, longing to just get the hell out of there. "I really need to go. I'll see you."

Hugging me, he pressed a kiss in my hair. "Okay."

Once he released me, I fled, my heart fighting valiantly to stay intact.

Chapter 3

I paced the empty condo, unsure what to do or what to think. It was unsettling having such little control over a situation. Never had I had someone apologize to me the morning after and with it being Collin – it really sucked.

Of course I'd been stupid to, well, seduce him the way that I had. He had a point that Spencer would be upset if he found out and I didn't want that. Suddenly I had an inkling of a clue as to what Irelyn had gone through last year.

My headache had subsided to a weak throb but my stomach was still sour. What I needed and craved was a huge, greasy cheeseburger and an extra large soda. And I knew just where to find those things.

"Hey, Bailey. What are you doing here?" Irelyn asked as I plopped into a chair, folding my hands on the table. "And, no offense, but you look horrible. Did you stay up all night drinking?"

A tiny grin threatened to appear. "Something like that. I really need a cheeseburger, fries, and the biggest soda on the planet."

"Sure," she said slowly and dashed off to place my order. She checked on her only other occupied table – it was still a little early for the lunch crowd – and returned to me. "What happened?"

"Nothing," I said as I fiddled with the salt shaker. "I just sat up and matched Collin shot for shot. Of mescal."

She crinkled her nose in disgust. "Yuck. Is that the stuff their uncle brought back from Mexico? That nasty stuff with the worm?"

"That's it," I said. "I crashed there – I was a little too drunk to drive."

"Well, at least you weren't too drunk to use your head."

I dropped my eyes in guilt and set the shaker spinning. "Yeah, guess so."

She glanced over her shoulder before sinking in the chair across from me. "Is something wrong?"

I couldn't tell her. I trusted her implicitly but I had a feeling she might tell Lucas and I couldn't have that - couldn't do that to Collin. Instead, I turned the tables on her. "I'm a little concerned about Morgan. Do you know something that I should know?"

"Well," she said, drawing out the word. "I think – I'm not sure, mind you – that she has a crush on someone. Maybe a little more than a crush."

"Who?" I asked, my curiosity aroused.

Biting her lip, she leaned across the table to whisper in conspiratorial fashion. "Collin."

Just wonderful, my heart railed. *Could my life get any better?* I swallowed my shock, hoping I wouldn't regurgitate it "Oh? Did she tell you that?"

"No, but she's been acting really strange every time she's around the boys," Irelyn admitted, her cheeks flushing as she awkwardly fiddled with her order pad. "I kind of think that she fantasizes about all of us being with a member of Out Back."

I snorted. "You sound like one of your stories."

Grinned sheepishly, she shrugged. "Maybe that's not entirely true but I'm pretty sure she likes Collin."

I shook a couple grains of salt on the table to run my finger through, biting back the words I longed to spew. "Why doesn't she just tell him?"

"Come on, you know how shy she is."

I nodded in agreement as my aching head spun. "Did you tell Lucas?"

"Yeah," she sighed as she slid her elbows on the table. "I did. I thought maybe he might talk to Collin or something but Lucas said it was a bad idea."

A spark of hope lit up my heart. "Really? Why?"

She blew a long puff of air at the hair falling out of her pony, hanging in her face. "Well, Lucas said that Collin sort of has a thing for Tori. He said that Collin's been spending a lot of time with her lately."

Wonderful. Just wonderful. Well, that explained a whole lot. That explained his plea to keep our evening a secret from Tori and not just Spencer. I suppressed the urge to bang my head on the table.

"How adorably sweet," I said, a bit of a bite in my voice. "Our little Collin is in love."

A deep groove formed on Irelyn's forehead as she stared at me, frown pulling at her lips. "Don't you like Tori?"

"I don't know," I sighed. "I don't know her that well so I can't really say."

"I like her," Irelyn defended.

"I know you do," I said. I heaved another huge sigh and wished for a cigarette even though it'd been at least a year since I last smoked.

"Let me go check on your food," she said and nearly fled to the kitchen. I would have laughed if I hadn't wished I could flee, too. But, I didn't and I wouldn't. I didn't run from things – they ran from me.

I swept the grains of salt off the table, wishing I would have asked Irelyn to bring my drink. I drummed my fingers on the table as I waited for her to come back – hopefully with the soda.

"Well, well, well," a voice drawled behind me. "It's the other party animal."

Groaning, I pasted a sarcastic grin on my face as I turned to Lucas. The grin slipped ever so slightly as I noticed his brother standing next to him.

"Kiss my ass, Lucas."

Lucas smirked and took the seat Irelyn had vacated. Collin shifted his feet uneasily before slipping into a chair between us.

"You both look like hell," Lucas continued, ornery glint in his eye. "I saw the bottle of mescal - you two should have just finished what was left and ate the damn worm."

Wincing, my stomach rolled as I avoided Collin's eyes. "I didn't see your wimpy ass drinking any of it."

"I told you, bro," Collin said quietly, avoiding my eyes like I was doing to his. "I spilled it."

I could feel a blush creeping up my cheeks and it pissed me off. I never blushed. And I definitely didn't need any reminders of the spilled liquor on Collin's shorts.

"So, finish off the damn bottle," Lucas shrugged.

"Let's not talk about eating worms, okay?" I suggested. "I'm about to eat real food."

Lucas tossed his head back and laughed, deservingly earning a reproachful glare from me. He grinned and winked just as Irelyn slid a plate of food under my nose. She wrapped her arms around Lucas and kissed his cheek.

"Do you guys want something to eat?"

"Yeah, bring us what Bailey has," Lucas said, pointing at my plate. "I think her drinking partner needs the same remedy."

"Okay," Irelyn laughed. "I'll be right back."

Silence descended upon us when Irelyn walked away and tension hovered over my head. I didn't dare look at Collin – I couldn't. I wanted to desperately but I didn't want to remind him of what we'd done and shower him with more guilt.

Still, I wished I could shake him and punch him or something. How could he love Tori? What was it about her? And then Morgan's face floated in my mind and I wanted to punch him for her. I wondered and speculated how things had turned around so quickly. What happened to my simple life?

"Luke, Bailey's coming with us when we go to Chicago," Irelyn said after she placed their order and finished with her other customer. She stood next to him, placing a hand on his shoulder.

Collin's head shot up and he looked at me with what resembled horror in his eyes. My heart clenched and I pretended not to see.

"Um, that's not a definite, Irelyn," I said. "I might go home that weekend."

Her brow furrowed. "I thought you were going home next weekend?"

"I'm not sure yet," I said as I bent my head over my plate. "Haven't decided."

"Come on," she wheedled. "Don't leave me high and dry."

"You should go," Collin said in a low voice. "It'll be fun."

I turned my face to him, confused. I longed to ask him what he meant but didn't - I'd figure it out on my own. "Like I said, I haven't decided."

He nodded and massaged his temples.

"You two suck at drinking," Lucas chided.

I picked up my burger and took a huge bite. "Damn, this is good."

Lucas stretched across the table. "Want a shot to go with that?"

I chewed and swallowed. "Maybe when I'm done."

Lucas chuckled. "That's the spirit." He glanced at Collin. "How about you, bro?"

"Never again," Collin groaned, his fingers still rubbing his head. "Ever."

I snorted – couldn't help it – and he tilted his head enough to raise a brow at me. "Told you I could drink you under the table."

He cracked half a grin that made my stomach trembled. "Yeah, whatever."

"I think you both are idiots," Irelyn chastised. "I think you both need to eat something and then go back to bed."

It was like *I* was Collin's twin for a moment as we both turned identical horrified glares at her. It took me a second to realize what she'd actually meant.

I drew a long drink of my soda and covered my mouth as I burped quietly.

"Excellent idea," I smirked and faked a yawn. Collin studiously ignored me. I just finished my food and asked Irelyn for the check.

"Sure. I'll go see if their food is ready and bring back your check," she said as she hurried away.

Lucas grinned at me and I had an urge to punch him – just for good measure. He slapped Collin on the back and the look Collin gave him made me believe Collin was thinking along the same lines as me.

"Lucas, you know I love you and I'm glad my best friend shacked up with you – but you're an ass," I said as I pushed my plate away.

Laughing, he stole a leftover fry. "I know. It's all part of my charm." He chewed furiously and grinned again. "You two are far too tense. Maybe you both should go get laid."

My jaw fell as Collin scooted away from the table and made a mad dash toward the bathroom. My stunned eyes followed him.

"He's going to puke," Lucas said, amused.

"Aren't you going to go check on him?" I asked, my heart thumping.

"He's a big boy," he shrugged.

Groaning, I shoved away from the table. "Fine. I'll do it."

"He's in the men's room, you know," Lucas smirked.

"So?" I said as I marched down the narrow hall to the restrooms. I pushed the men's room door open and the sound of Collin vomiting echoed off the walls.

"Collin? You okay?"

"Bailey, I'm fine. Go away," he groaned.

I frowned, ignoring his words. They hurt, true, but I needed to make him stop this stupid guilt trip of his.

"Not going anywhere, sorry." I peeked under all three stalls until I found him in the last one – the handicap stall. Perfect – more room for two. I kicked the door open, grateful it was unlocked, and stood over him.

He flushed the toilet and rose shakily to his feet. He wiped his mouth with the back of his hand and turned to me. "Why are you here?"

I shrugged. "I had to pee."

With a loud groan, he tried to brush past me but I stepped in front of the door.

"Bailey, I don't want to talk about it."

"Too bad, because we are," I said, anger riling up my digesting cheeseburger. If I wasn't careful, I'd resume his position and hunch over the bowl, losing my entire lunch. "Look, Collin, get over it. I'm sorry – I shouldn't have started it. If I would have known you'd be this upset over it I would have just left."

His bloodshot eyes finally found mine. "You mean, you intended to sleep with me last night? Is that why you stayed when everyone else left?"

"No," I said slowly. "Not at all. I just wanted to hang out. But I shouldn't have…um…I shouldn't have started things and once they did start, I should have stopped. I'm sorry. Please, quit taking the blame and feeling all guilty."

"I can't help it. I could have stopped it but I didn't want to," he said as his eyes dropped to the floor.

A little bit of arrogance tickled my heart at his words. My hand shook as I reached out and lifted his chin. "Collin," I said, my voice soft. "This is ridiculous. We were drunk and got carried away. No harm – no foul. No one has to know therefore no one gets hurt."

"Lucas already suspects it," he said, his eyes boring into mine.

"So? He doesn't know for sure," I told him. I stepped closer, an urge to kiss him so strong it was hard to suppress.

"Come on," he said with a dark laugh. "He's not an idiot. He knows you and I were the only ones in the apartment last night."

My heart shriveled as anger stirred up the tears that seemed so close to the surface lately. "Oh, so since I was there that automatically means that someone was getting laid?"

"No, Bailey," he said, horrified.

I dropped his chin and yanked the stall door open. "We need to make sure Spencer doesn't know I was there alone with you or else he'll know what happened. Same with Tori. And Morgan," I ranted as I stormed for the door.

Collin snatched my arm before I could get out of the room. "That is not what I'm saying," he said through clenched teeth. "Not at all."

"Don't try to sugarcoat it, Collin," I said with a snarky laugh. I jerked my arm out of his grip. "I know what people think and do you know what? I really don't give a damn."

I spun on my heel and pushed through the door, nearly plowing over a middle-aged man with a shocked face. I composed myself as I approached the table and dug a twenty out of my purse.

"Give this to your woman for my bill," I told Lucas as I threw the money at him. "I'll catch you later."

"What's going on?" he asked, standing to take my arm. "Is Collin all right?"

"Yeah, he's fine, don't worry," I said with a forced smile. I needed to keep cool or else I'd blow this whole secret – if it was still a secret – by my angry reactions. "I just remembered something I need to do. See you guys later."

Lucas released me with a nod and glanced toward the hall that led toward the bathrooms. With a wave, I shuffled out of the diner before Collin reappeared.

***

I had calmed down somewhat by the time I got home and managed a cheerful smile for Morgan when she greeted me.

"Where have you been?" she asked, worry on her face. "I called your cell and it went straight to voice mail."

"It's probably dead," I mused as I fished my phone out of my purse. "I should probably charge it more often, huh?"

"Yes," she said as she cocked her head. "Are you all right?"

"I'm fine, Morg," I said as I moved past her to get to the kitchen. I fetched a bottle of water out of the fridge. "I got a little drunk last night, crashed on Collin's couch and then I had lunch at the diner."

"Oh," she said, relief in her voice. "You look upset."

"Not in the least."

I twisted the cap off the bottle, took a slug, and then replaced the cap. I walked back into the living room, glancing at the television. Morgan had some news program on and I strained to read the ticker on the bottom of the screen. When that no longer amused me, I turned toward the bedrooms, deciding a nap would probably be a good idea.

"You seem agitated, Bailey," Morgan said as she lingered nervously behind me. "Are you sure nothing's wrong?"

"Yep," I said as I trotted down the hall to my room. "Just going to put my phone on the charger and take a little nap."

"Okay," she said. I glanced at her over my shoulder. Her sweet face was puckered in concern and it pissed me off. Why should she worry about me– the one who slept with the man she was crushing over – perhaps in love with? I felt like a total slut.

"I'm fine – just hung over and tired," I said softly. "We'll grab some movies and Chinese tonight, if you want. Okay?"

Her face brightened. "Sure."

I entered my bedroom, shut the door, and plugged my phone into the charger. I collapsed to the bed, staring at the ceiling.

I couldn't fathom Collin's guilt. So, we had sex – who cared? No one had to know. It obviously hadn't meant much to him and I wouldn't stalk him and demand that he love me just because we'd hopped in the sack. We both needed to move on and get over it. Maybe Tori would continue to deny him – if she was denying him – and he could hook up with Morgan. They'd be an excellent couple. They were both nice, quiet people. They both had good, decent hearts. Collin didn't belong with somebody like me. If it were to ever happen, we'd be the couple people passed on the streets and whispered about, asking what's he doing with her.

I closed my eyes wearily. Yeah, Morgan was more suited to him. And she'd look positively adorable on his arm. They'd make each other deliriously happy, get married, and fill a house full of kids.

Me – I wasn't the type to marry. I'd just enjoy life and have fun – flit from man to man. No one wanted to settle down with me because no one saw me as that girl. Hell, even Spencer knew better. He wasn't in the least bit upset that I'd ended it. He knew all along how things would work.

A tear escaped my closed eye and I wiped it away hurriedly – not wanting to take the chance of someone seeing it. It was time to end the self-pity party and take that nap. I was certain that I'd feel like myself when I woke and that was exactly what I wanted. I'd spend the evening with Morgan – possibly Irelyn, too – and forget all about men. Maybe I'd even boycott men for awhile. Nothing wrong with that.

Another idea hit me and I sat up to process it. Maybe I just needed to get away from this place. If I wasn't around, maybe Collin could get over his guilt trip. Perhaps I'd spend a week at home with Daddy and Steffi instead of just a weekend. Nothing heals a broken heart like a good spoiling by a girl's daddy.

My phone rang on the nightstand, still plugged into the charger. I groaned and flipped it open, ready to curse whoever insisted on interrupting my nap.

It was Collin.

With a heavy sigh, I answered. "Yes, Collin?"

"Bailey, don't hang up, okay? Just listen to me," he pleaded.

Rolling my eyes, I couldn't suppress a smile. "What?"

"I didn't mean to sound the way I did earlier. I didn't mean to hurt you," he said in a heartbreaking voice, his accent more pronounced. It made my heart ache. I hated feeling this way.

"It's okay, don't worry," I said. "Thanks for calling, though. I'm going to go take a nap."

"Bailey…"

"No, Collin, just stop. I don't want to hear another word about it," I demanded. "I'm thinking about going home for awhile- go see my father. I know you feel pretty shitty about what happened, even if it's not your fault, and I think it might be better if I'm not hanging around so much."

"You don't need to do that," he said, his voice a whisper. "Don't avoid me because of what happened."

"I'm not avoiding anything," I protested. "I just really want to go home. It's been awhile and I'd like to see my father."

"Are you, um, still going to Chicago with us? Er, with Irelyn?"

I snorted. "I don't know. Maybe. Maybe I'll just hang out at my dad's place and then shoot over there and meet her. My dad only lives an hour from Chicago."

"That's two weeks away," he said. "You're going to stay with your dad for two weeks? What about Morgan and Irelyn?"

I laughed. "They're big girls – they can take care of themselves. Besides, I don't know what I'm going to do yet. I'm just making it up as I go along."

"Well, um, okay," he floundered. "I guess I'll see you when you get back."

"Sure."

"I hope you go to Chicago, Bailey. You and Irelyn will have fun," he said quietly. "Don't not go because of me and what we did."

"Don't flatter yourself, sweetheart," I said with a grimace. "I gotta go."

"Okay."

"Thanks," I whispered and hung up. I set the phone on the nightstand and curled into a ball. Pushing everything out of my mind, I allowed my body to shut down until I finally dozed.

Chapter 4

I waited a few days before I left for Dad's. I avoided people as much as possible – and with quite a bit of stealth. I always had something to do so I had an excuse not to hang out and I always answered my phone, making sure to speak personally to people so it didn't seem like I was avoiding everyone.

Maybe I had a future as a spy.

I left Thursday while Morgan was at work, knowing that she intended to drive to her own folks' place that night and return Friday in time to see the boys play. Her folks only lived about forty-five minutes away but I had a little over two hours to drive. I put the top down and relaxed as the wind whipped my hair and the sun beat down on my head. A burden lifted from my shoulders and for the first time since Friday night, I felt good.

My father lived in an exclusive beach community in a small Indiana town right on the shores of Lake Michigan. You had to have at least a six figure salary to afford a home in my neighborhood and better than that to live right on the beach. My daddy did quite well.

I parked in the drive and hopped out of the car without even opening the door. I knew Daddy was probably at work but I was certain Steffi was lurking about somewhere.

I greeted Tilda, Daddy's loyal housekeeper, as I entered the house. I kissed her cheek as she squeezed me tightly, informing me that Steffi was on the beach. I thanked her before breezing through the house, kicking off my shoes when I reached the deck that overlooked the lake. I bounded down the steps and to the sand, wincing slightly at the how hot it was.

I spotted Steffi immediately in her modest navy blue bikini. She was sitting in a beach chair, sunglasses shielding her eyes, reading a book. That was the number one reason why I loved Steffi so much more than I could ever imagine loving Stepmother Number One – Steffi didn't care what others thought of her and had no problem sitting on the beach reading a book. And not some new fad diet book or gossip stories – she read the classics. She loved Dickens and Austen and had an extensive library in which she often let me browse.

I plopped in the sand next to her, startling her from her page. "Bailey!" she gasped. "I thought you weren't coming home until Saturday!"

I shrugged as a grin spread across my face. "I was bored."

She draped an arm around my shoulder and hugged me. "Good. I'm bored, too. Want to do something?"

I laughed. That was reason number two why I loved her – she was fun and not in the 'I'm much younger than your father so let's you and I be best buddies' way. She was fun because she was mature for her age but not so mature that she couldn't cut loose once in awhile. She honestly loved my father – not just his money – and he was crazy about her. And we genuinely liked each other – not pretended for my father's sake.

"Yeah, let's hit the mall," I said with a smile. "I need some new clothes or something."

"Well, let's go," she said as she got up and wiped the sand from her legs. I helped her gather her things and carried them to the house. She rinsed off in the beach shower then dashed inside to change. I chatted with Tilda to get all the latest gossip while I waited.

"Okay, I'm ready," Steffi announced fifteen minutes later. She was beautiful – long, blonde hair, slim figure, soft skin, and pretty eyes. She was taller than me by a few inches but never wore heels.

We took my car and hit our favorite stores immediately. She chattered on about what Daddy was doing and about a wedding they had to attend. She described all the stuffy people that would probably be there and chastised me gently for not going so she had someone to dance with. By the time we hit the shoe stores, she'd run out of gossip.

"Bailey, tell me what's going on," she said softly as she tried on a pair of sandals. "I know that's why you're here."

"Nothing is wrong," I insisted.

"Don't lie," she said. "I know better. Usually you're chatting right along with me, telling me what Irelyn and Lucas are up to or telling me about Spencer. You're far too quiet."

Sighing, I dropped the shoes I had tried on back into the box. "I'm not seeing Spencer anymore," I said. "I broke it off with him - for good this time. I just didn't like him that way."

"Well," she said, looking at me fully with a slight frown. "There's nothing wrong with that. You've been upfront and honest with him the whole time. Is he upset?"

"No," I said. "He doesn't seem to be."

"Does that bug you?" she asked.

"Hm," I pondered. "Maybe it does. But that's crazy – I don't want Spencer to be hurt."

"Of course you don't," she said as she draped an arm around my shoulders. "But us women, well, we like our egos stroked every once in awhile and a boy mourning over us is a huge boost."

I nodded vaguely.

"It's not Spencer that's got you all upset," she said as she leaned back to study me. "You're in love, aren't you?"

Snorting, I turned my head. She laughed and squeezed my shoulders.

"How can you tell?" I finally asked.

"Because you look miserable. Most of the people I know who fall in love for the first time look that way because they don't know what to do next or they're afraid their beloved doesn't feel the same. Which one are you?"

"You are far too perceptive for your own good," I muttered as I picked up the shoe box and placed it back on the shelf.

"And you're far too evasive," she countered. "Just tell me what happened, Bailey."

Damn tears formed in my eyes. Damn tears that hadn't really fallen since I was five and my mother died.

"Not here," I said, shaking my head.

Taking me by my hand as if I was a child, she led me out of the store. We wound up at the food court where she parked me at a table and disappeared. I took that opportunity to compose myself and by the time she returned, I had myself under control.

She slipped me a soda and smiled softly. "Tell me."

I started out slowly, telling her my revelation by the pool but I was like a snowball rolling down a hill by the time I got to what happened Friday night and then Saturday in the men's room.

She remained quiet and thoughtful until I finished. She handed me a tissue and I looked at it questionably until I touched my moist cheek.

"Damn. I'm turning into a crybag," I muttered.

"No, you're not," Steffi said. She patted my hand. "You're in a mess, I'll agree. I don't know what to tell you, for once."

I barked out a laugh. Steffi always had an opinion. "Not much you can say. I just need to get over Collin and get on with my life."

"I don't know, Bailey," she said. "He must like you somewhat if he was willing to sleep with you." I flashed her a pointed look and she rolled her eyes. "I know some men will sleep with just about anyone but the way you've described these boys in the past – I just don't think Collin would take you to bed like that since you dated his cousin and you are one of his friends."

I shrugged. "Of course he would take me to bed," I scoffed. "We were both liquored up and I was all over him."

"And you love him," she commiserated.

"I don't know," I said. "Maybe I don't. Maybe I just think I do."

She shook her head sadly. "I don't think so. But you are in a rotten place. Your best friend loves him and he's your ex's cousin. Yes, I know you and Spencer weren't serious but still – it's a tough situation. And then you say Collin likes some other girl?" She snickered then smiled apologetically. "Sorry, but this is worse than the trashy talk shows those snobby broads from your father's country club watch."

I snorted then laughed. She was right. I could see us all on a talk show stage, professing our love to each other and each one of us leaving in a crying fit. It was downright pathetic.

"Well, I don't want to dwell on it. Let's just hang out for a few days, huh?"

"Sure," Steffi said. "How about if we hit the spa tomorrow? Massages, facials, manicures….sound good?"

"Excellent," I smiled.

Daddy was over the moon to see me and showered me with affection. He ordered an elaborate spread from my favorite Italian restaurant and had it delivered. We sat around the table eating until we were stuffed.

The conversation was light and fun and for once, all the crap from Dalefield was gone. I was grateful I'd decided to come home for awhile – it was exactly what I'd needed.

"So, pumpkin," Daddy said as he wrapped an arm around my shoulder. "What are you doing this summer? Anything interesting?"

"No. Just hanging out with friends. But they all have jobs – even Morgan – and I get bored."

"Maybe you should get a job," Steffi suggested with a shrug. "Something part-time to give you something to do."

"I've thought about it," I admitted. "I've even considered coming back home for the summer."

"Now why would you do that?" Daddy asked.

"You don't want me home?" I demanded.

"Of course I do," he said with a fond smile. "But I'm really proud that my girl is out on her own."

"Not really," I corrected. "You're paying all my bills."

"Yes, and I'll continue to do so until you finish college. I don't want you worrying about anything but school."

I shot Steffi a quick look and she smiled.

"A part-time summer job wouldn't hurt her, Grant," Steffi said. "She could give it up when school started again. Let her get a taste of the working world."

After studying me for several minutes, Daddy finally nodded. "Okay, pumpkin, if that's what you want. But, if you'd rather come home, you have that option, too."

"Thanks, Daddy," I said. Home never sounded better.

***

I managed to forget all about my friends and the mess I'd made as I gave in to massage therapists and facial experts and relaxed. It was wonderful to be pampered and when we left hours later, I was totally loose.

It wasn't until my phone rang while I was out on the deck with Steffi, enjoying a bottle of wine while we waited for Daddy to get home, that I thought of everything again. I glanced at my ID and groaned.

"Hey, Irelyn," I said. "What's up?"

"Where are you?" she demanded. I could hear the din of a crowd in the background and glanced at my watch. She had to be at Rusty's.

"I'm at my dad's house," I said. "Chilling out with the stepmom."

Grinning, Steffi refilled my glass.

"You didn't tell us you were leaving early," Irelyn whined.

"Didn't know I had to," I said with a laugh. "Sorry – I guess I should have told someone, huh?"

"Yeah," she said a little impatiently. "We were worried about you."

"No need," I said as I sipped my wine. "I'm just here recharging the batteries and reconnecting with the parental units." Steffi chortled, hand pressed to her mouth. I winked. "Hey, why don't you give me the name of the place where this shindig is going to be next Saturday? I'll look up directions and shoot over there if I'm still hanging around here."

"Okay," Irelyn said and gave me the name. "You don't think you'll be back this week?"

I heard Lucas and Collin talking in the background and my heart nearly stopped. Morgan giggled at whatever they said and I wondered if Irelyn was speaking the truth – apparently the show went on without me.

"I'm not sure," I said as I chased away my self-pitying thoughts. Did I really think they wouldn't play this Friday because I ran off with my tail between my legs? Did I think they'd drop what they were doing and come get me? If I did, I was more pathetic than Dustin thinking he'd win Irelyn from Lucas. "Depends. I haven't really spent a lot of time here since Christmas. I'll let you know."

"Okay," Irelyn said. "Hey, Luke is getting ready to go on stage so I won't be able to hear you but I want to tell you something."

"Shoot."

"If something is going on, please, please talk to me. I swear I won't say a word to anyone – not even Lucas."

"Thanks but I'm fine. Go enjoy the show and tell everyone I said hey."

I hung up quickly before she could make me feel guiltier or worse – more pathetic.

***

I decided to stick around for awhile – my reasoning being that the more time I spent away from Collin the better my chances of getting over him. Besides, he needed to deal with what we'd done and move on without me being a constant reminder.

It wasn't until Wednesday night that any of my old high school friends called. I couldn't really be too pissed – I hadn't called them either.

"Bailey! It's Kora. What are you doing tonight?" Kora Zimmerman cooed into the phone.

"Nothing special," I mused as I floated on the tiny raft in our pool. "Why?"

"Daddy just told me that your father told him you were in town. And I'm throwing an awesome beach party tonight for my boyfriend's birthday. You remember, Todd, right?"

"Sure," I said. "I remember him. Anyone good coming to this party?"

She laughed bitterly. "Oh, a couple of our mutual friends and a few other people that might interest you."

"My curiosity is aroused," I said with a grin. "Who?"

"Veronica Lindgren."

My skin crawled as bile crept up my throat. Veronica was the bane of my existence and I longed for the chance to smash her face in the sand.

"Party starts at six," Kora said.

"I'll be there," I smirked.

***

I dressed rather modestly that night. I wore a one piece white bathing suit, bikini cut with a low neckline that emphasized my generous curves and hinted at nice breasts. I pulled a simple pink skirt and white tank over it and slipped my feet into flip flops before I drove to Kora's house.

The music was blasting and people were already on the beach, hitting a volley ball over a net and consuming alcohol from the many coolers on the deck. Kora rushed over and hugged me, exclaiming how pretty I looked. I smirked and asked for a drink.

I drew loads of male attention that day as I splashed in the water and played volleyball with my old friends. It was just what my bruised ego needed and by the time it grew dark enough to light a bonfire, I had my fair share of admirers vying for my attention.

"Oh, look," a droll voice said from somewhere behind me. "The slut has returned."

Chuckling, I turned slowly. Veronica Lindgren stood amidst a group of her friends with a knowing grin on her heavily painted face.

"And the pathetic, spiteful bitch has arrived. That really sucks – the party was going so well," I said with a sarcastic smile plastered on my face.

Veronica gestured at several of the males gathered around. "How many of them have you screwed tonight, Bailey?"

"Why?" I asked, folding my arms over my chest. "Jealous? Wish just one of them would do you?"

She sputtered a little as her neck turned red. "I wouldn't waste my time."

I snorted. "You mean they wouldn't waste their time. None of them want to sleep with a butt-ugly wretched loser like you."

Kora eased beside me and placed a hand on my shoulder.

"She's right," Kora said.

"You're both nothing but a couple of whores," Veronica continued. "You know the only reason why guys date you is because they know they'll get lucky."

"Maybe," I said as I finished my drink. "But I'm honest about it. If I want someone then I tell them – I don't play coy like you. I know what I want and I go out and get it."

But that wasn't entirely right, was it? I wanted Collin and yet I ran away.

But you had a reason my conscience tried to tell me. And it was right. I'd had to leave because he didn't want me and he felt bad about what had happened. And I really didn't need to go through the entire list of reasons why I fled from my friends like a coward. I had other things to deal with at that very moment.

"Just stay away from me, Bailey Foxworth, and stay away from my boyfriend," Veronica ordered.

I laughed. "Why? Afraid I'll steal him from you? Where is he? Let me see if he's doable and maybe I'll give him a shot."

Standing on my toes, I glanced around the crowd, totally pissing off Veronica. She fisted her hands and jammed them on her hips as her entire face turned redder than a baboon's backside.

"He's not here so don't even think about it," she said, her eyes spitting nails and other sharp objects. "And he wouldn't have anything to do with the likes of you."

"Who is he?" I demanded. "Let's just see if you're right."

"You are a whore," she said. "You really would try to sleep with him, wouldn't you?"

I shrugged, a lazy smirk on my lips. "Depends – is he hot?"

Huffing, she spun away from me, allowing the crowd to swallow her. I wasn't exactly proud of myself, but it was a shallow victory for me. Especially after what the little bitch had done to me in school. And I hoped she worried that I'd come after her boyfriend. I'd even ask around at the party to find out who he was. I wouldn't mess with him – had no desire- but I'd let her think I would. Screw it – I wasn't winning any popularity contests around here.

Guy Fargo, a boy I remembered from high school, wrapped an arm around my shoulder and pecked my cheek. "How tall are you, Bailey?"

I shrugged. "Five four – five four and a half. Why?"

He squeezed me. "I've always heard dynamite comes in small packages."

"Please," I scoffed as I rolled my eyes. "She had that coming and a lot more. So tell me, who is her boyfriend? I may have to give him a call."

Guy laughed and slid his arm down mine to grab my hand. "I can think of a better man for you."

"I bet you can," I said, as I raised a brow. "But I'm really not interested right now." Actually, my heart wasn't into it – it was miles away back in Dalefield.

"Your loss, babe," he said and kissed my cheek again. I smiled apologetically and wandered to the deck so I could replace my empty beer bottle with a full one.

I sat on the deck steps, watching the inebriated people try to dance and hook up and wondered if I was destined for this sort of life. If I didn't want to go to school, I certainly didn't have to go. I had a hefty trust fund that I'd be able to live off of once I turned twenty-five. Plus, Daddy always gave me what I wanted and had done so ever since my mother had died and he was forced to raise a little girl while running a successful chain of department stores.

There'd been nannies, of course, and Daddy tried to make it to the important things, but he'd always been so busy. That's when he'd shell out the money or bring home presents to make up for all the time he spent away from me.

The first stepmother arrived on the scene just after I'd turned nine. She and I clashed like water and electricity. She'd only been interested in Daddy's money and the 'in-crowd'. She hadn't lasted very long. Nor did she get any money – thanks to the prenup agreement.

Steffi came when I was thirteen and immediately put me on guard. She was young and beautiful and I thought she was just another woman out for a sugar daddy.

But she hadn't been. She'd genuinely loved my father and had actually reminded him several times that he needed to let delegate some responsibility so he could spend time at home with his daughter. In six months' time, we became a family. A real one.

My phone rang, dragging me out of my visit down memory lane. I flipped it open without a glance, thinking it was Steffi checking to make sure I was sober enough to drive home.

"Yeah?" I said as I watched Guy flirt with a girl I didn't know.

"What are you doing, Bailey?" Collin asked. My heart stilled.

"Um, sitting on the beach, drinking a beer and watching some idiot try to pick up a girl who definitely isn't interested. What are you doing?"

"You know what I mean," he sighed. His breath hit the phone and sounded like a wind tunnel.

"No, I don't think I do," I said as my brow puckered. "I mean, I thought I did and I even told you what I was doing but apparently that wasn't the right answer."

"Bailey," he groaned, his voice dripping with impatience. "Are you going to the party Saturday in Chicago?"

He'd obviously given up on his previous question yet I didn't really have an answer to the current one. "I don't know yet. Maybe."

"You should," he said quietly. "We'll talk."

"We'll see," I said sadly as I considered the beer in my hand. "Look, I have to go – the party is pretty lame and I'm tired. If I don't see you Saturday, I'll see you when you get back."

"Fine," he muttered. "Drive safe." He hung up without another word.

I flipped my phone shut, jammed it in my pocket, and dumped out my beer. I definitely wasn't in a party mood any longer. I slipped quietly to my car and drove to Daddy's.

Chapter 5

I parked in the lot of the charming hotel around three on Saturday afternoon. For such a squat building of about ten stories, it was rather impressive. The grounds were well maintained - the grass looking soft enough to sleep on - and the flower beds were overflowing with wave petunias in bright pinks and purples.

I walked up a cobblestone stone path to the lobby and approached the desk. The smiling young lady directed me to the block of rooms that Collin's parents had reserved for us, handing me a key after I handed her my credit card.

My room was small but clean and as charming as the outside. I dropped my bag on the bed and pulled out the outfit I intended to wear. I changed quickly into the pale yellow capris and matching top. The neckline was fairly modest, only showing a hint of cleavage, and the material wasn't as clingy.

I arranged my hair in a long braid that hung down my back and sprayed my favorite perfume on my neck and wrists. I slipped on my flip flops, glanced at my reflection once more before grabbing the keycard and hurrying out of the room.

The gardens were lovely: more petunias and plenty of other floral species I didn't know. The colors complimented each other - their sweet aroma was so summery that I wanted to close my eyes and run through a field like the tampon commercials on television.

The stone path wound around trees and to a surprisingly large courtyard cut into the perfectly cut green grass. Several covered tables littered the lawn and a stage – complete with instruments – was set up in a corner. My eyes grazed the partygoers, anxious to find someone familiar but I couldn't find Irelyn or Lucas or Spencer or…(swallow)…Collin.

I shrugged, not overly concerned, and meandered to the bar where I requested a bottle of water. The uniformed bartender handed me one with a smile. I returned it flirtatiously and turned back to the crowd. I heaved a huge sigh as I twisted the bottle open and took a sip.

"Bailey!" Spencer called as he appeared beside me. He hugged me and dropped a kiss to the top of my head. "Irelyn was worried that you wouldn't come." He held me at arm's length and allowed his gentle eyes to bore into mine. "Darling, what's going on?"

Forcing a grin, I pecked his cheek. "Nothing, Spence, honest. I just wanted to spend some time with my family."

"Well, you look outstanding," he said, though doubt still lingered in his eyes. "Come on, the others are over here."

He steered me to a table and Irelyn hopped up to hug me. "You did come!"

"Yeah," I said as I hugged her back. I glanced over her shoulder and found Collin fighting a smile. My heart lifted. My time away had done nothing to quell my crush – it had only enhanced it.

"Wow," Irelyn said as she stepped back to look at me. "You look fantastic!"

Shrugging, I plopped into a chair. "The stepmom took me to the spa – full treatment."

"It's working for you," Collin said, a roguish glint in his eyes. Heat crept up my neck and I fought to keep it off my face. "So, what did you do?"

"Not much – shopped, spent Daddy's money, hung out on the beach, went to a party." An evil grin broke out on my mouth. "Got into a pissing match with an old enemy of mine. It was classic." I snorted and took a sip of my water. "She thinks I'm going to seduce her boyfriend."

"Bailey," Irelyn groaned.

I narrowed my eyes at Irelyn as my stomach swirled. "She deserves a lot worse. And I'm not actually going after her boyfriend. I don't even know him."

"What's the deal with this chick?" Lucas asked as he sipped a glass of iced tea, amusement flooding his eyes.

"Nothing," I said as I turned my head to watch the crowd. "Long story – very boring."

"Did you get something to eat?" Collin asked. "There's a ton of food."

I didn't want to look at him but I knew it would be rude if I didn't. When I twisted to face him, my heart gasped. He was so beautiful and so out of reach.

"Nah – I ate before I left."

Nodding, he dropped his eyes to the table. It was obvious he was still feeling guilty. I wished I could smack some sense into him but I doubted it would work. I'd have to wait until we had a chance to talk and hope that whatever I said would chase the guilt from his heart.

The party droned on seemingly endlessly but I did have the opportunity to meet the Newton boys' parents. Patrick and Sandy Newton were fun people and I could easily see where the boys inherited their good looks and easy going personalities. Sandy fussed constantly over her boys, and Irelyn also, throwing hints that she'd like the next big event to be a wedding. The strain in Irelyn's eyes was visibly pronounced – the girl was not ready to marry.

Spencer was nearly as preoccupied as Collin and my stomach dropped to my flip flops. I wondered if he'd somehow found out about me and Collin and if he was hiding his pain. I'd have to ask Collin – if we ever were able to talk.

The guys finally left us to prepare for the first set so Irelyn took that opportunity to pounce on me like a cat on a mouse. I set my mouth in a straight line and prepared for her assault.

"Okay, fess up," she said, her eyes on Lucas as he strapped on his guitar and stepped up to the microphone.

"What am I fessing up to?" I asked in total innocence. "I did nothing wrong – that I can think of."

"Bailey, I'm not entirely stupid," she pleaded. "I can tell something is going on and it's killing me. Why won't you talk to me?"

Sighing deeply, I took a drink of my water, wishing for something stronger. I wouldn't drink, though – not with Collin's parents around. I'd wait until I got to my room.

"Irelyn," I said in defeat. "It kills me, too, that I can't talk to you about this."

"So there is something going on," she said as she scooted closer to me. "What?"

I bit my lip and ducked my head, trying to figure out what to say to her. I didn't want to launch into the whole story, as much as it pained me to keep it from her. And I didn't think she'd be too impressed with my recent behavior.

"Can you just give me a little more time to work things out?" I asked. "I'll talk to you, I promise. I just need a little more time, okay?"

"Are you in trouble?" she whispered, her eyes wide.

"No," I laughed. "Not at all."

Her eyes continued to scrutinize me carefully, looking for cracks in my façade. "Okay, I'll give you some space. But promise that you'll call me if you need me. Please?"

"Of course," I chuckled as I smiled at her. I really was grateful that I had her. I knew she'd come over in an instant if I called her – no matter what time. And I'd do the same for her. "Thanks."

"Sure," she said and managed a tiny smile that didn't quite reach her eyes. She wasn't appeased but she'd honor my request.

Jennifer, the graduate, and her friends danced in front of the stage while the guys played. Irelyn amused me greatly as she watched the girls like a hawk, making sure none of them were flirting with Lucas. I couldn't believe she was still so insecure – couldn't she see how much Lucas loved her? Didn't she realize how lucky she was to know she loved him and he loved her?

My gaze left Irelyn and wandered to the stage where it finally landed on Collin. I could see beads of perspiration on his brow reflecting the lights as he pounded on the drums. My heart thumped in time with his beat so hard that I was afraid I'd break a rib.

Lucky Tori, I thought. She's an idiot if she doesn't realize what's right in front of her face.

A lump formed in my throat which irritated me. I scowled and folded my arms over my chest earning a curious look from Irelyn. I pretended not to see as I concentrated on the dancers. I was so tired of feeling teary-eyed and emotional all the time. This being in love crap totally sucked.

When the boys finished playing around eleven, Irelyn and I jumped on the stage to help them tear down their equipment and pack it up in the cases. We hauled it to the van Collin had rented and once we finished, Spencer suggested we go up to the rooms to have a drink. Collin pulled me aside as everyone headed back in the hotel.

"What room are you in?" he asked.

My skin tingled from his touch. "Three-twelve," I said. "Why? Thinking of grabbing a bottle of mescal?"

I cringed, cursing my runaway mouth. But he laughed and squeezed my arm.

"No, not tonight. I was thinking that I'd stop by later and maybe we could talk."

"Oh, sure," I said, excitement shooting throughout my body. "That's fine."

"Great," he said with a grin and dropped my arm. We hurried to catch up with the others.

We ended up in Irelyn and Lucas's room and sprawled out on the furniture. Lucas fell on the bed, tugging Irelyn into his arms while Collin and I took the two chairs tucked under the table. Spencer passed out the beers then perched atop a dresser.

"Hey, Collin," Lucas called. "I thought you invited Tori to come?"

"I did," Collin confirmed, squashing all the wonderfully tingling feelings that I'd been experiencing. "She didn't want to come."

A worry line creased his forehead and I wondered briefly what that was all about.

"Is she sick or something?" I asked.

"Nah," he said, flashing me a feeble smile. "She just didn't want to come."

I really didn't want to spare Tori another thought but I couldn't help it. She irritated the hell out of me for being too damn stupid to not see how devoted Collin was to her.

Deciding he needed to think about someone else, I brought up Morgan's name.

"Where is Morgan?" I asked Irelyn. "Why isn't she here?"

"Her cousin's wedding was today, remember?" Irelyn reminded me.

"Oh, yeah," I said as I peeled the label off my beer bottle. "I think I remember seeing that written on the calendar she has posted on our refrigerator."

I peeked at Collin out of the corner of my eye but his face was unreadable. I sighed as I finished off my beer. Suddenly, I wasn't in the party mood and really wanted to just crawl in my rented bed and sleep. But I didn't – I accepted a fresh beer from Spencer and cracked it open.

My body refused to relax – even with the alcohol. It was far too aware of Collin sitting just a couple feet away from me. It yearned to move closer – to touch him – but I concentrated on the various colors woven into the carpet to keep from jumping over the table. I had to behave now and especially later when he came to my room.

I followed the conversation but didn't contribute much. I patiently waited until the appropriate amount of time passed when I could excuse myself and go to my room. I was eager to have a conversation with Collin but dreading it at the same time. I wasn't entirely sure that my heart would remain whole.

Spencer was the one who finally broke up the party. Standing to stretch, he claimed he was tired and going to turn in early. He waved distractedly as he hurried out of the room.

"Okay, is it just me or is Spencer acting a little weird?" I asked.

Collin shook his head. "He's been a little off for the last few days."

"Damn," I mumbled as I stared anxiously at the door. "Is it because of me?"

"I don't think so," Lucas said slowly. "I mean, I know he really liked you and all but I think something else is going on. He's not talking, though."

"Like someone else I know," Irelyn muttered.

Rolling my eyes, I got to my feet. "Whatever, Irelyn." She grinned. "I'm heading off to bed, too. See you all in the morning."

I escaped before Irelyn could protest and walked the short distance to my room. Once I let myself in, I set my beer down, and paced, wondering how long Collin would wait until he made his excuses.

For something to do, I went into the bathroom and released my hair from the braid, shaking it out so it could hang down my back. I was reaching for my brush when I heard the light knock on the door.

My heart fluttered and flipped as my jelly legs led me to the door. I peeked through the peephole and my nervousness increased. I opened the door to let him before someone could spot him lingering near my room.

"Thanks," he said as he brushed past me. I closed my eyes as a whiff of his cologne floated in front of my face. I dashed to the bed and sank to it as he pulled out a chair. "So, let's talk."

"All right," I said with a shrug, deciding that I would be honest with him. Mostly. "Okay, so I did leave to sort of get away from you and this whole mess. But I told you I was going to do that, remember?"

"That's what I thought," he said as a smirk toyed in the corner of his mouth. "I'm sorry you felt you had to leave, though."

I held up a hand. "I only did it to give you a little space, Collin," I whispered. "I knew you were feeling bad about what happened."

"Bailey," he said and my heart thrilled to hear my name roll off his tongue. "Yeah, I felt bad, but it had nothing to do with you. And you shouldn't have had to run off somewhere because of it."

Nodding, I stood and fetched the beer I'd set on the dresser. I took a long drink before turning back to face him. "It's not a big deal. It was nice to hang out at home for awhile."

His eyes roamed over my entire body and spread heat throughout my stomach. "It agreed with you. You look gorgeous."

I fought a blush and gave him a wry smile instead. "Thanks."

He crossed the room, stopping in front of me. Taking my free hand, he squeezed it. "And I swear, I didn't mean what I said in the men's room that day. I didn't mean to make it sound like you were ... you know...how do I say this... damn!" He ran a hand through his hair.

"Collin, don't worry about it – I know. I was very hung over and oversensitive."

"Don't make excuses for me, Bailey," he said as he squeezed my hand again. "I was acting like an insensitive prick."

I had to smile. "Maybe."

Laughing, he pulled me into his arms. I closed my eyes and inhaled his scent as I rested my cheek against his chest. I didn't want the talk to end – I wanted him to stay in the room all night.

And my body was reacting indecently to his innocent hug. My blood was boiling and my pulse was racing through my veins. As I wrapped an arm around his middle, I could feel the muscles in his back and my insides caught fire.

Then his lips were in my hair. I forced my head to stay put and not turn up so his lips could land on mine. His hands rubbed my back lightly, coaxing a contented sigh to escape my mouth. Reluctantly, I pulled away to smile up at him.

"Thanks, Collin."

I thought I spotted a flicker of desire shoot through his eyes but I couldn't be sure. I probably imagined it.

He lifted a hand to stroke my cheek and my eyes fluttered shut. I stepped closer, clutching his shirt. His finger trailed my jawline making goosebumps jump out on my arms. He lowered his head and kissed me softly – so softly I barely felt it. My heart surged as he cupped my cheek and his kiss increased.

I was vaguely aware that I still held a bottle of beer and wanted desperately to put it down so I could free my hand, but I was afraid that if I stepped away, the kiss would end and I wouldn't get another one.

He applied more pressure and my knees buckled. The arm around my waist tightened to support me, easing me closer to his body while his other hand tangled in my hair.

Feelings like I'd never known raced up and down my nervous system, wreaking havoc with my organs. Everything I thought I knew about guys and how to handle them flew out the window and that was fine. I allowed my body to shut down so I could concentrate only on his kiss.

I wanted him – true – but more than that, I loved him. I loved how I fit in his arms. I loved how when I stood on my toes and he bent his head, we met perfectly. I loved how his fingers twisted and twined in my hair. And I loved how his hand was gentle yet firm on the small of my back. Nothing about his kiss made me feel like he was anxious to just get me in bed. Instead, it made me feel ... cherished, in a way.

Finally, he ended the kiss, his lips lingering briefly on mine. I opened my eyes and he smiled sheepishly at me.

"Sorry," he said, his cheeks a little red. He inched back and rubbed the back of his neck. "I didn't intend to do that when I suggested we talk."

I shook my head. "It's okay." I took a long drink from the bottle before handing it to him. His smile widened as he finished it off and tossed it in the trash can.

"I should go," he said. He strode to the door and rested his hand on the knob. "Um, are we cool?"

"Yep," I said as cheerfully as I could. "Everything's fine."

"You're not going to hide anymore, are you?"

Snorting, I punched his arm playfully. "Nah. You guys are stuck with me again."

"Good," he grinned. "I missed you."

My heart cheered and I swallowed to settle it down. "Sweet talker," I teased with a wink. "Get the hell out of here – I need to get to bed."

He nodded, his brows dipped slightly. "Get some sleep. I'll see you at breakfast."

"Okay."

As soon as he left, I fell to the bed and draped an arm over my eyes. I was an idiot to think I might have a chance with him – even if one of my best friends wasn't in love with him. It was obvious he was attracted to me – but that was where it ended. He could never love me – I wasn't the type of girl guys fell in love with. And that was fine – I'd deal.

Chapter 6

I decided that Steffi's idea was brilliant and that a part-time job might be good for me. And the notice on the pool house bulletin board was just the thing. The condo association needed a part-time lifeguard at the pool Tuesday through Thursday mornings.

I could do that – I'd received my lifeguard certification in high school. Plus the job wouldn't interfere with my weekends.

The head of the condo association hired me on the spot which sort of amused me. He was a fifty-something man with a wolfish demeanor and the way he leered at me indicated me that if I wanted a pay raise, I could get it with little effort.

Good thing Daddy was rich.

I wish I could say things settled down and returned to normal but that wasn't the case. Morgan was jittery, constantly watching me out of the corner of her eye. Spencer was preoccupied and quiet. And Collin was concerned and a little overbearing. Oh, not with me. No, not at all.

Tori started showing up at Rusty's on Friday nights which was like a massive kick in my gut. And she always tagged along with whatever we'd decide to do after the guys finished their set. The funny thing was that she didn't hang all over Collin and he didn't treat her as a girlfriend, per se. I wasn't sure if they were a couple or not. Not even Irelyn or Lucas knew, either.

As much as my heart crumpled and fell into a pile of litter at my feet, I felt ten times worse for Morgan whose face was a constant mask of anxiety and hurt. I would have loved to tear into Collin for what he was doing to Morgan, but the poor guy had no clue. Maybe if Morgan would speak up she'd have a chance. But then, Collin was so into Tori that I don't think he would hear a word.

Yeah, life was pretty crappy all around.

As the Fourth of July approached, the Newton boys decided that they would throw the First Annual Newton Brothers Barbecue. Irelyn was not thrilled since it was up to her to call everyone and write down what dish they would like to bring to share with everyone. Being the good friend that I am, I told her I would just bring all the food if the guys would provide the booze. Irelyn agreed and hung up before I could change my mind.

The party was going to be at Collin's place since there was a nice-sized yard behind the house – with a privacy fence. He also agreed to cook the meat on the grill.

Being the daughter of a chain-store owner, I was privy to all sorts of deals. Daddy's department stores had wonderful grocery sections in them. I just called my daddy, told him of the party and he made a list of all the things I needed. The day of the party I stopped at the nearest store and the manager had everything ready to load in my car.

I arrived a little early but I didn't want to wait until two o'clock – I had a car full of food that I didn't want to spoil. I wandered around to the back yard, looking for someone to help me with the all the bags. I paused near the gate and gaped. Collin was standing before a huge grill – his back to me – hefting a huge bag of charcoal. He was wearing cargo shorts and no shirt. My mind rewound to that night and a shiver hurtled up my spine. I was totally mesmerized and it took all I had to shake out of my stupor before he caught me ogling him.

"Dinner and a show? Wow, I am impressed," I said, my voice strangely strained.

He nearly dropped the bag as he swirled to the sound of my voice. His face relaxed in a slow, heartbreaking smile and I leaned against the gate to support my wobbly legs.

"Hey, Bailey. You're early."

"I have all the food – would you rather I be late?" I asked with a smirk.

"Not in the least," he said as he set the bag on the ground and brushed the dust off his hands. "Need help?"

I pointedly eyed his arms. "You're the one with the muscles."

He snorted, his cheeks a little pink, and playfully pushed me out of the yard toward my car. My heart was clamoring in my chest as I stumbled, feeling like a total idiot. I opened the trunk and started loading his arms full of bags.

"Geez, Bailey," he said as I followed him into the house. "There's not going to be that many people here."

"Daddy owns a chain of stores, remember? I don't pay full price for anything."

He set the bags on the table, shook his head in amusement, then went out for the rest. I pulled food out of the bags and began sorting it as Collin brought in the last of it. He peered over my shoulder and his nearness caused another shiver. Towering over me, he reached around to pick up a package of meat. I closed my eyes to still the spin in my head.

"Steaks? Bailey, this is unnecessary," he said, his breath tousling my hair.

"I told you – this stuff came from Daddy's store. Don't worry about it," I said, trying to steady my voice, my breathing, and my heart.

"Thanks," he whispered as he dropped the steak and wrapped his arm around my waist. He gave me a little squeeze and pecked the top of my head. I leaned into him, shutting my eyes, welcoming the contact. My body came to life as every nerve was on edge.

"Collin!" Tori shouted from the backyard.

He moved away from me quickly and strode to the back door. "In here."

I slipped a cool mask over my face and finished sorting the food while Collin shot me anxious glances as he held the door open for Tori.

Tori was pretty – taller than me with sandy blonde hair that curled on top of her shoulders into a stylish bob. She had hazel eyes and a sweet smile - and she irritated me immensely.

"Hi, Bailey," she greeted, her smile growing. She carried a ceramic bowl to the table and cleared a spot. "I made a fruit salad."

"Lovely," I said with a fake grin. "Collin, do you have any bowls that I can throw this stuff in?"

Tori's smile faltered slightly as Collin gathered a few bowls from the cupboard. He set them in front of me, looking curiously into my eyes. Raising a brow, I motioned for him to get out of my way. His brow furrowed as he moved to stand near Tori.

I worked quietly, transferring the potato salad from the store containers to the bowls and then proceeded to do the same with the macaroni salad.

"Do you need help?" Tori asked in a small, uncertain voice.

"Sure," I said, not looking at her. "You could find some spoons, I guess."

"Um, I'm going to get the grill going," Collin said as he slinked out the door.

My heart was torn – mad because Tori interrupted and hurt because he'd let her. Then the guilt emerged when I remembered Morgan.

"I hope Lucas hurries with the alcohol," I mumbled.

"Collin probably has a beer in the refrigerator," Tori offered.

"You know, that sounds good," I said. I smiled at her and she returned it, her eyes lighting up with hope. I brushed past her to get to the refrigerator where I dug out a beer. I took a long swig and studied the bottle. I'd been drinking quite a bit lately - that was not good.

The others arrived after Tori and I got the food sorted and stored in the refrigerator. Collin helped Lucas and Spencer set up coolers full of ice and filled them with all sorts of drinks – alcoholic and nonalcoholic. Irelyn and Morgan helped me with plates and silverware while the guys laughed around the grill.

A preoccupied Morgan seemed miles away. I hoped she'd loosen up as the party wore on but it wasn't looking promising -especially with Tori around.

Collin stomped back into the kitchen to grab the steaks out of the refrigerator. Opening the packages, he shot at glare at each of us girls.

"What?" Irelyn asked.

"You girls need to get out of here. I have to marinade these steaks and you're not going to see my secret recipe," he said, a smirk toying around the corners of his mouth.

I snorted. "Not a chance."

He lifted a brow. "Why not?"

"Because I don't trust you," I said. "Who knows what your 'secret recipe' is."

He leaned against the counter, folding his arms over his chest, a challenge glinting in his eyes. "You don't trust me? Do you think I'd poison you or something?"

"Not exactly," I teased. "But I do want to know what this 'secret recipe' is."

Barking a laugh, he pushed away from the counter. He bent in my face and my breath quickened. "Never gonna happen, darling."

"I bet I could get it out of you," I said, not backing down.

"Never," he said, his eyes brightening with the banter.

"Come on, Bailey," Irelyn urged, taking my arm. "Let's go outside and let him work."

With a shrug, I grabbed Morgan's hand. "Fine," I grumbled but I glanced at Collin over my shoulder and winked. His grin morphed into a sexy smile that got my heart all worked up again.

As soon as we stepped onto the porch, Tori nearly knocked us out of the way as she hurried past us toward the kitchen. Reaching out, I snagged her arm to stop her. Her face was pale and drawn and her lips a tight, frightened line. My heart jumped for a moment, remembering the night Irelyn fell down the stairs and I wondered if something bad had happened again.

"Um, Tori, are you all right?" I asked.

"Yeah, sure," she said, her eyes darting from my face to the back door. "I just need to see Collin about something."

Figures. Maybe she'd just realized she was in love with him. Maybe she'd had an epiphany like I'd had. Maybe she wanted to declare her feelings. Maybe I wanted to puke.

"He doesn't want anyone in there right now," Irelyn said rolling her eyes. "He's working on his secret marinade."

Tori brushed my hand off her arm, her face flushed, her tone haughty. "He won't care if it's me. It's fine."

Pushing past me, she darted up the few steps and disappeared into the house.

Her words sliced my heart like it was a hunk of deli meat on a meat slicer. I chanced a quick glance to gauge how Morgan was doing but she appeared off in space as was usual for her lately.

I shrugged at Irelyn, adjusting the mask on my face to make sure it was perfect, and made my way to the drink coolers. Grabbing a beer, I glanced around at the new faces. I recognized a couple guys that did the sound board for the band at Rusty's but the guy talking to Spencer was someone I'd never before met - although he did look a little familiar.

A tight blue t-shirt stretched across his well-defined chest while his blond, spiky hair reflected the sun. When he turned my way, his green eyes sparkled as they darted up and down my body.

I had to meet this guy. Maybe he'd take my mind off Collin.

I stepped toward Spencer but Irelyn snatched my arm. "What are you doing?" she hissed.

"Going to talk to Spencer and meet his friend," I said. I raised a brow at her. What – did she want to hog all the gorgeous guys?

"That's Owen and he's not very nice," she said.

Owen - right. I'd heard Spencer talk about him several times and, if I remembered correctly, he'd attended the little party Spencer had thrown at his place last year. I might have met him that night but I couldn't be sure. The thing I remembered most about that party was Irelyn falling down the stairs and having to be taken to the hospital by ambulance.

Snorting, I glanced at her. "Is that what you're worried about? I can handle him." Shaking her hand off, I approached the guys peeking at the charcoal in the grill. "Hey, Spence. Who's your friend? I don't think I've met him."

"This is Owen," Spencer said, peering at me curiously. "Haven't I ever introduced you to him before?"

"Yes, I think so," Owen said as his eyes traveled very deliberately up and down my body. "Briefly, at Spencer's birthday party last year. How I could I ever forget someone like you?"

I rolled my eyes as I clutched Spencer's upper arm. "Like you'd know what to do with me if you ever had the chance."

Laughing, Spencer pecked my cheek. "She'll tear you up, dude."

"Great. I love a challenge," Owen leered.

I knew his type at once. I'd seen it plenty of times with the pretty boys from high school – the ones that were good looking and knew it. They'd play around with a girl – get what they wanted out of her and throw her away when they grew bored. And they thought they were it – that everyone wanted to be like them and that no one would ever tell them no.

"I eat worms like you for breakfast," I said, narrowing my eyes.

"Oh," he said as his lips curled into a lecherous grin. "I like how that sounds. Maybe you can get your little friend, Irelyn, to join us."

I laughed as Lucas glared and took a step toward him. "I told you to stay away from her," he growled.

Owen held up his hands, chuckling. "Just getting a rise out of you, man, that's all. Perhaps the little shy one will join us instead."

"How about not," I said in a near growl. I glanced over my shoulder at Morgan, standing close to Irelyn. "How about you keep the hell away from both of them?"

"That's fine, baby," Owen said, advancing on me, his handsome face drawn into a look of lust and arrogance. "You want me for yourself. You want Owen to teach you a thing or two?"

I shook my head in disgust. "Thanks but no thanks. I've learned all I need to know in life from better men than you – and worse."

Just then Collin appeared on the porch, Tori clutching the back of his t-shirt. His eyes were dark and full of raging anger. It startled me to see him look that way – he was usually so laid back.

He padded down the steps with his lips pressed together so tightly, they were turning white. Tori kept hold of him as they joined the group.

"Who're you hitting on now, Owen?" Collin asked, a hint of anger in his voice.

Owen either didn't hear or just ignored it. He nodded at me. "This lovely young lady but I think I've met my match."

A touch of pride flickered in Collin's eyes as he glanced at me. But the darkness returned when his eyes fell on Owen. "Yeah, well, I think you're right. She does have taste."

I laughed, my heart rejoicing. The moment would have been so much better if Tori didn't have a death grip on Collin's arm.

I waved toward the grill, my tone bored. "I'll leave you boys to your …whatever. I know how you like to compare things: who has the fastest car; who can build the best fire; who has the biggest…steak."

With a wink, I walked away, hurrying toward Irelyn and Morgan.

"He's an idiot," Irelyn said.

"He's an arrogant prick," I agreed. "He needs to be put in his place." I glanced at Morgan who was staring at the pack of guys. And Tori. Spencer was whispering something in Collin's ear and Morgan's eyes were glued on the two of them. Or maybe on Tori standing so close to Collin – I couldn't tell which. My heart ached for her and I had an irresistible urge to go punch Owen and 'accidentally' knock Tori off of Collin with my backswing. Childish? Yes. Immature? Absolutely. Satisfying? Without a doubt!

Collin finally deemed the steaks ready to grill and before long, a delicious aroma floated in the air. I shook Morgan out of her stupor by suggesting that she help me select music to play in the CD player in the garage. Lucas and Spencer had dragged the rather large speakers near the door so the music would filter out into the yard.

"Morg, what's the matter?" I asked as we flipped through the collection of CDs. "Aren't you having a good time?"

"Yes," she said as she dodged my eyes and picked up a Coldplay CD. "Play this one next, please."

"Sure," I said as I took it from her. "Morg, I'm worried about you. You haven't been acting like yourself lately. Talk to me, please."

"Nothing is wrong, Bailey," she snipped.

Taken aback, I could only blink stupidly at her. She had the most even temper out of all of us.

"Fine," I mumbled. "But you know that both Irelyn and I are here for you – you know, if anything is wrong."

She nodded her bent head and picked through the CDs. "Thanks. I appreciate that."

After we ate, we sat around drinking, talking, and listening to music. It would have been perfect and relaxing if it wasn't for the fact that Tori shadowed Collin like a two year-old following her mommy and the fact that Spencer hardly noticed I was there.

Throw in Morgan's mopey mood and we had one hell of a party. Good times.

I was trying to figure out if Spencer was pissed at me for what I said to his friend or if he was just tired of acting like I hadn't hurt him when I'd ended things. Either way, he was definitely avoiding me.

I was tempted to just say something – just stand up and blurt out the truth about what the hell was going on around here. I wanted to yell at Collin that Morgan liked him and he was hurting her.

I wanted to scream at Spencer that if he was upset with me then he needed to let me know so we could hash it out.

I wanted to chastise Irelyn and Lucas for being so disgustingly happy that they made the rest of us miserable. Okay, so maybe not miserable, per se, but envious at the very least.

Maybe it would piss a few people off but at least they'd show some life and maybe work things out.

But as I pondered this, I wondered would I scream out the biggest truth? Would I stand in the middle of my friends and admit that I'd slept with Collin and it had been the best and worst night of my life? Would I tell them that I was finally in love with someone but that someone regretted sleeping with me and in fact had taken an extended guilt trip over the whole matter?

What would Spencer say to that? And Morgan?

The only person showing any real life at the party was Owen. I thought for sure the idiot would leave when the sound guys had but no, he stuck around. He kept leering at Irelyn and Morgan like they were pieces of succulent meat hanging in a meat market window and he hadn't eaten for months. If Lucas didn't do something about it – I would have to soon.

Right around nine that evening, when the sky should have been dark, fireworks lit up night as everyone in the neighborhood tried to outdo everyone else.

Collin lit a fire in the fire pit and we all scooted our chairs in a circle to watch the show. I maneuvered my chair as close to Owen as possible. Someone needed to keep an eye on him.

After the fireworks died down, our party continued. It seemed the more alcohol consumed, the more people wanted to talk. Especially Lucas.

"Hey, bro," Lucas said, his eyes twinkling in the fire light. "Grab that bottle of mescal. Let's finish it off."

Collin's eyes whipped around to me, brimming with horror. Smiling, I gave him a shrug. "Get it, Collin. Let's see if I can drink the other Newton brother under the table."

Collin's face relaxed and his answering smile was grateful. But Tori was still too close to him for my liking.

"Lucas, I swear if you drink that stuff and puke all over the apartment, you're cleaning it up," Irelyn threatened.

Lucas kissed her softly. "You know you'll take care of me, love."

"Aren't they sickening," Owen whispered as he bent his head close to my ear. "She needs a good, hard lay by a real man."

"So that doesn't mean you, right?" I said as I pushed his head away from me.

He chuckled as he reached out to stroke my cheek. "Want to find out?"

I batted his hand away. "Not particularly. I do have some standards."

"That's all right," he said, his lips stretching into a creepy grin. "Maybe I'll take a shot at Morgan. Those shy, innocent types really get my blood pumping."

Rolling my eyes, I moved closer. "Morgan has too much class for the likes of you."

"Bailey," Collin called, stilling my heart. "I don't remember where you put the bottle. Come help me find it."

I lifted a nonchalant shoulder at Owen as I got up to follow Collin into the house. As soon as we reached the kitchen, he spun and grabbed my shoulders.

"Stay away from him, Bailey," he warned, his voice low and his eyes narrowed. "He's bad news."

Sure, he can dictate my love life while he has a girl hanging on his arm all day – a girl waiting for him to rejoin her.

Sighing, I twisted out of his hold and opened the cupboard above his head. Rolling to my toes, I fumbled around until I found the bottle. I shook it in front of him, making the little worm dance, then opened it. I took a long swig and winced before handing it to him.

He eyed me curiously as a slow smile graced his face. My heart warmed and it wasn't from the liquor. He took a drink and grimaced. "This shit is nasty."

"Yes, it is," I agreed. I grabbed his shirt, yanked him closer, pressed a hard kiss on his mouth, then took the bottle from his hand. He was frozen – stunned.

I pecked his lips again. "And I can take care of myself."

Turning on my heels, I bounded down the stairs, to the yard, and handed Lucas the bottle.

Chapter 7

I settled in the lifeguard chair, adjusted my sunglasses, and watched as the kids splashed each other with as much racket as they could muster. It was mostly younger children with their parents in the mornings – the older kids didn't show up until the afternoons and I was usually done with my shift by then.

The Fourth of July party had been a total flop – in my humble opinion. No one else was brave enough to admit it. But it didn't matter, really. It was over and done with and time to focus on what to do next.

As I sat in my chair I did wonder what to do next – and not with parties or get-togethers. I wondered what to do about the Tori-Collin-Morgan love triangle.

I probably should have thrown myself into the equation but I didn't think I really factored in there. I didn't stand a chance with him – not with Morgan crushing on him.

Another nagging little worry decided to join the rest of the mess in my head and that was Owen's remarks about Morgan. Was he all talk or did he actually think he could get Morgan to go out with him - or any other nasty thing he had in mind? I didn't think it was possible as according to Irelyn, Morgan was in love with Collin.

But what if she got desperate? What if she decided to try to make Collin jealous?

I shuddered at the thought.

My first impulse was to talk to Spencer but he seemed to be drifting farther and farther away from me. It bugged me - hurt, too - because he said we'd always be friends. And he'd broken up with me before - it's not like it was the first time this had happened.

 Maybe it just wasn't possible for us to be friends. Maybe we were the type to either be on or off - nothing in between. Maybe he was really into me and I'd tossed him aside like yesterday's garbage.

Everything began spinning and twirling inside my head to the point where I wanted to climb down from my chair, sprint to the end of the diving board, scream 'what the hell is going on?' and jump.

Of course that was a terrible idea for not only would it not solve anything but it would most likely get me fired and possibly committed in the local mental institute.

With a yawn, I shifted in the chair, trying to get more comfortable. It would have been so easy to doze as my eyes were hidden by my sunglasses, but I was actually serious about the responsibility of my job. What if a little kid fell in the deep end and no one noticed? I would not be the one to let something that horrible happen. Ever.

As my short shift approached the end, someone came to visit me – nearly shocking the hell out of me.

"What are you doing here?" I asked. "How'd you get in?"

"Morgan let me in," Collin grinned as his eyes quickly grazed my bare legs. Smugness raided my heart. "She was on her way out."

"Oh," I said, trying to think of something clever to say but my mind refused to help. His presence was affecting everything. "I see."

His grin turned into a smirk as he glanced at his watch. "How much longer are you on duty?"

"About a half an hour," I said as I turned my gaze from him to watch a little boy toddle near the edge of the pool. I started to get out of my chair to direct him to the kiddie section but his mother got to him first. I sat back down and raised a brow at Collin. "Don't you have to work?"

"I went in this morning but the boss let me leave early," he said mysteriously. "Hey, I have something for you. Do you mind if I hang out here and wait?"

I lifted my glasses from my eyes to glare suspiciously at him. "What is it Collin? I swear if it's mescal I'm going to tie weights to your body and throw you in this pool."

He laughed, his entire face lighting up. "No, I promise."

I nodded and jammed my glasses back on my face.

He slipped off his shoes and socks and sank to the edge of the pool, dipping his feet in the water. "So, if I fell in, you'd have to save me?"

I snorted and held back my smile. "No. I'd let you sink and have the maintenance guy fish your dead body off the bottom."

His eyes grew as he gaped at me, mouth wide open. When my smile escaped, he relaxed and laughed.

"You'd rescue me," he said with confidence. "You know you're dying to do the mouth-to-mouth thing on me."

My heart froze along with my face as it was my turn to gawk. "And I thought Lucas was the arrogant one. What happened?"

Collin kept his eyes on the water as he shrugged. "Maybe I'm tired of being the good twin."

My heart skipped a beat as I stared at the top of his head. "Collin?"

He jumped to his feet, pulled his shirt over his head, and winked at me. "Sure hope I don't drown."

Bending his knees, he dove beautifully into the pool. I watched as he swam the width and surfaced on the other side. Water flowed effortlessly down his chest as he pushed his wet hair back. My heart could hardly take it and nearly jumped in the pool after him.

He heaved his body on the edge on the opposite side of me and leaned back, propping his body with his arms. He winked at me and nearly finished my heart.

Why did Morgan have to love him?

My relief came only a few minutes late and I was finally able to climb off the chair. Collin had stuck around, goofing off in the pool while he waited for me.

"Done?" he asked when I stood beside him. He'd been watching a couple middle school kids show off their newly found swimming skills.

"Yes," I said with a grin. "Want to go get drunk?"

He removed my sunglasses as he edged closer. My heart thumped wildly.

"You look hot today, Bailey," he whispered, indeed raising my body temperature. He touched my cheek, a smirk lurking in the corners of his mouth. "Very hot. Let's cool you off."

He pushed me into the pool before I had a chance to recover from his touch. Shrieking, I cursed him when I surfaced but couldn't find him anywhere until his head popped up closer to mine.

"You're dead, Newton," I threatened but it did no good – he just smiled.

"Come on, Bailey," he said as he hands gripped my waist under the water. "Just having a little fun. It is hot, you know."

I wound my arms around his neck and pressed closer. A smug smile filled my lips when I caught his eyes darting down to check out my breasts that I had smashed into his chest. Yes, Collin Newton was indeed a boob man.

"I forgive you," I whispered as I inched my face closer to his.

His pupils dilated as I grew nearer. I brushed my lips very lightly on the corner of his mouth and, grinning, I hoisted my body up and forced his head underwater, very effectively dunking him. I swam to the side and hopped out before he could exact revenge.

He climbed out after me and I cringed.

"We're even," I declared.

He approached me slowly and when he was close enough, he spit a stream of pool water in my face.

I held my hands in front of my face. "Collin, you're an idiot."

He chuckled and grabbed my waist again, pulling me gently to his chest. He gazed into my eyes briefly, sighed, and pressed a kiss to my forehead. "Yeah, you're probably right."

He released me and ran to fetch his shoes, socks and shirt.

"Now come on – I told you I have something for you."

I ducked into the pool house to grab us some towels that were technically supposed to stay in the pool area. I wrapped one around my waist as Collin did the same before taking him back to the main building.

"What do you have for me that's so important?" I asked.

"You'll love it – trust me," he said.

As I unlocked the condo door, I paused. "Hang on. You have something for me and it's in my condo? Wouldn't it technically be mine already?"

Laughing, he ruffled my wet hair. "I told you, I ran into Morgan and she let me in. I brought the …thing…here before I came down to the pool."

I shrugged and pushed open the door. Instantly, a whine rent the air and I stepped back into Collin. He wrapped an arm around my waist and his laughter tickled my ear.

"Relax, it's fine. Stay here."

He slipped away from me and marched into the kitchen as I shut the front door.

"I know that's an animal, Collin," I called after him.

The whine turned to excited squeals and I wondered if he had a pig in my kitchen.

"You're right," he said as he returned to the living room with a large box. "Sit," he ordered.

I sank to the floor as he set the box down and produced two squirming brown and black furballs. He placed them both in my lap and they immediately jumped at my face, their little tongues licking my skin. My heart swelled as I wrapped them in my arms.

"They are …so…adorable," I cooed. "Why are they here?" I stilled as I eyed his smug face. "Oh, no, Collin. I can't have two puppies."

"Oh, I know," he said as he scratched one of the puppies. "I'm taking one."

"No, you're taking two," I said. The smaller one sat on my leg, his little black snout pointed up at me and his big brown eyes so expectant. "And that's so not fair," I said to the puppy. "Do not look at me like that."

"That one is Otis," Collin said as he lifted the lighter colored one out of my lap. "This is Milo."

"Milo and Otis?" I asked as I tickled Otis's ear. "Original. Watch children's movies much?"

His cheeks pinked. "It was a good movie. And I thought the names fit them."

"Where did you get them?" I asked as I scratched Otis's chin. He eagerly stretched his neck out so I had better access and promptly fell off my leg. I giggled and picked him up, holding him in front of my face. He licked my nose and I was in love.

"We found them out behind the shop," he explained, referring to the auto body repair shop where he worked. "There were three but one of the other guys took one. My boss was going to call Animal Control but I told him I'd take them."

"And you immediately thought of me?" I asked, lifting a brow at him. I cuddled Otis to my chest and he didn't seem to mind the wet bathing suit. I kissed the top of his furry head.

"Yeah," he said gently as his soft eyes found mine. "And look at you."

"What about Irelyn and Lucas?" I suggested, ignoring the frantic pounding of my pulse.

"They can't have dogs in their building," he said.

"Tori?" I asked weakly, although I knew I wasn't giving the little guy up anytime soon.

"She's more of a cat person," he said sourly.

"Yuck," I said. "Fine, I'll keep him."

Collin kissed my cheek as he scooped the other pup up in his arm. "Let's take them out to do their business then we'll go shop and buy them all the puppy stuff they need."

My heart tremored as I nodded at him and carried my new baby outside.

***

I made Collin wait as I showered quickly and changed. When we were ready to go, he placed both puppies back in the box and locked them in the kitchen. They jumped on the sides, whining and yelping and I nearly caved.

"They'll be fine, Bailey," Collin said, amused.

"Are you sure?"

Grabbing me by the arm, he dragged me out the door. "Yes. Let's go."

We piled into his SUV and I pulled my cell phone out of my pocket. I called Daddy and told him what we needed – hinting that I should set Collin up with the same kind of account that I had at all the stores. He agreed, naturally – anything I wanted.

"Oh, pumpkin," Daddy said before I ended the call. "I'm planning a little party for Steffi this weekend – for her birthday."

"Kind of waiting until the last minute, huh?" I laughed.

"Well, you know me," he said sheepishly. "I hope you'll come. Bring your friends home, you know Steffi wouldn't mind them being at the party and we'd both like to meet them."

"Sure," I said. "I'll ask them." An idea came to mind and I looked fleetingly at Collin. "What are you doing for entertainment?"

"I thought about hiring a DJ service," he said. "Do you have any other suggestions?"

A smile snuck across my face as I looked at Collin. He glanced at me with a furrowed brow. "Possibly. Book the DJ and maybe I can come up with another form of entertainment."

Grinning, Collin reached out to take my hand. That stunned me nearly speechless but I wouldn't let go.

"Okay, pumpkin. Take care of the new puppy and I'll see you soon. I love you," Daddy said.

"I love you, too, Daddy." I flipped my phone shut and smiled at Collin. "It sure does pay to have a father who owns a department store chain."

"Why?" Collin asked.

"Because we'll get everything at cost," I smirked. "He told me to set you up with an account and they'll give you a card."

"That's not necessary," Collin tried to protest.

"Yeah, whatever," I scoffed. "Do you want to spend tons of money on the puppy or would you rather get a discount." I didn't give him time to answer. "That's what I thought."

He rolled his eyes and squeezed my hand. "Was there something you wanted to ask me?"

My brow puckered as I watched his face, straining my brain to remember. "Huh?"

He chanced a quick glance at me then turned his eyes back to the road.

"Something about entertainment?"

"Oh," I said as I rolled my eyes. "Yeah. Duh. Daddy's throwing a party for the stepmom this weekend. Do you want to go?"

"Um," he stammered. "That's what you wanted to ask me?"

I smirked. "Well, that's part of it. Daddy said you all can come up for the party. They want to meet my friends. Oh, and maybe you and the guys could play a short set or something. Daddy will pay you."

His smile widened as he gave my hand another squeeze. My heart flipped and I wasn't real crazy about how much I was getting into the hand holding thing. "I'll ask Luke and Spence but I'm sure it won't be a problem. We're not playing this Friday because Rusty is having some sort of open mic night."

"Well, that's kind of cool," I said casually even though my heart was in my throat. "You can come up with me Friday night."

"Okay," he shrugged. My heart danced. "But I think Irelyn works Saturday morning so they probably won't be able to come up until Saturday afternoon. I don't know about Morgan and Spencer."

"I'll call Spencer when we get back," I said as Collin pulled into the parking lot and stopped the truck. "Let's go shop."

I stopped at the office and greeted Len, the store manager. He set Collin up with the same discount card that I carried. Collin kept up a steady stream of protests as I guided a shopping cart to the pet department.

"Collin if you don't shut up then I'll get you drunk again and this time," I said as I grabbed his arm and stood on my toes to look into his eyes, "I'll kick your ass instead of taking you to bed."

A flush washed over his face but a smirk followed so I knew I hadn't crossed the line too much. Cupping my face, he kissed my nose. "Bring it, little girl. I think I can take you."

My pulse raced and I was tempted to shove him on the display of pet beds and have my way with him. I just lifted a cool brow as his eyes lingered on my lips.

I smiled. "I don't think you have the balls."

"Just wait," he said and moved away. I was frozen, my heart still. It took several seconds for it to start again. "What kind of food should we get?"

I hurried after him and we spent a good twenty minutes browsing puppy food brands, comparing ingredients. We bickered constantly and I was sure that the other customers thought us a couple.

"Oh, these collars are cool," I said after we finally decided on food. I picked up a leather collar with an intricate design etched in it. "There are two so we they could match."

"No way," Collin objected as he took the collars from my hand and set them back on the shelf. "No way in hell those puppies are wearing anything matching."

"Why not?" I asked, my curiosity level at its highest.

He folded his arms over his chest and cocked his head. "I'm a twin, remember?"

I rolled my eyes. "Duh. I'm not totally stupid. But you and Lucas are twin people – not twin dogs. What's that got to do with anything?"

He fought a smirk as he grasped my shoulders. "Can you imagine the horror of your mother dressing you exactly like your brother?" He shuddered. "It's not pretty."

My eyes nearly bulged as I clamped my lips shut to hold in my laughter. It escaped in a snort and I pressed a hand to my mouth.

"Laugh it up," he said, his eyes shining. "It's damaging. I still have nightmares about it."

"Hold on," I said, tears from my suppressed laughter leaking out of my eyes. "I'm picturing you and Lucas in matching sailor outfits with those cute little hats."

He dropped his hands and rolled his eyes. "I don't think she ever dressed us in anything like that…"

"Sure," I laughed. "Wait until the next time I see her. I'll ask."

He groaned and rifled through the collars hanging from hooks. "I'm getting Milo a blue collar."

"Fine, fine," I said as I shuffled next to him, still snickering. "I'll get Otis red. Happy?"

"Ecstatic," he said sourly but I could see his lips twitch.

Collin carried my purchases in the house, opting to leave his in the truck. I unlocked the door and found Morgan on the floor playing with the puppies.

"Aren't they cute?" she asked as we stepped into the living room. She picked up Otis and peppered kisses all over his head.

"Yes, they are," I said. I took two bags from Collin and carried them into the kitchen. I dug out the toys and returned to find Collin sitting close to Morgan. My heart stopped in my chest when they looked at each other at precisely the same time and smiled. I discreetly slipped back into the kitchen and leaned against the door to catch my breath.

That's what you wanted to happen, remember? my conscience reminded me. And I had to agree. The sweet smile on Morgan's face was a welcome change from the mopey look she usually carried.

I unpacked the bags, giving Collin and Morgan a little privacy, and found a suitable spot for the dog dishes. I'd purchased a crate and a little bed but both those items were still in the living room. I'd wait to get those.

I set the dog food on the floor and put away the dog treats. All that was left were the toys, the collar and the leash. I cut off the tags, trying to stall. What if I waltzed back in the room and they were sharing a moment or...kissing?

"Hey, what are you doing?" Collin asked as he strolled into the kitchen with the crate and the dog bed.

I forced a smile. "Putting things away."

I grabbed the crate by the handle and situated in the corner. I opened the door and shoved the bed inside.

"There," I said, hands on my hips.

"I need to get out of here," Collin said. "Um, I'll call Spencer and Luke and let you know about Saturday. I already asked Morgan and she said she'd like to go but she can't until Saturday – she's working late Friday night."

"Okay," I said, my jaw aching from the fake smile. "Thanks."

"You okay?" he asked, his brow creased. He stepped closer peering in my face.

"Yes, I'm fine," I said. "Thanks for the puppy."

"Sure," he said as he kissed my forehead. "I'll see you later."

After he left, I remained in the kitchen, not walking him out. I wasn't sure if Morgan might want another private moment with him – maybe bond or whatever. And far be it from me to stand in the way of true love.

Chapter 8

I was mildly surprised when Collin called me Thursday night and suggested we drive up to my father's house together. I had assumed that he'd ride with Morgan – even though Morgan hadn't made any indications that she'd hooked up with him.

Maybe it hadn't happened yet. I fought off the hope and agreed to Collin's plan.

Irelyn and Lucas were indeed driving up Saturday afternoon as well as Spencer. He'd already had plans to hang out with creepy Owen Friday night.

Collin picked me up Friday afternoon in a rented van and we set off with the windows down.

He'd left Milo with Tori, the cat lover, and I'd left Otis with my neighbor, the elderly Mrs. Wesley, who'd fallen in love with him the first time she saw him.

I avoided mentioning Morgan – quite frankly, I didn't want to hear about it – and kept the conversation casual. We mostly talked about the puppies – just like proud parents. Once we grew bored with that, I filled him in on my dad and Steffi before giving him a brief description of my old high school friends.

"So, who is this enemy of yours that you got into a, and I quote, 'pissing match' with last time you were home?" he asked, amused.

I snorted. "She's a spiteful bitch. I don't think Steffi is friendly with her family so I don't know if they'll be at the party. But, who knows – if Daddy set up this party, then your guess is as good as mine who'll show up there."

He grinned his sexy smile and my heart flew out the window. "Well, it will be fun, I'm sure."

"It won't be boring," I mused as I glanced out the window.

When I directed him to my father's house, he let out a low whistle. I gave him a puzzled look which made him laugh.

"You live in Dalefield when you could live here?"

"It's not all that you would think," I said as he parked in the horseshoe drive.

I got out of the van and waited for him to join me before I walked into the house. Tilda embraced me as if she hadn't seen me in ages before I introduced her to Collin. He greeted her warmly as I scouted out the living room for signs of Steffi. I was eager for her to meet Collin but she was nowhere to be seen.

"Mrs. Foxworth is out on the deck, on the phone," Tilda said. "And I have the guest rooms ready if you'd like to take your stuff upstairs."

"Thank you so much," I said and gestured for Collin to follow. He admired the tasteful art Steffi had purchased and listened as I explained each piece. I showed him to the guest room right across the hall from my room and stood in the doorway as he dropped his bag, his eyes sweeping the room.

"Damn, Bailey, this is nicer than my whole apartment," he said.

"Come see my room," I said as I grabbed his hand and dragged him across the hall. My room was large with French doors that opened onto a deck with a wonderful view of the lake. A set of steps led to the main deck directly below on the walkout level.

"This is beautiful," he said as he stepped out on the deck. I followed him and stood at the rail, watching a sailboat graze the water. "Do you sail?"

"Yeah, right," I scoffed. "I do have a jet ski, though. Want to try it?"

He grinned at me. "Hell yeah."

I returned his grin and grabbed his hand. "Let's go see Steffi first then I'll take you out on the lake."

I could see the approval in Steffi's eyes as soon as she shook Collin's hand and it meant more to me than I could ever explain. Too bad it would never happen between Collin and me, but I respected her approval nonetheless.

After we changed into bathing suits, we hit the lake. He helped me drag the jet ski to the water and I climbed on front, making him perch behind me and wrap his arms around my waist. It took all my concentration to maneuver the damn thing through the waters but I managed. And once I was sure he could handle it, I switched places and let him drive.

By the time we got back to the house and showered, Daddy was home. He greeted Collin as warmly as Steffi had, shooting me a discreet wink of approval.

We dined out on the deck and it just felt so natural – like everything was right. I was beginning to feel all warm and fuzzy and let me tell you, it was a strange concept.

Daddy and Collin talked about the band and Steffi quizzed Collin about what songs they'd play. She made several requests in which Collin informed her they could do if she wanted. His approval rating rose and I had to suppress my laughter.

After dinner, Daddy and Collin enjoyed a glass of scotch and a cigar.

"Hey, Steffi," I asked as I sipped a glass of wine. "Any parties going on tonight that Collin and I can crash?"

Daddy chuckled and gazed upon me fondly. "Pumpkin, don't you want to show Collin the town?"

"Not really," I snorted. "I would rather find a good party."

"I think Janie Baker is having a party tonight," Steffi said. "I heard her mother say something about it at the salon today."

"Excellent," I grinned, eyeing Collin. "That's just down the beach. We don't have to drive and Janie is intimidated enough by me that she won't say a word if we show up."

"Oh, Bailey," Daddy groaned.

"Grant," Steffi gently chastised. "They're young. Let them go. Bailey is smart enough not to get in any trouble, you know that."

I got up and kissed my daddy's cheek. "We won't be terribly late but don't wait up." I kissed him again. "I love you, Daddy."

"I know," he sighed. "I love you, too."

"Thanks for dinner," Collin said. "And the scotch. Excellent, by the way."

"You're very welcome. Take care of my little girl," Daddy said.

"Always," Collin said with a smile.

Taking Collin's arm, I dragged him down the deck steps to the beach. We walked a short way in silence but I knew it wouldn't last.

"Okay, Bailey – fess up. What kind of trouble are you walking me into?"

I stopped to laugh – even wiping the tears from my eyes. "Geez, Collin, it's not that bad. Janie doesn't hate me, per se, but she's not what I'd call a good friend." I tucked my hand in his arm. "But some people who do actually like me will be there so all is good."

He patted my hand dubiously. "I'll take your word for it." When I grinned, he untucked my hand and laced his fingers through mine. "Let's go."

We hadn't walked far when we spotted the bonfire and heard the music. I tensed a little, knowing that Veronica more than likely would be there, and he felt it.

"What's the matter?"

"Nothing," I shrugged. "We're almost there."

My apprehension increased as we neared the crowd and that was puzzling in itself. These people never, ever scared me before and I knew I could handle them. I had to chalk it up to Collin's presence.

Once we reached the others, it didn't take me long to find my old high school gang – including Kora.

"Bailey!" Kora exclaimed. "I thought you wouldn't be back until tomorrow!"

She hugged me and I endured it briefly until I drew back to stand next to Collin. "This is Collin. Collin – Kora."

"Oh, hi," she said coyly, her eyes appraising him. "Um, Janie's around somewhere. I'm sure she'd like to see you."

"I bet," I said. I glanced at Collin. "Let's find something to drink."

It wasn't hard to find the alcohol stash and I supplied both of us with a cold beer. As we stood near the coolers, surveying the party, I pointed people out and made him laugh at my narrations.

"Why is this Janie intimidated by you?" he asked.

I barked out a hollow laugh. "That's probably Veronica's fault. Veronica likes to run her mouth and I guess she doesn't paint the greatest picture of me. Janie's like a little mouse. If she only had a spine she'd be all right."

"This Veronica sounds intriguing," he said as he sipped his beer. "I'd love to meet her."

I lifted a shoulder. "Okay."

He reached out to grab my arm. "I'm joking, Bailey. Don't approach her – she'll just think you're looking for trouble."

"Maybe I am," I whispered as I looked into his eyes.

"Then we can find it elsewhere," he said as he stared unblinkingly at me.

My heart stammered as it pondered his words. Was he suggesting we slip away and...well, repeat our last performance?

He moved closer so that he towered over me and I had to crane my neck to see his face. He lifted a hand to trace my jaw with his index finger and I had to lock my knees to keep from collapsing.

I thought about the tall beach grass that grew on the dunes and how wonderfully concealing it could be. My cheeks burned and I was sure Collin could feel the heat but I didn't move away from him. I couldn't.

"Who invited the whore?" a nasty voice called and broke me out of my trance.

I stiffened and turned, angry not only at the words but for them interrupting what could have been an awesome moment.

"Don't you ever get tired of running your mouth?" I asked as I stepped away from Collin and approached Veronica. "Because everyone sure gets tired of hearing it."

"I really doubt that," she scoffed. "And I know that you were trying to find out about my boyfriend so you could try to seduce him. Everyone told me."

Laughing, I inched closer, my hands fisted at my side. "Scared? Think he'll dump you for the chance to be with me?"

"No," she snorted, nose scrunched up in disgust. "He'd rather be with a classy woman than a tramp."

"Then what the hell is he doing with you?" I asked, brow raised. I took another step toward her and gently patted her cheek. "Don't worry – I don't want your boyfriend."

"Good," she said smugly, pulling her head away from me. "Because I was about to show you what it's like to have someone go after your boyfriend – but wait – you don't have one! That's right – boys don't want you for a girlfriend. They just want you for sex."

"That's not entirely true," Collin said as he stepped behind me and wound his arms around my waist. "Not true at all."

"Who the hell are you?" Veronica asked.

"Collin Newton," he said as he pecked the top of my hair. "Bailey's boyfriend. And I guarantee that I'm not just using her for sex."

My heart shot out of my chest and danced across the lake like a stone skipping the water. I shifted so I could wrap an arm around his waist as a victorious smirk slipped across my lips.

"If you'd like to show me what it's like to have someone try to sleep with your boyfriend, go ahead," I challenged.

Collin shot me a reproachful look. "I think not." He bent his head and kissed me softly, causing my stomach to twist. "I have everything I want here."

I rolled my eyes at him and earned a grin but inside I was melting. Oh, I knew he was just putting on a show but it didn't matter at that moment. I'd play along for as long as I could.

"He's a little cheesy but he's all man and all mine," I said. His grin widened and his face brightened. "Let's get another drink and mingle."

"Let's," he said, laughter rolling in his eyes. Lacing his fingers through min, he dragged me away from Veronica and back to the drink table. He snagged a couple beers, twisted the top off of one and handed it to me.

"Thank you," I whispered, meaning for more than just the beer. He nodded, understanding in his eyes. I took a drink. "That was Veronica, by the way. My biggest fan."

"I could tell," he said with a laugh as he glanced over my shoulder. "And she's watching us like a hawk." He took my beer out of my hands and set it down along with his. "It's show time, Bailey – don't let your fans down."

He wound one arm around my waist and cupped my cheek with his other hand. Drawing me closer, he pressed his lips lightly to mine. My hands flew to his shoulders and slowly snaked around his neck as his lips grew more demanding. I melded my body to his, eager to erase any space between us, and he held me tighter. I could feel his arousal against my leg and it made my desire shoot up off the charts.

He pulled back only slightly and didn't let go of me. "Damn, Bailey, you don't know what you do to me."

With a tiny smirk still on my lips, I kissed him chastely. I nodded down at our flush bodies. "I think I have an idea."

He laughed and hugged me to his chest – I suspected so he could hide the light flush of his cheeks. "They're playing our song – let's dance," he whispered in my ear.

I shuddered and moved my hands to grip his shoulders. "You dance?" I asked.

He lifted a shoulder and watched the group of kids dancing on the packed sand near a portable CD player.

"Not a whole lot," he said. His eyes were full of mischief. "But I'd do it for my girlfriend if she really wanted me to."

"Okay but it has to be a slow one," I said.

"You got it," he said as he handed me my drink and latched onto my hand. He eased us toward the dancing group and tapped the shoulder of a girl sitting by the CD player. "Play something slow, would you?"

She shrugged, her body slightly swaying. I wondered if she'd be able to find something slow in her state. But she did – pushing the skip button until she found a laid-back tempo.

Collin's sexy smile melted my heart – again. He took me in his arms and I rested my cheek against his chest as my body moved in perfect harmony with his. Every so often, he'd drop a kiss on the top of my head.

When the song ended, he waved at the inebriated DJ girl who gave him a thumbs up. He lifted my chin, pecked my lips, and then raised a brow.

"Now what?"

"Well," I said slowly, pressing my body into his. "We can either make out here in front of everyone or we can go make out in the beach grass."

A slow smile spread across his mouth and my pulse picked up speed. "Think you can score a blanket? I'd hate for you to get full of sand."

Excitement shot through me like electricity. I reluctantly ripped my body away from his and my heart cried out in protest. I stood on my toes and kissed the corner of his mouth.

"Let me see what I can do."

It wasn't hard to find Janie and even easier to convince her to give me a blanket from the deck. I thanked her, promising to get it back to her someday, and hunted for Collin. He was talking to Guy and a couple other boys I didn't know so I grabbed his arm and pulled him away.

"Sorry fellows," I said, not the least bit apologetic. "But he has places to go and people to do."

Collin shrugged at the guys and wrapped his hand around mine. He allowed me to drag him away from the group and remained silent until we were out of earshot of the party.

"People to do?" he asked.

I squeezed his hand. "Let them think what they want – they will anyway."

He didn't say anything else. When we neared my house, I stopped and turned to him. "This is Daddy's property. Well, not the beach, but all that," I said as I waved to the sandy yard near the house.

We were far enough away from the house where no one would see or hear us if they were out on the deck so I walked through the loose sand and spread out the blanket in a patch of high dune grass. I sat and patted the spot next to me. Collin dropped beside me.

"You didn't have to do that at the party, you know," I said as I plucked a piece of grass and began shredding it.

He propped an arm behind me and cupped my cheek with his other hand. "Yes, I did. I didn't like what they were saying about you."

"I'm used to it," I whispered. "It doesn't bother me anymore."

He inched his face closer. "It bothers me."

I clutched a fist full of his shirt and eased us both to the blanket. He hovered over me briefly before brushing his lips softly over my mouth.

My eyes fluttered shut as my arms wound around his neck. He applied a little more pressure and outlined my mouth with his tongue. I moaned and parted my lips. He shifted his body slightly over mine and trailed his fingers down my side as he continued to kiss me. I twined my fingers in his hair and pulled him closer even though it was no easy feat – there wasn't much space left between us.

His fingers found the hem of my shirt and ducked underneath it. They worked their way slowly up my skin, drawing tiny moans of pleasure from me, until they found my bra. I lifted slightly so he could unhook it and he grinned in my mouth.

It was his turn to moan when his hand slipped under my loosened bra and found my breasts. He ripped his mouth from mine and pushed my shirt up so he could kiss them. I squirmed underneath him as lust blazed through my veins.

"They are so spectacular," he whispered.

"So you've mentioned," I said, my voice hoarse.

He dragged his lips away from my breasts and up my throat and back to my mouth. His arousal was evident once more and pressing into my leg. And, damn, did I want him.

I swept a hand down his back and over his side to brush the lump in his shorts. He moaned in my mouth and I broke the kiss to smile.

"What's this? Is someone a little excited?"

His breath was uneven and his eyes chock full of desire. "Maybe a bit. Do you want to take care of that for me?"

I yanked his mouth back to mine, squeezed my eyes shut, and sent out a telepathic message: *I'm so, so sorry, Morgan. I really am. But I'm only human and so very weak.*

I kept my mouth firmly on his as I answered: "Most definitely."

I tugged his shirt over his head and before I could find his lips again, he did the same with mine and my bra. He kissed me quickly and then moved his mouth to my throat and my chest and my breasts. I wiggled in anticipation and reached for his shorts.

"Anxious, are we?" he grinned as he made his way back to my face. He brushed my hair behind my ear then worked my shorts off my hips and helped me remove the rest of his clothes.

Then he swore rather loudly.

"Yeah, we're getting there," I said, smiling.

He tried to laugh but couldn't muster one. He kissed my forehead, his naked body covering mine. "I don't have a condom, Bailey."

"You never were a boy scout, were you?" I rolled my eyes and swiped at the sand on his shoulder. "I'm clean and on the pill. It's your choice."

A slow smile spread across his face as he kissed me again. "Oh, I'm clean."

I hooked a leg around his waist and he shuddered. "Then what are you waiting for?"

He captured my lips with his and eased into me slowly. Both of us sighed and the desire level rose. I arched into him but he took his time and I could only cling to him and kiss him and writhe in ecstasy.

When he finally picked up the pace, I was nearing the edge and so desperate to take the plunge. I could tell he was, too. I buried my face in the crook of his neck and bit down on his shoulder. He held me as close to his body as possible as we finished and shuddered in each others' arms. He lowered me to the blanket and rested his forehead on mine, panting heavily.

"Damn, Bailey," he huffed. "You are unbelievable."

I yanked his face to mine. "You aren't so bad yourself, stud."

He smiled as he dropped next to me, wrapping me in his arms. We stayed still as our bodies settled and when they did, he kissed me tenderly, helped me find my clothes, and brushed the sand off my body. Once we dressed, he shook out the blanket and draped it over his arm. He held my hand all the back to the house.

When we entered through the French doors to my room, the bed loomed before us. I stepped into him.

"Do you want to stay here tonight?" I asked.

I could see the indecision and torment in his eyes. He kissed me softly. "I better not. It is your dad's house."

I snorted. "They're on the top floor – they won't know."

He kissed me again. "I don't think I should." He held me tightly against him and stroked my hair. "Get some sleep."

I nodded and stood on my toes to press a quick kiss to his lips. "Good night."

After he left, I hurried to my bathroom to shower and remove all the sand. When I finished, I curled in my bed, allowing my mind to think about what had just happened and what it meant. I just didn't have a clue.

Chapter 9

I woke slowly the next morning, relishing the feel of my bed. As I yawned and stretched, I realized that I'd done it again. I'd slept with Collin last night.

Jumping out of my bed, I paced up and down, gnawing on my lip. Okay, so I screwed up again – maybe. We'd both been sober – relatively. Sure we'd had a few drinks but not nearly as much as the first time. We had both been totally aware of what we were doing.

So, what did it all mean? Did Collin want to be with me? Or did he just want me? I knew I'd never find answers pacing the floor so I jumped in the shower and dressed. By the time I got down to the kitchen, Collin had already eaten breakfast with my father and was outside helping him to set up things.

"Morning, Bailey," Steffi greeted. She looked far too radiant and young to be turning thirty-six. "How was the party?"

"Interesting," I smirked, pushing the after party activities out of mind. "Collin pulled one on Veronica..." I stilled – my hand halfway to the plate of muffins sitting on the breakfast bar. "Damn. Damn."

"What?" Steffi asked, her perfectly plucked brow nearly in her hairline.

"Damn it," I cursed. I sank to a chair and explained how Collin had played doting boyfriend the night before. "But you see, some of those people will be at your party today."

"So?" Steffi frowned.

"So, me and Collin are going to have to continue the charade. And," I said, massaging my temple. "Damn. Morgan will be here. So will Spencer. How do you think they'll like seeing me and Collin all snug and cute and touchy-feely?"

Steffi sniggered. "I'm sorry, Bailey, honest, but damn, you do know how to get yourself into a mess, don't you?"

"That ain't the half of it," I groaned as I caught a glimpse of Collin out on the deck with Daddy. "And I'll tell you about it later."

I stood and headed for the French doors but Steffi grabbed my arm.

"Did you sleep with him last night?"

A smirk slipped on my lips. "I plead the fifth."

I slid out of her grasp and escaped to the deck.

"Good morning, sunshine," my dad greeted.

I rolled my eyes at him and peeked around the yard. "Where is Collin?"

"Unloading equipment from the van," Daddy said as he consulted with a caterer. "The DJ guy was here earlier and he talked to Collin about where to set up the stage and the sound stuff and everything technical that I'm too old and too stupid to understand."

"You're not the only one," I commiserated. I pecked his cheek. "I'm going to go see if Collin needs help."

I walked around to the front of the house and spotted his legs peeking out from under the open cargo doors of the van. My heart picked up an extra beat as I approached him.

"Need any help?" I asked.

When he spun around, his face brightened when he spotted me. I was so relieved to see no guilt in his eyes that I almost jumped in his arms. It was my guilt that was stopping me.

"Sure," he said, his sexy smile slipping into its rightful place. "You can carry the bass drum."

"Yeah, that's not going to happen," I smirked. "I was thinking more along the lines of carrying your drumsticks."

His smile faltered and he reached out to touch my hair. "Are you okay today, Bailey?"

"Sure," I said with forced cheerfulness. I'd spent a remarkable evening with the man I loved even though he didn't know I loved him and he probably didn't feel the same way. "I'm fine. How about you?"

He lifted a shoulder and grabbed my hand, tugging me closer. "I'm fine. And I know you're probably not anxious to let the others know about this so we can keep it to ourselves."

"Collin," I said as I placed a hand on his chest. "You're not going to go on another guilt trip, are you?"

"No," he said. "Promise."

I nodded and bit my lip. "Oh, hey. Guess what I realized this morning?"

He creased his brow. "What?"

"There are probably going to be quite a few people from the party last night at the party today. And since they think we're a couple..."

He nodded, smile on his face. "So I must play the attentive boyfriend, huh?"

"Yep," I said rolling to my tiptoes. "In front of them...and in front of Spencer."

I almost added Morgan's name but since he wasn't aware of Morgan's crush, I kept my mouth shut.

"Damn, I forgot," he said. He sat on the bumper and crossed his arms over his chest. "We'll just have to let them in on it when they get here," he said with a careless shrug. "We'll tell them it's just a ruse."

My heart plunged straight past my stomach. "Yeah, they'll understand."

He pulled on the collar of his t-shirt and pointed to the bite mark on his neck. "Of course I should probably keep this hidden from them like I had to do your dad."

"Damn," I said, only a little abashed. "Um, sorry?"

Chuckling, he ruffled my hair. "Are you going to help me or what?"

"Sure," I said with a faux smile. "As long as you don't give me anything heavy. I don't want to get all sweaty and smelly."

He laughed and a smile stayed on his face as I helped him unload his equipment. He carried all the heavy stuff, causing his muscles to strain and my pulse to quicken, although Daddy did come out to assist when he could.

Once we got everything on the stage, I helped him set up the drum kit, listening carefully as he explained the purpose of each piece and how it all went together. Once that task was finished, he patted the stool behind the drums and I sat down. He shoved the drum sticks in my hand and grinned.

"What am I supposed to do with these?" I asked as I held them in front of his face.

"Duh," he said. He squatted behind me and placed his hands over mine. "Here. Hold them like this."

He situated the sticks the proper way and guided my hands over the drums. We played a beat I recognized from one of the cover songs they did at Rusty's. His lips were very close to my ear making it hard for me to concentrate on his count.

"Awesome," he said when we finished. "You'll be a drummer yet."

I snorted. "Only if you do that for every song."

I took him into town for lunch and a brief tour. I wanted to get out of Daddy's hair because he was getting a little stressed at all the preparations and I knew only Steffi could calm him down.

We got back in time to see Irelyn and Lucas pull up followed closely by Morgan and Spencer in Morgan's car.

"And, here we go," I said as Collin parked the van.

I hopped out to greet my friends, perhaps a little more cheerfully than usual. I gave them all a tour of the house and showed them to the guest rooms.

Steffi and Daddy were in the kitchen, going over final plans when I gathered everyone together and introduced them. I watched Steffi's eyes as they shifted ever so slightly when I mentioned each person's name. She was matching the faces to the stories and figuring if she'd pictured that person right. I couldn't wait until later to find out how well she'd done.

"Let's go kick back on the deck before all the idiots get here," I said but caught Daddy's dark look. "I mean, all the guests."

Collin laughed and held the door open for us. Actually, the whole reason why I wanted everyone outside was so we could let them in on the joke. Or, so I could force Collin into telling everyone.

"This place is amazing," Morgan said. "Oh, I wish my parents lived up here."

"It is a great place," Spencer agreed. He gave me a wink and I had to draw courage from the deepest pit of my stomach.

"Okay, here's the deal," I said attracting everyone's eyes. "So, Collin and I crashed a party last night – a really lame party and not worth the effort –but still, it was a party."

Collin laughed in agreement. Irelyn's eyes darted from Collin to me and there was no doubting the speculation. Collin had mentioned once that Lucas had suspicions. Well, it seemed as if Irelyn had them, too.

"Anyway, my 'friend' was there..."

"She was no friend of yours," Collin interrupted. "A right bitch, this one," he explained to the others. "Thought I was going to have to throw Bailey over my shoulder and haul her away. She was ready to rip this Veronica in half."

I rolled my eyes. "Thanks for the rendition, drama queen."

Lucas cracked up and smacked Collin on the back.

"What Bailey is trying to tell you guys is that some of these people from the party last night will be here today," Collin said.

"So we need to keep a close eye on Bailey?" Morgan asked, her eyes sparkling. I made a mental note to ask her later what had happened while I'd been gone. Her moping mood had vanished. "That's not an unusual request."

"True," Collin frowned. "But actually, this Veronica said some pretty terrible things about Bailey and I sort of stepped in and told her I was Bailey's boyfriend."

Lucas snorted. "Dude..."

"What did she say about you?" Spencer asked.

I turned my eyes toward the lake. It was enough that Collin had to hear it, I didn't need the rest of them to know. "It doesn't matter."

Collin placed a hand on my shoulder.

"It wasn't nice," he told them, nearly growling. "So, anyway, they all think Bailey and I have a thing and we figured we'd better tell you guys before they all arrived and started talking about it."

"Sure," Lucas drawled.

Irelyn gave a curt nod as Morgan frowned.

"Okay," Morgan said.

Spencer couldn't stop laughing. "This is too funny."

"Try it on my end," I said, faking irritation.

Spencer's laughter increased as he strolled across the deck to take me in his arms. I buried my face in his chest and wrapped my arms around him, taking shelter in his embrace. It felt so safe and familiar. Once again, I wished that I'd have fallen in love with him but as safe and comforting as he was, he lacked the excitement and heart-pounding chemistry that I found just standing near Collin.

Spencer dropped a quick kiss to the top of my head. "We got your back, Bailey, don't worry."

I lifted my head to smile at him. "Thanks, Spence."

He winked, pressed a chaste kiss to my lips, and stepped back. "So, what time does this shindig start?"

"Soon," Collin said as he pulled a folded piece of paper out of his back pocket. "Here's a list of songs Steffi asked us to play."

The guys went over the list while I took the girls upstairs to freshen up for the party. Irelyn's lips were in such a tight line, she couldn't even apply her favorite lip gloss. And Morgan's peppy mood suddenly went into overdrive.

Guilt flooded me again and I was absolutely dying to confess, but I didn't want to hear the torrent of moral lectures that would come from Morgan's mouth and possibly Irelyn's. I knew I should just encourage them to speak their minds and get it over with but I didn't want them to rant and rave and put a damper on the party. I'd wait and let them do it tomorrow.

"Girls," Steffi said as she breezed into my bathroom. "I have to prepare you." She took a deep breath and fretted at me. "Your father just told me that he invited everyone in the neighborhood."

"Damn," I swore as I slammed my brush on the counter. "That means Veronica's dumb ass will be here."

"I know," Steffi said as she gave me a brief hug. "And Bailey please try to refrain from beating her up until after the party. Not that I would mind – I'd love to see her get what she deserves – but it would upset your father."

"Is she that bad?" Morgan asked, her eyes wide.

"She's a bitch," I spit as I leaned against the counter.

"Bailey's right," Steffi agreed.

"We'll keep Bailey out of trouble," Irelyn said with a too bright smile.

"Good luck with that," Steffi said doubtfully. She flashed a megawatt smile and breezed back out of the room.

"Let's go," I said as I flicked my hair over my shoulder. "All the idiots should be arriving."

***

The food was good, the DJ was great, and the guys were outstanding. They alternated with the DJ and hung out with us between sets.

Although quite a few people from Janie's party showed up – Veronica remained absent. That suited me just fine because I'd had more than my fair share of confrontations with her lately. And I was already on edge because of Irelyn and Morgan. Then, Collin would have to sit close to me – all part of the charade – and throw my equilibrium further off balance.

I couldn't even enjoy being Collin's fake girlfriend because every time he touched me, Irelyn stiffened and Morgan frowned.

Parties were really starting to suck for me.

Kora and her gang oohed and aahed over Lucas, Spencer, and Collin, dancing right up in front of the stage. Their antics only caused more tension for Irelyn and even more peppiness for Morgan.

And a huge headache for me.

The only bright spot was how much fun Steffi – and Daddy for that matter – seemed to be having. Steffi's friends raved over the band and even though they were quite a bit older than the guys, they eyed them just as flirtatiously as the younger girls. And the more alcohol they consumed, the friskier they became.

I slumped in a chair at the table I was sharing with Irelyn and Morgan as the guys played their final set, sipping a whiskey and coke, bored out of my tree.

My mind kept wandering back to the previous night when Collin and I were hidden in the dune grass, kicking up sand...

"There she is," Veronica whined in a nasally voice.

I yawned, swirled the liquid in my glass, and turned lazily to face her. "I knew I smelled something."

"Who are these girls?" Veronica asked, an evil smirk lurking on her lips. "More whores?"

That was all I could take. I jumped from my chair and snarled in her face. "You can mess with me all you want but don't mess with my friends, bitch."

Irelyn and Morgan were at my sides in an instant, each clutching an arm.

Veronica just laughed and waltzed away to the food table.

Shaking them off, I marched toward the house. They followed behind me and I sighed in exasperation as I strode into the kitchen to rip open the refrigerator door. I grabbed a beer and viciously twisted off the cap. I drank about a quarter of it before slamming the bottle on the counter.

"Stop looking at me," I growled. "I'm fine. I'll be good. I'll kick the shit out of her later."

"What is the deal with her?" Morgan asked, her face as pale as the white kitchen tiles.

"She's nothing more than a jealous, spiteful bitch, that's all." I picked up my bottle and sucked down some more. "And I'm tired of her mouth."

When the music stopped, I heard Lucas thank everyone and wish Steffi a happy birthday. I sighed as I finished the beer. I tossed the bottle into the recycle bin and headed for the door.

"The guys are done. Let's go back outside."

The girls nodded and trailed behind me.

"Bailey!" Lucas shouted as he yanked me into a hug. "You were about to kick some ass, weren't you?"

I wriggled out of his grasp and ignored Collin's pointed looks. "No. I'll bide my time."

"For what?" Veronica asked as she joined our group. "You'll bide your time until you can give the other two a turn?" She pointed at Spencer and Lucas.

"Nah," I said as my lips curled over my teeth. I looped an arm through Spencer's. "I already gave him a turn and Lucas there is in love with my best friend so he's out of the question."

She laughed wickedly. "Has that ever stopped you before?"

"Listen here, bitch," Spencer said as he took a step toward Veronica.

I placed a hand on his chest and shook my head. "Don't waste your breath on her – she's nothing. That's why she verbally attacks everyone – to make them look bad and herself look good."

'So, do your new friends know about your old nickname?" she asked as if I hadn't just insulted her. "Easy Lay Bailey?"

I laughed. "No, I didn't tell them."

She lifted a brow. "Too ashamed?"

"No," I snorted. "The nickname just sucks. You'd think that with your grades you would have more imagination and could come up with something better. Oh, wait – your father had to make a huge donation to the school to keep you from flunking out. Damn, almost forgot."

She puffed up like a stuffed turkey, turned on her heel, and nearly fled. I cracked a satisfied smile as I watched her through narrowed eyes. "What a dumb ass."

Collin squeezed my shoulder and a wave of tranquility washed over my body. "Are you okay, Bailey?"

"Sure," I said as I smiled at him over my shoulder. "Fine."

"Bailey, if you don't beat the living hell out her, I'll be highly disappointed," Lucas said as he held Irelyn against his side.

"I'll get her," I said as I pointed at the drink table. "Now let's drink."

The rest of the party went okay and Veronica pretty much disappeared. Irelyn and Morgan lightened up and we actually enjoyed the DJ's music. I relaxed after a few drinks and cherished Collin's subtle boyfriend act.

When the party finally wound down, we all retired to our rooms. Daddy's house had six bedrooms, besides the master suite, so no one had to double up. Of course, that didn't stop Irelyn and Morgan from storming into my bedroom as I was pulling on my pajamas.

"Problem with the accommodations, ladies?" I asked.

"Bailey," Irelyn hissed. "We saw the mark on Collin's neck. Just how much did you two act last night?"

"Oh," I said, scrambling for a lie while my face flushed in pleasure at the memory. "That was an accident. We were just horsing around, is all."

"Spencer saw it," Morgan said, her big eyes worried. "I can only imagine what he's thinking."

"Geez," I said, rolling my eyes. "He knows what's going on."

"Yeah, but he's not the only one who is going to be hurt by this," Irelyn said between clenched teeth.

Damn. Morgan. Damn. I sighed and plopped on the bed.

"We were dancing and Veronica was watching and we were laughing. I hid my face on his shoulder and I accidentally bit him. No big deal."

Morgan nodded, her brow furrowed. Irelyn just set her lips and left the room. Morgan shrugged apologetically before she followed.

"Damn," I swore. I shut off my light and fell into the bed. I stared at the ceiling, wondering what the hell to do. Twenty minutes later, a soft knock bolted me upright.

I heaved another sigh, this one in frustration, and stormed to the door. I ripped it open and gasped. "Collin?"

He pushed me into the room and shut the door. His eyes quickly roved over my rather revealing pajamas before he spoke. "So, yeah, I caught a little razzing from the guys about your bite, darling."

His eyes were teasing even though he wore a serious face.

"Bet it wasn't as bad as what I got from the girls," I said as I returned to the bed. "I'm in trouble."

"Why?" he said as he sank beside me, all teasing gone. "Bailey, what's the deal? They both seemed sort of pissed all night."

I shrugged and tucked my legs under my body. "They think all this is going to hurt Spencer. I can't blame them – they're probably right."

"Nah," Collin said. "I talked to Spence and he said it was cool – especially after he met Veronica."

"Don't worry about it," I said with a smile. "I'll talk to them both tomorrow.

I'll assure them that everything will go back to normal once we leave."

His eyes darkened as he nodded his head. "Okay. I'll let you get some sleep."

"Sure," I said. I stood and walked him to the door. "Thanks, Collin, for everything."

Cupping my face, he kissed me softly. "Get some rest, Bailey. Everything will look better in the morning."

With a wink, he slipped out the door.

I crawled back in my bed, feeling as if I could cry as hard as I had the day my mother died. I resisted and eventually drifted off into a restless slumber.

Chapter 10

The next morning was anything but cheerful. Everyone seemed eager to go back to Dalefield – except me. I kind of liked the nice little game of deception I had going here with Collin as my loving boyfriend and my friends ignorant of the whole scheme while they went on with life miles and miles away.

But, I was my father's child and I would not hide from my problems. I'd go back with the rest and meet all this conflict head-on. I'd start with Morgan.

"Morg," I said as we gathered on the deck for a quick breakfast. "Do you mind if I ride back with you? I mean, you are going back to the condo, right?"

If I hadn't been watching her so intently, I would have missed the quick look she gave Spencer before smiling warmly at me. "Sure, but Spencer rode up here with me and he needs a ride back home."

"He can ride back with me," Collin offered. "He can help me unload all the equipment and take me to drop off the rental van." He punched Spencer playfully in the arm. "You don't mind, do you?"

"Not at all," Spencer quipped. He fluttered his lashes at Collin. "Will you buy me lunch?"

Collin chuckled. "Sure, big guy. We'll stop on the way back and I'll buy you a kid's meal with a toy."

Irelyn sat silently next to Lucas, hardly touching her food or saying a word. She would be the easiest to crack, I knew, for I could see the restraint in her face. She was doing everything in her power to not blow up at the table.

Yeah, I'd have to deal with her later tonight.

We packed up our belongings, hung out with Daddy and Steffi for a bit, and finally hit the road late that morning. Steffi hugged me extra long so she could whisper in my ear.

"Tell them all the truth, Bailey. Tell each one of them the truth," she said. "You all need to hash this out and figure out where to go."

I nodded, composing my face before I stepped back, and pecked her cheek. "I'll call you later."

***

Morgan chattered happily as we drove, sandwiched between Collin's van and Luke's truck in our own little convoy. She talked about how cute Otis was and wondered what he'd weigh when he was full grown and how we should enroll him in obedience classes. I let her words wash over me as I tossed things around in my head, wondering if I should just ask her outright if she had a thing for Collin. I needed to tell her what had happened but I couldn't stand the thought of hurting her. She was so sweet – even if she had been suffering from a long, drawn out bout of PMS lately.

In the end, I decided it would be best to wait until we were home. I told myself it was because she was driving and I didn't want to distract her but in all actuality, I wanted to be in a position where I could escape if I had to. I would stand up to any fight and not back down from any bully – but I couldn't stand to see hurt on Morgan's gentle face.

Spencer called my cell when we reached the halfway home mark and suggested we all pull over at the nearest fast food joint to eat. I consulted with Morgan and we agreed.

Morgan parked in the lot of a burger joint. Everyone got out of their vehicles, stretching their legs. It was only a two and a half hour drive but for some reason, it seemed like a lot longer.

Collin's eyes sought mine after we got our food and found a big table. I raised a brow before dropping my head over my tray. The t-shirt he was wearing was loose and old – one he probably wore when he did heavy, dirty work – and occasionally, when I chanced a glance at him, I could see the bite mark peeking out from under the collar. My constant reminder of how good it could be if only I wasn't involved in a love triangle. No – it was more of a love circle – a vicious, blood thirsty one at that - and I was stuck in the middle like the little dot you placed the tip of your compass on when measuring circumference. And let me just say – I loathe anything to do with mathematics.

He sat there, all nonchalant with his brother and his cousin, and for some reason, it drove my heart insane. Just to watch him be – just to see him chatting normally with those around him made me love him even more.

I was seriously considering some heavy duty therapy.

We finished eating and hit the road again. The icy shoulder Irelyn had given me earlier that morning had worsened during lunch and made me long for a sweater. A thick one. And it was July!

When we finally got home, I dashed down the hall to fetch Otis. Mrs. Wesley wasn't eager to give him up but I promised her she could puppy-sit every time I needed her. She kissed Otis's furry head and reluctantly handed him to me. I cuddled him to my chest, stroking his soft fur while he wiggled and squirmed, wanting only to kiss my cheeks, and remembered the day Collin brought him here. I remembered how Collin and Morgan had shared that look and I wondered what had happened after that. Obviously nothing to make them a couple or else he wouldn't have…well, we wouldn't have had sex on the beach.

I sucked in a deep, cleansing breath as I stood outside the condo door, preparing to enter and fix this mess one way or another.

"Hello, sweetie," Morgan cooed as she eased the puppy from my arms. She sank to the floor and bestowed sweet kisses all over his face. I wandered to the refrigerator, stalling for time, and located a bottle of water from the back. I leaned against the counter, leg shaking in agitation, and pondered what to say to start the conversation.

"Screw it," I shrugged.

With a sigh, I went back into the living room and stood over Morgan. She glanced up at me, alarmed.

"Okay, Morg – cut the shit. You've been mopey for weeks then sunshine and rainbows all of a sudden. What the hell is going on?"

She dropped her eyes to Otis. "I don't know what you're talking about."

"Don't lie to me," I said. "We're friends."

She nodded slowly, patted Otis's head, and stood. "Yes, we are. Friends. And friends go out of their way to avoid hurting each other, right?"

"That's exactly right," I said, swallowing my guilt. "They try like hell, at least."

"So, why do you keep insisting on hurting Spencer?" she accused, her face glowing a bright red. "Do you know what you're doing to him?"

"Spencer?" I asked, stunned. "What about him?"

"Bailey, he was in love with you," she said. "And you just ended things without much of an explanation."

"Wait a minute," I said, holding up my hands. "Hang on – Spencer said everything was cool. He told me we were fine."

"Of course he did," Morgan said, her face growing a deeper, darker shade of red. "That's what he wants you to think. He doesn't want to hurt you!"

I rolled my eyes at her theatrics and gulped at my water. "If he's so hurt and so in love with me, then why does he act normal and all Spencer-like?"

"That's just it –it's an act," Morgan said.

"No, it's not," I said, anger brimming to the surface. "And I think I know Spencer just a little bit better than you."

"Maybe in the biblical sense," she said, her angry red turning into an embarrassed red. "But I've talked to him. I've talked to him a lot lately. He called me the day after you two broke up and cried on my shoulder."

"Seriously?" I whispered, stunned. She nodded. "Damn!"

My curse was so loud that it sent Otis scurrying under a chair, tail tucked between his legs.

"And then this boyfriend act with Collin over the weekend," Morgan threw in my face. "That was really the icing on the cake."

Pain deadened her eyes and weighed down my heart. Icing on whose cake – hers? Or Spencer's? Or both?

"I'm sorry, Morg," I said as I dropped my eyes from her face. "Really."

"Don't apologize to me," she said, her voice hard. "Bailey, I understand that you don't like Spencer that way and I think you were right to break things off with him. But when you said all that stuff about Collin pretending to be your boyfriend and then we saw that mark on his neck – that was going a little too far."

If only she knew...

"Why do you care so much?" I asked.

"Because I feel so sorry for him," she said. "He was so pitiful."

Just great. Heap more guilt on me – I can never have enough. "He should have talked to me. He should have told me how he was feeling."

"Why?" Morgan demanded. "Would you have taken him back?"

"Well, no," I admitted. "But I wouldn't have behaved certain ways."

"What ways?" she asked in a low, scary voice. "Like a whore?"

She could have hit me in the head with a crowbar and it wouldn't have packed quite the punch as her comment. I turned my head, bit back my retort, and then lifted my chin.

"Maybe," I whispered. "Maybe not. I need some air."

I grabbed my keys and my bag and stormed out of the condo.

***

Okay, so why was it a surprise to me to hear my best friend voice her opinion? Did I think that Morgan was the only person on the earth – besides my Daddy – that didn't think of me that way?

And what was this stuff with Spencer being in love with me? Surely, Morgan misunderstood. He'd never acted that way when we were together. He definitely never told me. There I was believing he was over me and that was one less person who would be hurt should anyone find out that I'd slept with Collin. Twice.

Running my hair through my fingers, I decided that I might as well confront Irelyn while I was on a roll. Maybe once she got all her yelling and screaming out of the way, I could talk to her and tell her what was really going on. I'd tried to help unburden her guilt a few months ago, maybe she'd help with mine.

I parked in front of her building, relieved that Lucas's truck was nowhere to be seen. It was getting close to dinner time so I didn't imagine he'd be gone long – all three of those boys had some sort of internal clocks that went off at meal times – never allowing them to miss a meal.

Irelyn met me at the door, phone in her hand. My heart fell to my feet – Morgan had beat me to her.

"I guess you've been talking to Morgan," I said as I brushed past her and entered the apartment.

"Yes," she hissed. "Damn it, Bailey, what is going on?"

"Go ahead," I smirked. "Get it out of your system."

"You knew that Spencer would be upset with this little Collin charade but did you even think about Morgan? I'm sure it broke her heart! And then the hickey…"

"It wasn't a hickey," I interrupted, trying to lighten the mood. "I did not suck on his neck. I just bit him."

"I'm glad you find this hilarious."

"Not particularly. My head has been a messed up jumble for a while now," I said.

Irelyn paused briefly in her tirade to study my face. I hoped she would see the sincerity and the guilt that had been hiding behind my eyes for weeks. I hoped she knew how truly sorry I was for everything that I had caused. I hoped she'd forgive me if I drew the courage to tell her about sleeping with Collin.

But her eyes hardened and gone was my understanding friend. Gone was the girl who'd been so confused and hurt and stressed last year – the very one that I'd done what I could to help. Apparently, she'd forgotten about all that in her anger.

"Why is your head all messed up?" she asked.

"It's a long story and you don't have the time," I said like a coward.

"I'll make time," she said. "I even chased Lucas out of the house after Morgan called because I figured you'd come here."

Hmm, maybe she might not totally side with Morgan. I sighed heavily. "It's not a pretty story and you might not like it a whole lot."

"Tell me," she said.

"Well, let's see. It started a few weeks ago when I discovered that I didn't really have feelings for Spencer any longer – that I sort of had them for someone else. Someone that I … well…I fell in love with," I said, avoiding her eyes.

But she was having none of that. "Bailey! You're in love with someone?"

"Geez, don't make it sound like a miracle. It could happen. It has," I said.

Giggling, she hugged me, easing me into a false sense of comfort. "Aww. Who is it?"

I drew back and bit my lip. "Does Lucas have any beer here?"

"Sure," Irelyn said. "Help yourself. But isn't it a little early? And do you know what - you've been drinking a lot lately."

"Don't preach," I growled. "I know I have been. I just need to sort things out then I'll concentrate on the drinking. Cut me a break."

"Okay," Irelyn said, softly. "Finish your story. Tell me who you're in love with. Does he love you, too? Does he even know?"

"Can I talk?" I asked, the bottle shaking ever so slightly in my nervous hand.

Irelyn nodded.

"Okay. So, I realize that things will probably never work between me and this guy but I know that I need to break up with Spencer because I don't want to lead him on."

I chanced a quick glance at her –not wanting to offend her after the ordeal she'd gone through with Dustin and Lucas, but wanting her to understand exactly why I'd ended things with Spencer.

"Okay, that's understandable," she said. "Go on."

"So, we all go to Rusty's the night after me and Spence split," I continued then took a swig of the beer. "And afterwards, we all went to Collin's place, remember?"

"Yes," she said slowly, narrowing her eyes. "I do. You stayed there after everyone left and got hammered with Collin."

"I'll say," I murmured under my breath.

She gasped as her hand flew to her heart. "No. Oh, damn. Oh, hell. Bailey, tell me you didn't!"

I lifted a shoulder and turned my head. "I could tell you I didn't but that wouldn't be true."

"Damn!" she cursed as she paced the living room. I could hear soft swears rumble from her lips and I knew Mount Irelyn was about to erupt. "Lucas said that you two slept together that night – he said he could tell by the way Collin was acting. But I didn't believe him. I didn't think you'd do that to Morgan."

"Hold on, now," I said as I reached out and grabbed her arm to stop her pacing. "In my defense, I had no idea that Morgan liked Collin at that time. If you'll recall, you told me the next day when I was scarfing down a greasy cheeseburger to cure my hangover. I didn't know until then."

Irelyn studied my face briefly then nodded. "Yeah, you're right. So, what, this night with Collin was just once – just a drunken thing?"

Before I could stop it, the truth fluttered across my face. Irelyn's eyes grew in horror.

"You've slept with him since?"

No use lying. "Once."

"After you found out that Morgan was in love with him?" she nearly screamed.

"Hell, yeah," I screamed back. "And I'm sorry, okay. So sorry. But she's not the only one who loves him!"

The silence was ten times louder than the cars that cruised the main strip with their rap music thumping and rattling windows. And the pause between us was like a tiny crack in our friendship. I wondered it if would expand or if we'd manage to seal it before it caused more damage.

"Irelyn, think about it," I pleaded. "Do you honestly think I'd do anything to purposely hurt Morgan?"

"I didn't think you would," she said avoiding my eyes. "When did you sleep with him again? Was it Friday night? Was it after he pretended to be your boyfriend?"

I refused to lie anymore. From now on, I'd be straight with both of them. "Yeah, it was."

"And you didn't think to use any restraint?" she said as she spun around to face me. "For Morgan's sake?"

"Did you?" I spit back at her. "Did you think to use restraint for Dustin's sake?"

I knew that was hitting below the belt but damn if I was going to let her do this to me. I'd been carrying enough guilt around with me to where I was going to need a wheelbarrow pretty soon. And even though I detested seeing the flicker of pain shoot through her eyes, I had to get my point across.

"My situation was totally different," she whispered. "And you told me you understood."

"I did," I said, my voice softening. "Now I'm asking you to understand. I love him, Irelyn. I truly love Collin. I'm not just messing around."

"Morgan loves him, too," she said, not budging from her earlier point. "Morgan who is too shy to say anything to anyone. Morgan who deserves to not have her heart broken."

"So that's just it, huh?" I asked as *my* heart broke. "That's the way you think this should go. You think I should just step aside and let Morgan take a shot at him?"

"Yes," she said, eyes on mine. "I do."

I nodded, my lips screwed up in thought. "I see. So, we'll all cheer on sweet little Morgan and hope that Collin feels the same way for her. It doesn't matter what Bailey feels though, right? Because Bailey's feelings don't really count."

"That's not true," Irelyn said, shaking her head. "That's not true at all. You and Morgan are two entirely different people – with different personalities."

"I got you," I said as my heart split down the middle. "I know, Irelyn, it's all right. I understand. Let's let the good girl get the good boy because everyone knows that the bad girl doesn't really love anyone anyway. Right?"

"Bailey," Irelyn tried to protest.

"Shut up," I barked. "Don't worry about me. You're right – sweet Morgan will never fall in love again but Bailey – shit, she'll have a new guy next week." I set the bottle down easily on the coffee table. "I need to get out of here for awhile. Don't worry, I won't say a word to Morgan or Spencer about when I had sex with Collin. We'll keep it a secret so no one gets hurt."

"Bailey, do not leave," Irelyn said. "We're not through here."

"I am," I said, my insides shaking. "I'm way through here."

I yanked the door open and jogged down the stairs, too agitated to wait for the elevator. I needed a real drink and a little space away from my friends. Things certainly hadn't gone like I'd thought they would and I needed to rethink my decisions. And my options. And my heart.

Chapter Eleven

Not sure what to do at that point, I returned to the condo. I braced for Morgan's explosion but all was quiet when I opened the door. Well, except for Otis's excited yips drifting in from the kitchen.

"Morg, are you here?" I called as I paused in the mouth of the hallway. Nothing.

With a shrug, I went into the kitchen to release Otis from his crate. He jumped on my legs, happy barks emitting from his mouth.

"How about a walk?" I asked as I located his leash. His barks grew higher in pitch.

I clipped the leash to his collar and let him pull me out the door.

As I walked, my mind wandered, rolling through recent events. I realized that everything had started falling apart after that first night with Collin.

"No, that's not true," I mumbled to myself as Otis paused to sniff a fire hydrant. "It started falling apart after I figured out that I was in love with Collin."

A wry smile drifted across my face. I'd known all along that love was nothing but a hassle. Look what had happened to Irelyn and that she'd gone through last year? And now this.

Tiring of the fire hydrant, Otis yanked on the leash, urging me forward. My feet followed while my mind was still lost in some crazy world.

I'd been stupid to think that I could easily fall in love and live happily ever after. I'd never been that type of person. People certainly didn't look at me that way. I was Bailey, the chick that flitted from man to man, never settling down. When I tried, I just wreaked havoc on those around me, leaving pain and anger in my wake.

"That's just it," I said as Otis finally found an acceptable spot to do his business. "I need to stop this insane idea that I'm in love and go back to the way I used to be. I'll go out tonight and find someone to help me forget Collin and everything else."

With a plan in mind, I dutifully cleaned up after the dog and coaxed him back to the condo.

***

After a long, pampering bath, I dressed in a short skirt and a white halter. I shoved my feet in two inch stilettos, painted my face, and brushed my hair into a sleek, dark curtain down my back. Satisfied with my appearance, I grabbed my phone, bag, and keys before heading out the door.

Not wanting to go to Rusty's, even if it was open on a Sunday, I decided to head to the outskirts of town. I had to use my phone to give me directions to the little club Spencer had talked about several times but had never taken me to it.

The Tail Feather Club was a story building with a gravel parking lot and not a whole lot of charm. The outside was sided like a house and could almost pass for one except for the gaudy neon sign of a chicken shaking its tail feathers blinking in the window.

It took my eyes a few minutes to get accustomed to the dim, smoky interior, but once they did, I was able to make my way to the horseshoe bar in the center of the room. Taking a seat, I turned to check out the dance floor near the back but several wood pillars obstructed my view. I had to lean to my left to see the sparse group out on the floor, enjoying the beat of some unfamiliar tune blaring from the jukebox.

To my right was a wooden staircase leading to the second floor. I could only wonder what was up there as a rope was stretched across the bottom step with a sign warning customers that only employees were allowed to cross.

"Can I get you something?"

Glancing over my shoulder, I smiled at the young guy tending the bar. He was sort of cute in a big, bulky way.

"Whisky and soda, please," I said with a wink.

The corners of his mouth turned up as he nodded. He mixed my drink with professional care and slid it to me. I paid him as I turned back to the bar to take a sip.

"Nice place," I said.

He lifted a shoulder. "It's all right."

"How is it open on a Sunday?" I asked.

He pointed over his shoulder at a door next to the staircase. "Kitchen. We serve a lot of food on Sundays."

"I see," I said. My eyes darted to the tables that were near the kitchen door. Several people sat, eating burgers and other bar type of foods. My stomach gave a tiny grumble but I wasn't interested in that sort of sustenance.

"What's a pretty girl like you doing here alone?" the bartender asked.

I lifted a brow, amused. "Is that a pickup line?"

"No," he said rather quickly. "I just hate to see nice girls in a place like this alone. A lot of sharks in the water, if you know what I mean."

Laughing, I reached over the bar to pat his hand. "I appreciate your concern but I can take care of myself."

He grinned as he plucked a cigarette out of a pack and lit it. "I'm sure you can."

I nodded at the pack he'd set on the bar. "Can I bum one? I haven't smoked in awhile but I think a cigarette would be mighty fine right now."

Picking up the pack, he offered me one. Once I pushed it in my mouth, he lit it for me, too.

"Thanks," I said. "What's your name?"

"Scooter," he said. "And you are?"

"Bailey."

"Nice to meet you, Bailey," he said, shoving an ashtray between us. "Now, are you going to tell me what you're doing here?"

"Slumming," I said, inhaling smoke that burned my chest. I tried not to cough. I'd never been a regular smoker and it had been awhile since I'd last had one, but this was really ridiculous.

"You're too pretty to be slumming," he said with such honesty that I actually believed he wasn't just trying to pick me up.

"Thanks. You're sweet," I said.

Before he could answer, a hand landed on my shoulder. "Well, look who decided to grace this place with her royal presence."

I set my cigarette in the ashtray before turning around to face Owen. "Like I told Scooter, here - I'm slumming."

Owen's smile lit up his face. He really was quite attractive - for a slimeball. "So glad you decided to slum in my place."

"Sure," I said as I rolled my eyes.

"Scooter, this beautiful young lady drinks on the house," Owen said. I didn't hear Scooter's reply.

"Thanks," I said as Owen took the barstool next to me. "I forgot that you own the place."

"It was my father's," he explained as he nodded to Scooter. "I take care of it now."

"Excellent," I said although I could care less. Still, he could probably prove to be a means to an end if I had the urge...

"Where are all of your friends?" Owen asked as his eyes scanned the bar. "Especially that cute, sweet quiet one? What was her name - Morgan?"

My skin crawled at the thought of him anywhere near Morgan. "She's not here."

His eyes danced in delight as he moved closer, a lecherous smirk on his face. "Is someone a little jealous? Huh? Does someone have a thing for little Owen?"

"I don't know who someone is but I'm guessing no," I said as I picked up my cigarette and took a drag.

He laughed as he placed a hand on my knee. "Ah, one of those hard to get chicks. That's okay - makes everything more fun."

I smashed my cigarette in the ashtray and blew the remaining smoke in Owen's face. "Where's the ladies' room?"

Still grinning, he pointed to the other side of the staircase. I waggled a couple fingers at him as I made my escape. I needed to regroup.

Once inside the sanctity of the ladies' room, I gripped the edges of the sink as I stared at my reflection in the mirror. My dark hair was immaculate but my hazel eyes held a look of sadness. I hated that. I needed to rid my body of all self-pity. Perhaps Owen was just the thing.

After washing my hands, I reapplied my lip gloss and reentered the bar. When I returned to my seat, Owen's glass was there but he was absent.

"Bailey."

I blinked as I met Scooter's worried eyes. He refilled my drink, glancing to the left and right.

"Stay away from him," he whispered as he leaned over the bar. "He's bad news. He treats women like crap."

I took the fresh drink from Scooter with a smile. "Thanks, hon, but I can take care of myself."

"I know you can," he said, anxiety all over his face. "But I've seen the girls that he's brought in here and I've seen what he does to them. He destroys them, Bailey. I mean, he really tears them up. He uses them in worse ways than you can imagine and when he gets bored with them, he just throws them away without a second thought."

Morgan flittered through my mind and I wondered, if Owen ever actually pursued her, if she'd be smart enough to stay away from him.

"Thanks for the warning," I said. "But I have no intentions of letting that man ever do anything like that to me. I'm not the one man sort of girl."

His frowned drew deep lines in his forehead. "I don't see that. You look like a nice girl to me. That's why I don't want you getting mixed up with...you know."

His lips tightened as he edged back, grabbing dirty glasses from the end of the bar. Just then, Owen sat next to me again, placing a hand on the small of my back.

"Everything okay, darling?"

"Just peachy," I said as I tossed back my drink. "How about a shot of something good?"

Owen's white teeth sparkled as he grinned wide. "That's my girl." He motioned at Scooter. "Give me a bottle of tequila and two glasses. And not the cheap stuff, either. Bring us something good."

Scooter nodded as he rushed off to do Owen's bidding. He returned a short time later, setting a bottle on the bar, pushing shot glasses in front of us both. Owen poured and then gestured for me to lift my glass. I did.

"To good times," he said.

"Good times," I repeated and then downed the shot.

"Smooth," Owen said, slamming his glass on the bar. He refilled us immediately.

It didn't take long to get my head spinning out of control - especially after countless shots. My wits definitely weren't about me but I knew, the longer I was around Owen, that I didn't want to use him in any way. He was just too creepy.

"Let's dance," he asked, tugging me off my barstool. I followed him to the floor and allowed him to pull me close. He wrapped his arms around me, his hands inching closer and closer to my hind end.

"Watch it, buddy," I tried to warn but the liquor slurred my words, making them ineffective.

"You are so hot, Bailey," he whispered, his breath warm on my cheek. "I wanted your friend, Morgan, but you are so much more woman than she could ever be."

"Nah, she's so much better than me," I said, fisting his shirt to keep from slipping out of his arms and crumbling to the dance floor. "Better."

He laughed as his hands slid further down. "I don't know about all that. Sure, those nice girls are fine, but when you want to have a good time, that's when you hook up with women like you."

My fuzzy mind wasn't sure exactly what he was saying. "What do you mean? Like...a whore?"

His laughter increased. "Call it what you will, but whore is an ugly word. I prefer 'fun girls'. I think it has a nice ring."

"So, I'm a fun girl and not a nice girl?" I asked.

His smile faltered. "I'm sure you're nice, too." He nodded over my head. "How about we go upstairs and you can show me how fun and nice you are?"

"But the sign said no one can go up there," I said.

His eyes crinkled in amusement. "Everyone knows that the upstairs is for those who want to have fun. Do you want to have fun?"

"I don't think so," I said as I wriggled out of his embrace. "I think I need to go home."

He followed me back to the bar where I located my bag. "Oh, come on, Bailey. You know you want to go up there. Spencer told me that the two of you were never serious - that you'd go out for awhile and split up and then get back together. I know girls like you get bored. I don't mind. I'll show you a good time and then you can come back anytime you want."

I had to get out of there. His words were tearing a hole in my already fragile heart. "Thanks, but I need to go."

"Suit yourself," he said with a shrug and an angry glint in his eye. He leaned closer. "But you'll be back. Girls like you always are." He stalked away, drink in hand, and I released a breath.

"Are you all right, Bailey?" Scooter asked.

I nodded as I retrieved my phone and keys from my bag. "Yeah. I just need to go home."

"I don't think you should drive," he said.

He was probably right. The problem was, who to call. My two best friends hated me, Spencer would have a fit, and Collin...well, Collin seemed to be my only bet. With a sigh, I dialed his number.

"Bailey," Collin said. "Where are you?"

"Tail Feather Club," I slurred. "Can you come get me?"

He swore vehemently, making me wince. "I'm on my way. Stay away from Owen, do you hear me? Don't let that bastard lay a finger on you."

"Yeah, okay," I said. I hung up my phone and slumped on the bar. "Here."

I looked up to see Scooter sliding a cup of coffee under my nose.

"Thanks, Scooter," I said as I sipped the strong brew. "You're too nice to work here."

He winked. "Did you call someone to come get you?"

I nodded. "Yeah. He's on his way."

"That's good. Just sit here by me until he gets here," Scooter ordered. "I'll keep an eye on you."

I was so tired of people - especially men- trying to take care of me. But Scooter, he was different. Sweet.

"Thanks, Scooter."

It took Collin nearly twenty minutes to get there but I still hadn't sobered up, although Scooter kept feeding me coffee.

"Bailey," Collin sighed when he found me. He lifted a brow at Scooter. "Does she have a tab?"

"She's taken care of," Scooter said. "Just get her home safely."

"Thanks, man," Collin said as he wrapped an arm around my waist. He helped me to his SUV and buckled me in. "How are you feeling?"

"Not very wonderful," I said as I rested my cheek against the cool glass of the passenger door window. "Not very wonderful at all."

"I'll take you to my place, okay?" he said. "I don't want to leave you alone in this condition."

"Sure," I said as I drifted on a wild sea of drowsiness. I slipped under for what seemed like seconds but the next thing I knew, Collin was shaking me gently, ordering me to wake up.

"Come on, Bailey," he said as he eased my body out of the car. "Let's get inside."

Once we stepped into the living room, my stomach rolled and I made a mad dash to the bathroom. I heaved nothing but tequila - everything burning my throat on the way up, tears slipping from my eyes.

Once I flushed, Collin materialized. "Better?"

"Not much," I admitted. I stood on wobbly legs. "I need a shower, I think."

With a slight nod, he closed the lid of the toilet, made me sit, and left the bathroom. He came back seconds later with two towels.

He turned on the shower, fiddling with the water until he got the temperature just right, and then turned back to me.

"Let's get you undressed."

"I like the way you think," I said, my head woozy.

"I know," he replied as he helped me up and undressed me.

He quickly shed his clothes and assisted me into the shower. Holding me up under the spray, he kissed me.

"Thanks for this," I said. "It's not very sobering but I've been fantasizing about showering with you for awhile now." I hiccupped. "Of course in my fantasies, I wasn't drunk and there was a lot more rubbing and suds involved."

"Some other time, then," he said, holding me closer. "Promise."

My hands slid up his chest to connect behind his neck. I rolled to my toes to press a kiss to his lips. "How about now?"

He kissed me back, a chaste kiss, and shook his head. "Now is not a good time."

My heart wilted. "I understand."

"No you don't," he said, giving me a squeeze. "I can see it in your face. Bailey, trust me when I say that I want you very much right now, but you're very drunk and I don't think it's a good idea. I'd rather not take advantage of you in this condition."

I tried to smile but my lips refused. Instead, a torrent of tears escaped my eyes.

"Bailey," Collin said, hugging me to his chest while rubbing my back. "Don't do that. I promise you that some other time, we'll definitely try the shower thing. I'm not putting you off - I just don't want to do anything like that while you're drunk."

"It's not that," I muttered between sobs. "I...this is all a mess."

"It seems like that now," he soothed. "But it's all right, really. We'll get this mess sorted."

I couldn't speak - could only sob. I was faintly aware of Collin shutting off the water and wrapping us both in towels. He led me to his bedroom where he dressed me in one of his t-shirts before tucking me in his bed.

My tears began to subside as he crawled in beside me. I burrowed into his side.

"Bailey, please don't cry," he said.

"Sorry," I muttered.

He stroked my hair as I tried to compose myself. "What's with the tears?"

I shook my head. "I'm not a whore, Collin."

"Of course not," he said, dropping a kiss to the top of my head. "I know you're not. All of your friends know you're not, too."

"I think deep down my friends *do* think that," I said. "I think deep down everyone thinks that there's not much Bailey wouldn't do."

He held me tighter, pressing my ear against his chest. I could make out every beat of his heart. "I don't believe that, Bailey. I don't think you're like that at all. I think there's a lot of fire inside of you, but I don't think you spread that fire out."

I had to chuckle at that. It was cute. And sort of sweet.

"Thank you, Collin."

"You bet," he said, kissing the top of my head again. "You need to get some sleep."

My eyes fluttered shut as my muscles started to relax. Collin's arms loosened but didn't drop away from me.

"I want people to know the truth," I mumbled.

"The people who are closest to you don't need to know the truth," he said. "We know the *real* Bailey and we like her just the way she is."

In the dark, I smiled as I drifted away in an alcohol induced slumber.

Chapter Twelve

Consciousness threatened to expose my very nauseous body to supreme torture. I grabbed a pillow and held it over my head to soften the blows that were hammering away inside it. I didn't know why I always thought drinking excessively would solve my problems – all it ever did was get me into more trouble and make me horribly ill the next day. Too bad I always forgot that important lesson when I hit the bars. What an idiot.

The previous evening rolled through my head like some stupid movie stuck on repeat. Another thing about my drinking binges was that I always remembered everything. That came in handy most times – but other times, not so much.

I remembered the shower with Collin and my heart leapt. I also remembered trying to seduce him but he'd turned me down. I hoped he hadn't been lying when he'd said it was due to the fact that I was totally shit-faced.

There was no getting around the headache so I decided to just get up and deal with it. Hopefully it would fade to a subtle throb if I got up and moved around a bit. I tossed the blankets back and stumbled to the bathroom.

I balked at my reflection and it didn't take a rocket scientist to figure out why Collin had chosen to not stay in bed with me. My hair was wild and tangled and just a mess. My eyes were bloodshot and puffy and my face splotchy. I didn't even want to think about my breath – I could taste it and that was nasty enough.

I turned on the taps, washed my face, and then dug a comb out of one of the vanity drawers. I had no clue where my clothes were – they were no longer on the bathroom floor. With a shrug, I exited the bathroom through the door that led to the spare bedroom and tiptoed through the living room. I stopped cold when I heard Collin's voice.

"..quit making excuses, Tori," he said, frustrated.

"I'm not," Tori whined. "Not at all. It's just that…well, geez Collin. I don't want to talk about this."

"Well I do," he said firmly. "I want to know what the deal is."

I plastered my back against the wall, hating that I was eavesdropping but unable to stop. It was morbid curiosity – kind of like a car wreck; you didn't want to look but you couldn't help yourself.

"Why is Bailey here, huh?" she demanded. "What's going on there?"

"I told you," he groaned. "She needed me last night and I brought her back here to take care of her."

"And yet you claim there's nothing going on there. That's the pot calling the kettle black."

"When you're done with the cliché sayings, can we get back to our discussion?" he asked.

I didn't want to hear anymore – I'd heard enough. I crept back to the bathroom and paced the small floor. What the hell was Tori doing there and what had I almost interrupted? And did I honestly want to know? It was obvious that he didn't think there was anything going on between us or else he was too ashamed to admit to Tori about our ... whatever kind of thing we had. Or didn't have.

I heard a door shut so I hurriedly turned the taps back on – just in time, too.

"Hey, Bailey," Collin called from the other side of the door. "You all right in there?"

"Peachy," I called over my shoulder, wincing as pain flashed through the front of my brain. "Be out in a second."

"Okay. I'll have the three T's ready for you," he said as his footsteps faded away from the door.

I had no clue what the three T's were but he had certainly aroused my curiosity. I dried my hands on a towel and made my way to the kitchen. I sank to a chair and Collin grinned as he slid a cup of tea in front of me.

"Okay, I'll bite. What are the three T's?" I asked as I blew the steam off the tea.

"Tea, toast, and Tylenol," he shrugged as he buttered the toast that had just popped in the toaster. He set it on a plate and dropped it in front of me. He pointed at a couple of tablets. "Eat your toast then swallow those. Afterwards, if you feel like you can handle it, I'll make you some eggs or something."

"This is fine," I said. "Thanks. Don't you have to work?"

"I took a vacation day." He held up a hand before I could protest. "I have accumulated a ton of vacation time – I need to burn some of it up."

He sat across from me, his eyes searching my face. His scrutiny made me fidget in my chair. I hated that he could see the blotches and the puffy eyes because I hated to cry. And the fact that I'd cried in front of him made me want to hide under my bed like a frightened child.

"So," he asked as he twirled a coffee mug on the table between his hands. "Do you want to tell me what the hell is going on?"

I froze, toast halfway to my mouth. "Um, what?"

"I know about the arguments you had with Morgan and Irelyn," he admitted. "Lucas told me. But neither one of us knows what these arguments were about." He smiled sweetly and it swept my heart up in a flittering bundle. "I do have an idea, though."

"Do you now," I said, unable to resist a smile of my own. "Tell me then."

"Well," he drawled as he sipped his coffee. "I think Morgan, being as moral as she is, wasn't happy with the fake boyfriend bit and went off on you. You, not wanting to argue with her, left and went to see Irelyn. Irelyn was probably pretty much on the same page as Morgan and was upset with you, also, because they both think that Spencer was upset by our little act." He pushed his mug out of the way and leaned over the table as his smile widened. "How did I do?"

I picked up the tablets, popped them in my mouth, and washed them down with my cool tea. "Not too bad. But you're missing a few facts. Pertinent facts."

"Oh?" he asked, brow lifted. "Care to share?" He tipped his chair back, considering me as I summoned the nerve I'd need to get through the entire episode.

"Morgan's pissed at me because of the boyfriend act," I started. "But that's not all." I pushed the half eaten toast away. "Can I have some coffee? Tea's not really my thing."

"Sure," Collin said, dropping his chair back to four legs. He got up to fetch a fresh mug from the cabinet and filled it for me. "Anything in it?"

"No, thanks," I said, smiling my thanks when he slid the cup to me. I wrapped my hands around it. "Morgan told me that Spencer called her the day after we split. She said Spencer more or less cried on her shoulder."

I ducked my head, sipping my coffee.

"Seriously?" Collin asked in disbelief. "Because, no offense, he just didn't seem that upset. Luke didn't think he was, either."

"According to Morgan he was and he was just acting like he wasn't for my benefit. I guess yours, too, if Morgan is right," I said.

"So, Morgan is mad at you because Spencer was hurt by your breakup?" Collin asked.

"Yeah," I said slowly. "But I think there's a little more to it than that."

"Like what?"

Loyalty urged me to keep my mouth shut and not betray Morgan. But, on the other hand, I didn't think it would hurt. Hell, maybe it would help if he knew how Morgan felt. Well, it would help Morgan, possibly. Me, though, it would definitely put me in a bad light. Would Collin think worse of me for sleeping with him while my best friend was in love with him? It was bad enough I'd done it while his cousin was still harboring feelings for me.

The only thing left to do was to put it all on the table – air the dirty laundry. I'd come clean – sort of. He really didn't need to know what my feelings for him were. I could keep that little secret to myself for the time being.

"Irelyn and I both think that Morgan…has…feelings…for you."

His jaw fell far enough that it nearly scraped the floor. His eyes bored into mine, incredulity blazing inside his pupils. "No. No way."

I lifted a shoulder and turned my head. "It sort of makes sense – if you think about it."

"Huh," Collin said as he ran his hands through his hair. He glanced nervously at me. "I don't, you know, like her like that. I mean, I think she's sweet and a great person but I never thought of her that way."

Inside my body, my emotions were waging a war. One part of me was mourning for my friend's lost love but the other part was celebrating. My stomach rolled and I nearly fled to the bathroom.

"Do you know what I always thought?" Collin continued, still recovering from the bomb I'd dropped. "I always thought she had a thing for Spencer."

It was my jaw's turn to fall. "What?"

He nodded, a helpless smile flitting across his lips. "Yeah. I caught her staring at him a few times – especially when you and Spence were still together."

"Oh, shit," I muttered. "Maybe you're right. Maybe that's why she's so mad at me for hurting him."

"Makes sense," he agreed. "So, what are you going to do?"

"No clue," I shrugged. "Try to talk to her again."

He offered no additional solutions. He stood to refill his coffee cup and brought the pot over to top mine off. "What happened with Irelyn?"

"That one was really ugly," I said. "Not pretty at all."

"So fess up. Tell me what happened," he said.

"She got on me about the boyfriend thing, too," I said. "A little harder than Morgan because she said not only had I hurt Spence but I'd hurt Morgan, too."

"Did you tell either of them that it was my idea?" he asked, a flicker of anger in his eyes. "And that I had a big part in this whole thing?"

My heart flipped at his chivalry. "Well, I think they blame me most of all because I had the lowdown on people's feelings and you didn't. You didn't know that Morgan had a thing for you."

"Still," he sighed. "It's not right for them to put this all on your shoulders. It's as much my fault as yours."

"Sweet, Collin, really, but I can handle it. It will all work out somehow."

His jaw tightened and his lips clamped together before he nodded. "What did Irelyn have to say?"

"She just reamed me for the mark on your shoulder," I said with a grin. "And she sort of figured out what happened between us."

He snorted a feeble laugh. "Lucas has been riding me – asking me what happened between the two of us. I didn't tell him anything but I didn't have to – he knew. I don't think he's said anything to anyone…"

"He told his suspicions to Irelyn. She told me that."

His lips puckered in thought. "Figures he would. Sorry about that," he said, his eyes grave.

"Nah, don't worry about it. When Irelyn asked me about it, it was hard to deny." I took a long drink of my lukewarm coffee. "She was pissed, of course – especially when she figured out that we'd slept together the night before Steffi's party."

"Who the hell is she to judge?" he asked, anger swiftly sweeping his face. "I mean, who judged her when she was screwing my brother and her boyfriend?"

I held up a hand to stop his rant, touched that he'd defend me so. "Yeah, I brought that point up, too, and it didn't go over well."

He shook his head in disgust. I didn't want that, though. I didn't want him angry at Irelyn for voicing her opinion. I knew Irelyn and I knew we'd talk once she cooled off. Besides, if Collin were to say anything to Irelyn it could possibly lead to an argument between the two brothers. It was horrible enough that there might be bad blood between Collin and his cousin if Spencer were to find out about all this.

"Collin, don't get all pissed at Irelyn, okay? She and I will straighten it all out. I said some things and she said some things – it wasn't just her."

"All right," he agreed reluctantly. "But I'm not liking this, Bailey. Not in the least. They're supposed to be your friends. Hell, I remember you defending Irelyn when she was still with Dustin and seeing Lucas on the side. She could extend you the same courtesy."

"The situations are a little different but I do agree," I said as I finished my coffee. "But I know Irelyn and I know that she won't be able to stay mad for long. She'll think about things and turn up and we'll talk. It will all work out somehow."

"I hope so," he said.

"Collin, please, for me, don't say anything to her or to Lucas. I don't want you and your brother fighting. Okay?"

He flashed a crooked smile. "Sure. Whatever you want."

I beamed. "What I want are my clothes so you can take me to get my car."

His smile morphed into an impish grin. "Maybe I hid them so you had to parade around my house in nothing but a t-shirt."

My heart ricocheted off all my other organs and my blood began to boil under my skin so badly I thought bubbles would form on my arms. I lowered my lids and plastered a seductive smile on my lips. "If I wasn't feeling so horrible, I'd slam you on this table."

His grin widened. "Interesting." Rising out of his chair, he walked around the table to plant a kiss on my forehead. "Your clothes are folded neatly in the bedroom. Go ahead and change and I'll take you to get your car."

***

I hated to leave him – his teasing had turned the key and unlocked my desire – hangover or not. But I needed to get home so I could talk to Morgan. I really wanted to settle things with her and I was especially curious to see if she did have feelings for Spencer and not Collin like Irelyn thought.

I unlocked the door and found her sitting primly on the sofa reading a paperback. She marked her page and set the book aside as I dropped my bag and sank to a chair.

"Hey, Morg," I said.

"Bailey," she said as if she were the reverend's wife being forced to greet the town hussy. "Are you all right?"

"Sure," I said, waving away her concerns. "Fine. I just went out and got loaded – partied pretty hard. I couldn't drive so I called Collin to come get me. I figured he was the only one not mad at me." Her eyes dropped guiltily to the floor. "And he let me crash at his place. But don't worry – I didn't sleep with him this time."

"Don't be so crude, Bailey," she chastised.

"Tell me, Morgan, exactly why you're so mad at me," I challenged. "Why do you care so much if I hurt Spencer?"

"Because he's a sweet person," she said, her eyes avoiding my face. "You didn't hear him on the phone."

"Why didn't he talk to me about it? Or Collin or Lucas? Why you?"

"I don't know," she said, finally finding my eyes. "I think he's too proud. He didn't want the other boys to know how hurt he was."

"So, he could have talked to me," I said. "I'm not a heartless bitch."

"He is so crazy about you," she shouted. "And you threw him away - again. You always do that!"

"How the hell do you know?" I asked. "Huh? Spencer is the only guy I've dated since you and I met! You don't know how I've been in the past."

"I know enough," she said.

"Oh?" I said, raising a nonchalant brow. "Really? How?"

"How?" she repeated. "Just listening to you talk. You're the one who brags about men you've been with."

Maybe I had told them about a couple of the guys I'd dated in high school but I never thought that I'd bragged. I'd only wanted to impress them, though. They'd both laugh me out of the room if they knew the honest truth – just how many there'd actually been.

"Are you in love with Collin?" I blurted.

"Collin?" she asked, blinking rapidly. "No. What gave you that idea?"

I laughed and drew a dark look from her. "Sorry but Irelyn was under the impression that you were in love with him."

"No. Not at all," she admitted in a small voice.

"So, it's Spencer. He's the one you're in love with, right?" I asked.

Her cheeks turned a lovely shade of pink – one that would make roses jealous. "Maybe."

"You're mad at me because I hurt the man you love," I concluded. "Makes sense but why the hell didn't you talk to me about this?"

"How could I? You were dating him!"

"I mean afterwards," I said. "We could have figured this out."

"No, we couldn't. It doesn't matter, anyway. He doesn't want me – not after having you."

My heart sank to my shoes. How unfair. I'd hurt Spencer and in turn hurt my best friend. Life couldn't really suck much more at the moment. "Morgan, I…"

"Oh, save it," she said. "There's really not much you can say."

"And what was I supposed to do? Huh? If I would have stayed with him to spare his feelings then he wouldn't have gone out with you, either – because we would have been together," I tried to explain. "And holy shit, why is he so upset? We weren't supposed to be serious."

"Well he was," she defended.

"That's not my fault," I answered. "Not in the least. I can't help the way he feels for me anymore than I can't help that I don't feel the same way."

"I know that," she said.

"Then why are we arguing?" I asked.

She paused like she had to remember what the point of the whole argument was. Her chest heaved as angry breaths shuddered her insides. She swiped at her brow and closed her eyes. "The point is not how you feel about him or whether you should be with him. If you don't have feelings for him then you did the right thing by breaking up with him." She opened her eyes and met mine. "But this whole act with Collin upset him – I could tell. And then the hickey…"

"Bite mark," I corrected.

She rolled her eyes. "Whatever. Well, tell me the truth, Bailey – did you sleep with him?"

I wouldn't lie. I had to tell her the truth and get it out of the way. There was no way in hell we'd be able to fix our friendship if I lied to her. "Yes, I did."

She scowled and flopped back into the sofa. She pinched the bridge of her nose as if stopping it from bleeding. "Does Spencer know?"

I snorted. "I'd think you'd know that before me."

She opened her eyes and glared. "That's not funny."

"Didn't mean it to be," I said in a firm voice. "I don't know if he knows. I just figured if he did, he would have told you. He's obviously been confiding in you."

"He hasn't mentioned it," she said.

"Both me and Collin agreed that he shouldn't know right now," I said.

"I'm not telling him," she snapped.

I softened. "You really love him, don't you?"

"It doesn't matter," she said and ducked her head. "Not now."

I chuckled and gained a confused look from Morgan. "Irelyn thought you were in love with Collin. She even convinced me you were."

She straightened as her brows dipped over her eyes. "You thought I was in love with Collin?" I nodded. She scooted to the edge of the sofa as understanding then hurt flamed in her eyes. "And you still slept with him?"

My heart freaked and pounded furiously as though trying to knock some sense into me. It needn't have worried – I realized how stupid I was to open my mouth. "Hey, I didn't know you were in love with him – Irelyn told me the next day."

Her lips pulled into a thoughtful frown as she slowly nodded. "So, that was the first time?"

"I…" I said as I gawked at her open-mouthed.

"But you slept with him the night before Steffi's party, didn't you? When you *bit* him." She cocked her head and waited for my answer.

I blew a long breath of air. "Yeah."

She jumped to her feet. "Damn it, Bailey. How could you do that?"

"Hang on," I said as I, too, stood. "You don't love him – you just said so."

"That is totally beside the point! You didn't know that. You thought I was in love with him and you *still* slept with him! How could you do that?"

My head was spinning wild circles. I could see exactly what she meant but then I couldn't. I was at a total loss for words and at a loss for what to do. "Morg…"

"Save it!" she screamed as she stormed across the room. "Just…ugh!" She jerked the door open and let it slam behind her.

I sank into the chair, my hangover headache reappearing with a vengeance. What the hell was I going to do now?

Chapter Thirteen

I mulled the argument with Morgan for the next few days - especially while I sat in the lifeguard chair and watched over the pool. Yes, I knew I had been wrong to sleep with Collin when I thought Morgan was in love with him but she was blowing things entirely out of proportion.

I tried to sort things out and find a place to put them all so maybe I could be better prepared when I next had the chance to speak to her, but I was failing miserably. And Morgan was totally avoiding me. She came and went while I was gone and didn't sleep in her bed. I wasn't sure where she was staying and I couldn't even call Irelyn to ask if she knew.

Life was definitely a bitch.

And to top it all off, I hadn't heard from Collin since he'd called Monday night to see how I was feeling and if things were better with Morgan. I'd given him an edited version of the argument – doing what I could to keep him from feeling like he needed to be involved. But once that conversation had ended, it was like he'd dropped off the face of the earth. Maybe he was tired of all the drama. I certainly was.

I was grateful for Otis's company for I'd have been extremely lonely in that condo by myself. I rained affection on him and took him with me wherever I went. He seemed to be the only friend I had left.

Thursday afternoon, I took Otis to the local dog park and watched him romp with the other dogs while I enjoyed the shade of a huge oak tree. My eyes glazed over as I stared out into the enclosure and contemplated – again – what to do. I briefly entertained the notion of calling Spencer and sitting him down for a nice little chat. Maybe if I straightened things out with him – gave him a little closure – maybe he'd take Morgan out.

I bent to rest my elbows on my knees and cradled my head in my hands. I couldn't force Spencer to love Morgan any more than I could force Collin to love me. What a sad, silly, pathetic mess this whole situation had become. What the hell was going on, anyway?

I sat back to tick points off my finger, not caring if the other dog lovers thought me strange. They could all bite my ass.

The first tick was Morgan. She loved Spencer. But, enter second tick, Spencer loved me. Then, thirdly, me – I loved Collin. And fourth, Collin. He loved Tori. Possibly. I wasn't totally sure about that at all. How could he willingly sleep with me if he loved another? Collin didn't work that way. At least, I didn't think so. Maybe he didn't love me, but I was beginning to wonder if he loved Tori.

I groaned and grabbed the leash that I'd dropped to the bench beside me. I wasn't solving anything here at all. I whistled for Otis and smiled when he lifted his head, pricked his ears, and happily loped over to me. I clipped the leash on his collar and led him out of the fence. He trotted beside me as we made our way back to the condo.

***

Morgan was once again sitting on the sofa when we returned. I nearly fell back out the door – almost as if she was some kind of spirit that had come to haunt me – but I managed to compose myself and unclip Otis. He ran to her and she greeted him warmly. I hung the leash on the handle of the coat closet, kicked off my flip flops, and sank to my favorite chair.

"What's up, Morgan?" I asked in a cool voice. "Haven't seen you all week."

"I've been around," she said, straightening as she watched Otis trot to the kitchen for a drink.

"Around where?" I inquired.

"I'm moving out, Bailey," she said stiffly. "I'm renting an apartment above the bookstore."

I blanched as my insides iced over and briefly stopped the flow of blood to my brain. I scrambled to think – to speak. "What?" was all I could manage.

"I'm leaving," she said, her confidence growing at the lack of mine. "I've already moved a lot of my things and I just came back to get the rest and to let you know."

"That's really crappy," I said. Her astonished eyes grew as she gaped at me. My voice returned and I wasn't about to pass up the opportunity to use it. "We have an argument and you just up and leave? You run? Why not stick around and try to settle it, huh?"

"You wouldn't understand," she muttered.

"So make me," I demanded. "Make me understand. Don't be a coward, Morgan – you're better than that."

She shook her head. "No, I am the coward. I'm not like you."

"Don't start that," I said.

"I'm not starting anything. This is more about me than it is about you."

Her words made no sense whatsoever. "That's sort of funny, Morg, when just the other day you were screaming at me for being a whore."

"No!" she said as she covered her mouth. "No. I didn't say that."

"Whatever. That's neither here or there. Why are you moving? The truth."

"I told you – you wouldn't understand," she insisted.

The door opened and Irelyn stepped shyly inside. She flashed me a weak smile as she shut the door and shifted nervously from foot to foot.

"Hey, Irelyn," I said in a sarcastically cheerful voice. "Come in and join the fray."

"Fray?" she asked as a crease furrowed her brow. "What's going on here?"

"Morgan is leaving," I said sweeping my hand toward the sofa in a grand gesture. "She no longer sees fit to live with me. Apparently she can't stand the sight of me anymore."

"That's not true," Morgan objected. "It's just that...well...it's hard to live here now."

"Why?" Irelyn asked as she sat gingerly next to Morgan. "What's the matter?"

Morgan nibbled on her lip and laced her fingers together on her lap. She crossed her ankles, uncrossed them, and then crossed them again. She glanced at Irelyn then dropped her eyes. "It's personal."

"And we're all friends here," Irelyn said, wrapping an arm around Morgan's shoulders. "Tell us."

"I don't fit in with you two," Morgan blurted.

I bolted upright, ready to rage. What the hell was she thinking? "What?"

"Hang on, Bailey," Irelyn said, holding up a hand. She turned to Morgan and gave her shoulders a gentle squeeze. "What do you mean you don't fit in?"

Morgan shook Irelyn's arm off and stood so she could pace, wringing her hands the entire time. A flush invaded her face and made her look so innocent and vulnerable it actually tugged at my heart.

"You two are so different from me," she explained lamely. "I'm not like you. I don't...do the things you two do."

"What the hell is that supposed to mean?" I demanded.

"I don't mean it in a bad way," she said. "I just don't relax the way you do."

"So, because Bailey and I have...well, we've engaged in sex without being in a proper relationship, that makes you totally different from us?" Irelyn said. I could see the struggle on her face to remain calm.

"Something like that," she mumbled. "You two have so much in common."

"So what you're saying is that Irelyn and I are a couple of whores and you're not," I said, angry.

"Bailey," Irelyn said, shooting me a look.

I ignored it. I was still mad at her, too, and even though Morgan lumped me and Irelyn together, it didn't automatically make us best friends again. "No, Irelyn, I want her to explain. Maybe we're not as moral as she is but that doesn't make us bad people."

"Bailey," Morgan said, astounded. "How can you stand there and say that?"

"Easy," I snorted as I narrowed my eyes and took a few steps toward her. "I opened my mouth and let the words fall out."

But Morgan didn't back down. She jabbed a finger at me. "See? That's what I mean. You don't care about my feelings at all."

"Of course I do," I said, my loose grip on composure slipping through my fingers. "Do you know how much guilt I've eaten because of you?"

"Apparently not enough," Morgan spit back, finally realizing she had a spine. "You slept with Collin after you found out I was in love with him. Well, supposedly in love with him."

"Oh, damn," Irelyn cursed, massaging her forehead. She lifted her eyes to meet mine. "You told her?"

I shrugged. "She figured it out. But relax, she's in love with Spencer – not Collin."

Irelyn's eyes grew to the size of hubcaps. "Really? Oh wow. I didn't see that. Well, that makes things easier."

"The hell it does," Morgan argued. "Don't you see, Irelyn? You two thought I was in love with Collin and Bailey still slept with him. After she found out that I was supposedly in love with him! She didn't care how I'd feel. She gave no thought to me whatsoever."

"But, Morgan," Irelyn said. "Okay, I can sort of see what you're saying, but what does it matter now? You don't love Collin."

"It's the principle of the thing. What if I had been in love with Collin? Can you imagine how I'd feel? Betrayed by my best friend."

"She's in love with him, too!" Irelyn exclaimed. "And I know what it's like. I know how hard it is to deny those feelings. They make you unable to resist. You just want to be with him all the time – no matter who gets hurt. That love is so strong that you'll move heaven and earth to be with him."

I had to grin at Irelyn – she finally got it. She finally had some sense knocked into her blonde head and realized that I felt for Collin like she did Lucas. Oh, I was still angry with her but she was trying to apologize to me in a way she knew I would approve – I hated sappy make up scenes.

"I knew you'd take her side," Morgan snipped. "I just knew it. You two always have it so easy – beautiful Irelyn and sexy Bailey who have men falling at their feet. You two can laugh and bond over all this while plain, quiet Morgan sits in the corner and laps it all up knowing it will never happen to her. But you two don't care. No, not at all. But when you need someone to talk to or someone to listen to you vent, then you call dependable Morgan who will listen and try to offer advice. But do you take it? Hell no! Because Morgan's advice is moral and you two would rather deal with it in your own way."

She drew a long, hard breath, her body shuddering. I could see the tears gathering in her eyes and sure enough, a couple tumbled to her cheeks. My heart ached for her.

"I don't fit in," she said, her voice quite a few octaves lower. She swiped angrily at her tears and picked up the bag she'd placed near the door. She slipped the strap over her shoulder. "I'm sorry."

She walked out before Irelyn or I could think to stop her.

"What..." Irelyn stammered. "What the hell just happened here?"

"Got me," I said as I got up to go the kitchen. I grabbed two bottles of water and returned to the living room. I handed one to Irelyn before I sat in my chair and twisted off the top. "She's a little emotional."

"What happened?" Irelyn asked. She fiddled with the cap of her bottle but didn't remove it. The bottle shook slightly in her hands.

"She told me that she wasn't in love with Collin that she was, in fact, in love with Spencer." I paused to gauge Irelyn's reaction and I wasn't disappointed. "And, Spencer's been talking to her. I guess she must have said something about the two of them and he told her that he couldn't be with her because of me."

"Damn," Irelyn muttered. "Damn."

"Yeah," I shrugged like I didn't care when in fact I actually did. A little too much. "Then, when she grilled me about Collin I admitted everything. But, I let it slip that we thought she was in love with Collin and she went ballistic when she found out I'd slept with him after the fact."

"Yeah, I got that," Irelyn said.

"So, I get the Worst Friend of the Year award," I said.

"Bailey," Irelyn pleaded. "No. I should get that. I'm really sorry about the other day. I…" she heaved a huge sigh and studied the carpet while she gathered her thoughts. "You were right about a lot of things. I guess I judged you before I took a long look at my past. Look what I did? What right did I have to say those things to you?"

"You were trying to protect Morgan."

It was her turn to snort. "A fat good that did, huh?"

I laughed.

"The thing is, I totally understand what happened. Maybe neither of us did the right thing, but I understand how you feel. How much in love you can be and how those feelings just take over and you can't think rationally. If you feel anything for Collin that I do for Lucas, then I know."

"Thanks," I said, shaking my head as I turned my face. I hated the awkward apology. I knew she hadn't meant what she'd said – hell probably knew it right after she'd said it. It was cool.

"So, what do we do now?" she asked.

"Kiss and make up?" I suggested.

She barked a shaky laugh. "I mean about Morgan."

"Hell. That's the million dollar question. I do not know."

"Did she say where she was going?" Irelyn asked, her face stricken and her pretty eyes full of concern. It was hurting her as bad as it was me. The fact of the matter was that even though Morgan was different than me and Irelyn, we were still friends. We all three meshed well together. And Irelyn and I weren't as alike as Morgan made it out to be. Hell, Lucas and Collin were twins but they were still two different personalities.

"She's renting an apartment above the bookstore," I said.

"Well, I guess we should let her cool off then maybe try again?" she asked more than stated.

"It's as good a plan as any," I said.

I finished my water and squeezed the bottle, relishing the crunching sound in my fist. Maybe I needed a gym membership so I could go beat the hell out of a punching bag – it might relieve my stress.

"What are you going to do about Collin?" she asked.

"Don't know," I said.

"I know you spent the night with him Sunday night," she said, trying to hide a smile. "What happened?"

"Ha," I laughed. "Nothing. I went out and tied one on and when I couldn't drive, I called him. He shoved me in a shower – no sex you pervert," I said with a grin. She blushed and smiled. "Then he tucked me in his bed and let me sleep it off."

I frowned as I remembered the next morning and his mysterious conversation with Tori.

"Is that all?"

"Yep," I said, not wanting to discuss the Tori scene only because I didn't want to relive it myself. "That's all. No hanky panky – just hangover cures."

She bobbed her head and finally took a drink of her water. I watched her but didn't really see her. A plan was sort of forming in my head. Well, maybe not a plan but an idea of where to get started.

"Hey, do you think I should talk to Spencer?" I asked.

"I don't know," she frowned. "What will you say?"

Another million dollar question. I wished fervently that I had answers for then I'd be able to quit school and live on my own and never have to ask my father for another cent. Hell, I wouldn't even need my trust fund.

"Well, I could probably start with Morgan. Maybe I could convince him that he should date her. I know you can't force people to feel things they don't but maybe he doesn't want to date her because he thinks I'll be upset."

"That's true," she said.

"Yeah," I agreed but it didn't really sound all that feasible. What if he was using me as an excuse so that he didn't hurt her? "Do you know what bugs me the most?" I said as a thought flew in my head.

"What?"

"Why he cried on her shoulder. Why didn't he talk to Luke or Collin?" I asked. Irelyn offered no answer and I didn't expect her to. "And is he really all in love with me? We both agreed that we'd keep things simple when we first started seeing each other. We both agreed that it wouldn't get serious. He said he didn't want a serious relationship."

"Maybe things changed," Irelyn offered softly.

"Then why didn't he tell me?" I asked.

She drew a deep breath and released it slowly. "Probably because of your agreement to keep it simple. Maybe he was afraid to tell you that he felt more than what you thought he did."

That made perfect sense – especially to me. Wasn't I the expert at hiding behind a mask? Didn't I want to keep people guessing at what I was really feeling? Would I want someone prodding into my heart?

"Should I speak to him, I wonder?" I mused aloud. "I don't really want to hurt Spencer anymore than I already have."

"I agree," Irelyn said. "But, I also agree that maybe you *should* speak to him. I just worry that he might figure out that you slept with Collin."

"Yeah, ya think?" I snorted. "I really don't want him to know but yet, I do. Damn, Irelyn. This really sucks."

"Tell me," she said with a grim smile. "Been in a similar situation, remember?"

"So, what's the right thing to do?" I asked, hoping she'd have a brilliant resolution. "I keep thinking maybe I should speak to Collin, first, but since I don't know what precisely is going on with us, I don't know what help he'll be."

"Um," Irelyn said, shifting uncomfortably. I furrowed my brow at her. I thought all the awkward moments were over between us. At least for now.

"What?" I asked.

"When's the last time you talked to Collin?" she asked, her darting eyes avoiding contact with mine.

"Monday night," I said. "I tried to call him Tuesday but I got his voice mail. I left a message and he never called back," I admitted, ignoring the twinge of pain shooting through my heart. "I haven't called since." I shrugged, acting as if I didn't really care. "I'll talk to him Friday night after their gig."

"They're not playing Friday," Irelyn said, her face suddenly going white.

"Why?" I asked as I narrowed my eyes. "What's going on?"

"Well," Irelyn said, scratching the back of her head. "Okay, I'm going to just tell you."

"Please do," I said dryly.

"Lucas told me that Collin took the rest of the week off of work. He left Tuesday evening. With Tori."

My heart crystallized into an icicle then fell to my feet and shattered into a thousand pieces.

Chapter Fourteen

My life was nothing but an agonizing hell. I couldn't even pluck up the ambition to go tie one on. I fought self-pity with strength and courage I never dreamed I had and I managed to keep it at bay – though it taunted me from the sidelines.

I didn't want to think what Collin was up to with Tori – it made me physically ill. It seemed as if Tori had finally succumbed to Collin's charms and they'd gone away together to celebrate their new found love.

I wanted to puke.

Irelyn called me frequently and prattled on mostly about nothing. I knew she had an ulterior motive – she was checking up on me. I appreciated it but it was really starting to wear on my last nerve - I just didn't have the heart to tell her that.

The condo seemed far larger than it really was now that Morgan was gone. I was happy to have Otis to keep me company – he was also keeping me sane. I showered him with loads of affection and he accompanied me everywhere he could.

I took Otis to the dog park Sunday afternoon and watched as he romped with another puppy about his size. Otis had grown quite a bit and when I'd taken him to the vet for a checkup and his puppy shots, the vet had informed me that Otis would probably get to be about forty pounds when full grown. The vet hadn't been sure what sort of dog Otis was – a combination of all sorts – but it didn't matter. Otis was perfect the way he was.

I rested on an iron bench and kept a close eye on Otis while I contemplated the events that had turned my life into such a messy thing. It had all started when I'd realized that I was in love with Collin. Things had gone strictly downhill from there.

What if I hadn't broken up with Spencer? Would things still be like they used to be? Would Morgan have left?

Groaning, I pinched the bridge of my nose. This whole business was giving me one humungous headache.

"Is anyone sitting here?" a soft voice asked.

I sighed and squeezed my eyes shut. "Um, no – if there was then certainly you'd see them."

The voice laughed and I opened my eyes in time to see a man plop down next to me. He smiled, a dimple indenting each cheek. He had blond hair with hazel eyes hidden behind the lenses of a pair of stylish glasses. He was quite handsome – in my opinion – but my heart just wasn't into flirting.

"I'm Craig Flint," he said, extending a rather large hand. "And you are?"

"Annoyed and irritated," I said.

He lowered his hand as uncertainty flickered across his face. Shame flooded my body.

"Sorry," I said with a hint of a smile. "Bailey Foxworth."

"If I'm disturbing you…"

"No," I said as a real smile floated across my lips. "Just having a bad week."

"I understand," Craig said as he stretched his arm across the back of the bench. "Been there myself plenty of times."

I scanned the park and located Otis near the fence, tugging on a rope toy with a Chihuahua. "Where's your dog?"

He pointed his long index finger at a tawny Boxer trotting the perimeter with his head raised regally. "That's Skipper. He's sort of an arrogant thing."

"I see," I said and smiled. It was sort of funny.

"So, Bailey," Craig said, drawing out each syllable of my name. "Do you have a husband? Boyfriend?"

I snorted a laugh – had to. I've had men try to pick me up in all sorts of places but never on a bench in an enclosed yard filled with dogs barking and crapping all over the place. Not the epitome of romance.

"No, I don't," I admitted with half a smirk. "No girlfriends, either."

He laughed. "Well, that's good."

"If you say so," I muttered and shaded my eyes as I followed Otis with my gaze. I knew I was being rude and Craig seemed like a nice guy, but I didn't want to encourage him. I didn't want to involve myself with anyone else. I couldn't handle the small circle of friends I'd once had.

"Look, I don't mean to pry, but sometimes it helps to talk to a stranger," he offered. I slowly turned my head to face him, my hand still above my eyes as if in a salute.

"That's nice of you – really – but I don't think it will help my situation. Thanks anyway," I said. I dropped my hand and contemplated whistling for Otis and making a graceful escape but I really had nowhere else to go except for the empty condo.

"Okay," he said with a shrug. "Suit yourself."

He relaxed against the bench, his arm still draped over the back of the bench. He was far enough away that it didn't stretch behind me and for that I was grateful – I'd hate to have to snap it in two.

"So," he said in a casual tone. "How about if we grab a cup of coffee or something?"

"I've sort of taken myself out of the dating pool," I said trying my best to sound aloof. "Men have been a total pain in the ass lately."

He laughed and winked at me. "Okay, understandable. How about this – I'll give you my number and if you decide that you'd like to grab lunch or something, you give me a call?"

I imagined taking him to Rusty's one Friday night and cuddling up next to him while we watched Out Back play and hastily swept the thought from my mind. I wouldn't use this man in my vain efforts to try to make Collin jealous. Not only was it wrong and I was tired of being the bad guy, but I didn't think Collin would care much. He'd more than likely be relieved.

"I guess that wouldn't hurt anything," I said. I pulled out my cell and programmed his number. "Just, don't hold your breath."

He chuckled. "I won't, I promise."

Grinning, I stood, whistling for Otis. He loped to my side, accompanied by the Chihuahua. I clipped his leash to his collar then shook Craig's hand. "Maybe I'll see you around sometime."

"Sure, Bailey. Take care."

I led Otis out of the enclosure and headed toward home. I'd no more than waved one last time at Craig when my cell phone rang. My heart nearly jumped out of my throat when Collin's name flashed on the ID. Taking a deep breath, I answered.

"Hey, what's up?" I asked as if he hadn't totally disappeared for damn near a week.

"Nothing," he said. "Just got back in town. What are you doing?"

"Walking Otis."

"Um, me and the guys are going to practice tonight. Care to come by?" he asked, his voice a little hopeful.

What the hell, I thought. It wasn't like my heart hadn't been broken over and over before. "Sure. I'll bring Otis and he can play in the backyard with Milo."

"Excellent," he said and I could almost see him grin. "Um, do you want to call Morgan and invite her? I'm sure Luke will bring Irelyn."

"Not on your life," I snorted.

"That doesn't sound good," he said apprehensively. "What's going on?"

"Nothing to worry your pretty little head about," I said. I was dying to ask him where he'd been and if Tori would be joining our little gathering but I didn't want him to know that I cared. I'd see for myself soon enough.

"Luke told me that you and Irelyn fixed things but something is still going on with Morgan," he said. "Did she really move out?"

"Yeah and do you know what – who cares?" I said as I drew closer to my building. "If she wants to be that way then let her. Irelyn and I both tried to talk to her and I'm not bending over backwards anymore."

"Relax," Collin said. "Chill. It's fine, Bailey, honest. I was just wondering."

"Okay. I'll be there later," I said as I entered the security code for the building. "See you then." I hung up before he could say anything else.

***

I stood before my closet wondering what to wear. Should I go all demure and mysterious or should I go slutty? Deciding it really didn't matter I went with denim capris and a designer t-shirt. I slipped on the flip flops, grabbed the dog, and darted out the door.

I contemplated calling Morgan on the drive but decided against it. Maybe one of the guys could call her – she probably wouldn't ignore them.

It was so tempting to just throw in the towel and say forget Morgan and her high horse. Who needed her anyway? But I just couldn't. I truly missed her. She'd been a good friend to both Irelyn and I since we all met last year. And it bugged me that she might be honestly hurting. I didn't like pain, either, and I could only imagine how she was feeling.

But I was sticking to my guns. I still thought she blew things way out of proportion and even though I could see why she'd be upset, I didn't understand why she didn't let it go.

I parked in front of the house and gathered Otis in my arms. The guys were already in the garage – I could hear them- but I skirted the huge doors and deposited Otis in the backyard where Milo greeted him excitedly. I watched the pups frolic for few minutes before draping Otis's leash over the gate and trudging to the garage.

I slipped in the door while the guys were mid-song and grinned at Irelyn. She waved me over to the chair she'd set up for me. I was vastly relieved not to see Tori anywhere.

As I sat next to Irelyn, I finally allowed myself to look at Collin. I caught his eye and he winked, sending a chill up my spine and making me feel like that pathetic lovesick little girl. I hated him for that but loved him all the same.

"He was asking me all about you," Irelyn whispered in my ear. "He wanted to know how you were taking Morgan's moving out."

I shrugged while inside I was a bit of a mess. Why would he care when he'd spent the better part of a week with Tori? Or was he hinting around to see if I knew? I leaned into Irelyn. "Next time, tell him to mind his own damn business."

She blinked rapidly and pulled away to flash me a puzzled look. I raised a brow and shrugged. Screw it. If he could be mysterious about Tori then I could be a bitch about Morgan.

The guys played a couple songs before taking a break and joining us. Spencer passed out the drinks but I shook my head when he offered me a beer. I needed to chill on that stuff before it got out of hand.

"Okay, ladies," Spencer said as he twisted the top off a beer and took a long slug. "Tell us what's going on with Morgan."

I rolled my eyes and grimaced in disgust. "What is this – some kind of jacked up intervention?"

"No," Lucas said as he sat on the cooler, dragging Irelyn out of her chair and into his lap. "But I know Irelyn has been upset about the whole thing. I imagine you are too, even though you'd rather act like a bad ass."

I clicked my tongue and released a long sigh. "Whatever. Look, if she doesn't want to live with me, fine. Not many people can tolerate me, anyway. And if she thinks she's so much better than me and Irelyn, let her. I mean, we're nothing but a couple of lowly whores in her opinion."

"Bailey," Irelyn growled in warning. "You know that's not true."

I lifted a shoulder, astutely avoiding Collin's eyes. "Whatever. If you guys want to know what's going inside Morgan's head, then call and ask her. I sure the hell don't know."

"She won't answer my calls," Spencer said. "I've even gone to the bookstore and she ignores me."

"Sorry, Spence," I mumbled.

"What happened?" he persisted.

"She's mad at Irelyn for supposedly taking my side. As for why she's mad at me," I paused, dying to glance at Collin but knowing as soon as I did it would give everything away. "That's between Morgan and me."

"Bailey," Spencer whined.

"No, Spence," Collin said quietly. "Let it go, man. Bailey's right — it's her business."

I could have kissed him — really wanted to — but I just offered him a grateful smile. He returned it but it didn't quite reach his eyes. Confusion flitted swiftly across his face and made me wonder what he could possibly be confused about — he pretty much knew the deal between me and Morgan. I was the confused one.

"Let's go through the songs on the list for Friday night," Lucas suggested as he scooted Irelyn gently off his lap. He pressed a kiss to her temple and jealousy raged throughout my body. How I wished I had that kind of relationship with Collin.

The guys went back to work and I sat silently by Irelyn, commenting here and there when she spoke to me. My mind was whirling, trying to figure out what to do next. I couldn't stand that my life was in such disarray.

When they finished for the night, Collin offered to throw some burgers on the grill and since everyone else was amiable to it, I had to agree.

Spencer and Lucas fiddled with the grill under Irelyn's keen supervision. Collin grabbed my arm and dragged me into the kitchen, mumbling that he needed my help with the food.

"Talk to me Bailey," he said as we entered the kitchen. He dropped my arm and opened the freezer. He retrieved a package of hamburger patties, tossed them on a plate, and set them in the microwave. Once he had them defrosting, he leaned against the counter and folded his arms over his chest. "You've been fairly quiet all night."

"What do you want me to say?" I asked. "You know what's going on — there's nothing new to report."

His shoulders slumped as he sighed and bent his head. "Are you pissed at me for some reason?" He lifted his eyes to me, very much resembling a lost little boy — it tugged at my heart.

"No," I whispered, unable to admit the real reason for my cold shoulder. "Just dealing with the Morgan situation. I was actually thinking about talking to Spencer. Think it will help?"

He straightened and screwed his face up in concentration telling me I'd successfully dodged a big bullet. "Maybe. I don't think it will hurt." He dropped his arms. "Are you going to tell him about us?"

What us? I wanted to ask. "No, I don't think so. I don't see the point."

"Yeah, you're right," he said as he turned to watch the patties spin in the microwave. A heavy silence descended upon us and I could tell he was struggling to chase it away much like I was. I hated the awkwardness – it unnerved me.

"So, um, where have you been?" I asked.

He shot me a brief, guilty look before concentrating on the defrosting meat. "Um, with Tori. She needed help with something."

I nodded and swallowed the huge lump in my throat. I could not let him know how much it hurt to hear him admit to me that he'd been with her and not offer any explanations.

I opened the refrigerator and gathered condiments, placing them carefully on the table. Sensing my unease, he fetched a stack of plates and silverware. Once everything was set, I escaped outside, claiming I was thirsty and wanted a water bottle from the cooler.

I relaxed somewhat as we all ate and even laughed a little bit at the puppies' antics. As the evening dwindled, I made my excuses to leave. I whistled for Otis and attached his leash.

"Hey, Bailey," Spencer called. I paused and lifted a brow. "Can you give me a lift home? I rode with Lucas and Irelyn."

"Sure," I said as I waved to everyone.

We barely got out of the driveway when Spencer started riddling me with questions. "I know something is going on that everyone is keeping from me and you're the only one who'll be straight with me."

I glanced at him, holding Otis in his lap, and decided to be as straight as possible – he deserved it. "Okay, Spence, here goes. Morgan is pissed at me because I hurt you."

"Bailey," he pleaded.

"No, wait," I snapped. "She told me that you called her the day after we split and cried to her – telling her that you were in love with me."

He sighed and lightly banged his head on the window. "Yeah, I did," he said in a low voice. "But I think I was just a little upset at the time. I don't think I was really in love with you but I did like you a lot. Sounds sort of childish, huh?"

"No," I said.

"I was more pissed at myself because you told me all along that you didn't want to get serious and I let myself get all into you. It was my fault, not yours."

"Spencer, why didn't you talk to me?"

"I couldn't, Bailey. I was embarrassed. And I didn't want you blaming yourself, like you're doing now. I didn't want to cause any problems but I did anyway. Shit."

I took a huge breath and released it slowly. "Spence, you didn't cause this – not knowingly at least," I said. "Um, well, I recently found out that Morgan has a thing for you. She's sort of in love with you and that's why she's so mad at me. She said that you told her you wouldn't date her because of me."

"Oh, hell," he said, running his free hand through his hair. "She asked me to some party with her and I told her it wasn't right because I didn't know how you'd take it. I thought she was only trying to be nice and cheer me up. I didn't know."

"I know that," I said gently.

"Didn't any of us learn anything from the whole Lucas/Irelyn fiasco?" he asked in a feeble attempt at humor.

"Guess not," I said, not wanting him to know just how much we hadn't learned. Look at the secret I was harboring – the secret we were all hiding from him. He needed to know the truth but the problem was, I didn't know who should tell him – me or Collin? And did it really matter since Collin was not interested in me – at least from a relationship standpoint?

"I don't know what to do," he said.

"You and me both," I said as I pulled in front of his building. "But don't sweat it, Spencer. I think this is something Morgan is going to have to work out for herself. I think she needs to know we're still her friends but I don't think there's much else we can do."

He cupped my chin and looked straight in my eyes. "Bailey, if there's someone else, don't be afraid to tell me. I care about you and I want to see you happy."

That pesky lump reappeared in my throat. Why couldn't I love him? "There's no one, Spence. But thanks."

He nodded and pressed a chaste kiss to my lips before setting Otis on the seat and exiting. I watched him climb the steps to his apartment then patted Otis's head and put the car in gear. I had to get my life straight and soon.

Chapter Fifteen

The end of summer break was rapidly approaching and I knew I was going to have to make a decision about dorm life. Seeing as Irelyn was now living with Lucas and attending Community College and Morgan wasn't speaking to me, I was low on roommate options. Besides, I wasn't sure what would happen to Otis. Collin probably would take him but I would miss the little furball too much.

I'd only signed a month to month lease on the condo and I could probably extend it – hell I could extend it for a year. But the condo hardly seemed like home anymore. Maybe I could find something else...

I went to Rusty's Friday night and sat like a statue beside Irelyn. We both ignored the empty chair that Morgan used to occupy and concentrated instead on the band. It wasn't as enjoyable as in the past but I managed to stick to soda. That is, until Tori showed up, grinning like mad and planting her butt in Morgan's chair.

"Hey, Irelyn," Tori said. My stomach churned. "Hi, Bailey."

"Tori!" Irelyn greeted. "Where have you been?"

"Oh, just had some things to take care of," she said as she motioned for the waitress. She ordered a soda and I ordered a beer. Screw the no booze rule. "So, have they finished the first set?"

"Yes," I said, as I accepted my beer. I sucked on it eagerly, ignoring the little voice in my head telling me to take it easy.

"So what brings you down here?" Irelyn asked, her body rigid. I cracked a smile – Tori's presence wasn't as welcome for her, either.

Tori shrugged as she toyed with her glass. "Collin kept insisting that I come down – he said I sit in the house too much." She lifted her head to flash Irelyn a shy smile. "He's right so I told him I'd come after work."

Wonderful, I thought. Front row seats to the lovefest. Just what I needed. I considered making my excuses and leaving before they finished playing. But of course I didn't. Curiosity – morbid as it was – forced me to stay. I was interested to see how they interacted together. If they fell all over each other like Irelyn and Lucas tended to do, I'd escape as quickly as possible.

"Morgan didn't show, huh?" Tori asked.

"Obviously not," I muttered. Irelyn glared at me, warning me to back off. I rolled my eyes and smiled brightly at Tori. "She doesn't associate with us anymore."

"Collin told me," Tori said. "I tried to call her but I got her voice mail. Collin thought she might talk to me but apparently she doesn't associate with me, either."

Too bad, I thought. They'd get along well together. They could compare notes on how they each had a thing for the guys I'd either dated or wanted to date. What a lovely little club that would make. Maybe they could call Veronica and she could be the club president. Oh, and they could name the club "Let's Make Bailey's Life a Living Hell." Catchy title.

They guys finished while I was mulling over the club so I nearly jumped when they plopped down at our table. Lucas squeezed in between me and Irelyn while Spencer sat next to me. Collin, of course, sat next to Tori but I didn't see any contact. Maybe they'd do that later.

"You seem out of sorts tonight," Spencer observed as he leaned in to whisper in my ear. "What's the matter?"

"Not a thing," I said as I smiled and patted his cheek. "Thinking about joining a new club."

His brow wrinkled in response but he didn't say anything. He motioned for the waitress and ordered a round of drinks.

As everyone discussed what to do with the rest of the evening, I kept to myself. I was trying to figure out how to leave without a million people asking me if I was okay or if something was wrong. I just couldn't take seeing Collin with Tori.

So he didn't hold her hand or kiss her or anything – that didn't matter. He was next to her. He'd invited her to be there. She came. That was enough. If I rammed a machete through my chest it still wouldn't hurt as much.

But what hurt the most were the little looks Collin kept giving me. Confused looks. Concerned looks. It took all I had to keep my mouth shut and not ask him what the hell his problem was. He was there with the woman he supposedly loved and I was here with Spencer, my good friend who I, for some reason, couldn't fall in love with. What a shame, too.

The conniving part of my brain came to life and urged me to go ahead with the others over to Collin's place. Maybe Tori would grow tired and head up to her apartment then I could seduce Collin and show him a real woman. I knew he had a hard time resisting me. He might not love me but he sure the hell lusted after me and I never, for as long as I'd known him, seen him look at Tori like he was aching inside to touch her.

That thought brought a smug smile to my face which did not go unnoticed by Collin. A slow grin crept across his lips as if he was thinking the same thing as I. Maybe he was thinking of the night on the beach – he did have a touch of fire in his eyes.

Then sweet little Tori, sitting next to him and looking so lost like she didn't belong, asked him a question and tore his attention away from me. I knew in that moment that I wouldn't try to seduce Collin. Maybe if Tori was a spiteful bitch like Veronica I could do it but I'd honestly never done anything like that in my life. I'd never slept with anyone else's boyfriend and I wouldn't start now.

Just as everyone was finishing their drinks and preparing to leave, Owen breezed into the bar with a cute little brunette on his arm. I froze – like everyone else at the table – until my burning anger thawed me enough to get to my feet.

"What the hell are you doing with her?" I demanded as Owen ushered Morgan to our table.

Morgan shifted nervously from foot to foot and wouldn't meet anyone's eyes.

"Jealous are we?" Owen taunted.

I narrowed my eyes and leaned across the table, my hands balled into fists. But before I could utter a word or throw a punch, Lucas and Spencer grabbed my shoulders and forced me back in my chair.

"That's better," Owen sneered as he dragged two chairs to our table. He motioned for Morgan to sit and she did. "I'm taking the little lady out for a drink. Is there a problem?"

"She's too good for you," I spit. Morgan lifted her head and glared. I fell back in my chair, amazed.

"Just mind your own business, Bailey," she said.

I turned my head, my anger still pulsating throughout my body. My eyes fell on Tori - she was white as a ghost and as stiff as a flagpole, her hand clutching Collin's arm. Something was definitely going on and it wasn't between Tori and Collin.

"Sorry we missed your set," Owen continued. "We were hanging out at my club when Morgan reminded me you guys were playing here."

So that's what this was all about. Morgan was playing a game. She was using Owen as some sort of pawn to either make Spencer jealous or make me and Irelyn worry that she was seeing such a pervert creep. Or both. Well, I couldn't speak for Spencer or Irelyn but she sure had me riled up.

"Pity," I said as I smirked openly at Morgan. "We were just leaving."

"Bailey," Irelyn hissed at me.

I raised a cool brow at her, wishing I could send her a telepathic message. If Morgan wanted to play games then I'd play along – only she wouldn't like it. "Well, we were. Weren't we?" I glanced at Spencer but he wasn't paying any attention whatsoever to me. He was watching Owen and Morgan closely, his brows knitted together in concentration.

"Okay, so maybe it was just me," I said with a shrug as I stood. "See you around."

"We're with you, Bailey," Collin said, anger seeping into his voice. He took Tori by the arm and nearly dragged her out of the bar, confirming my suspicions. Time for me to play good cop/bad cop and question the two of them.

"Irelyn?" I asked in a soft voice, trying to convey that it was all right with me if she stayed.

"We'll be there in a little bit," she said, clutching Lucas's thigh. Spencer moved to my vacant chair indicating that he was hanging out, too.

"I'll follow you two," I told Collin. He nodded and escorted Tori out of the bar.

The whole way to his house I wondered what could be going on. Did Owen do something terrible to Tori? Was Morgan in danger? I needed answers and I needed them fast. That bastard would not lay a hand on my friend and if he ever did, he wouldn't live to tell about it.

By the time I parked and stormed into Collin's house, I was a ball of rage. I found the two of them in the kitchen, Tori clutching a cup of instant tea so hard her knuckles were turning white.

"One of you tell me what is going on," I demanded. "Is Morgan in trouble? Is he going to do something to her?"

"Bailey, calm down," Collin said as he touched my arm.

I jerked my arm out of his way. "No, I will not. You need to tell me what the deal is so I know whether I need to go back down there or not."

"She'll be okay tonight," Tori mumbled. "I promise."

I took a long breath, holding it in so it could soak up some of my tension and release it slowly. I sat down across from Tori and look directly into her eyes. "What is the deal?"

"Owen is a jerk," she said.

"Tell me something I don't know," I said.

That brought a fragile smile to her lips. "I dated him for a bit," she continued. Collin dropped into the chair next to her and took her hand. That burned my heart but I ignored it. I needed to think about Morgan. "He was real nice and charming and swept me off my feet. I thought I was in love with him." She brushed a finger under each eye to clear the tears. "He really messed with my head, though. He would say nice things to me to get me in bed but afterwards he would tell me how horrible I was and that he'd had better.

"But I stayed with him. Oh, he never hurt me physically but he really screwed me up inside." She took a deep breath and sipped at her tea. "Then, I thought I was pregnant and I told him. I was scared and didn't know what to do. He told me that I was nothing but a slut and it probably wasn't even his."

I watched as Collin squeezed her hand and it didn't hurt me as much as the pain in Tori's voice. I didn't much like her but I didn't much like how she'd been treated, either. "What happened?" I asked.

She sniffed and rubbed her eyes. "Um, well, I wasn't pregnant. My period was all screwed up. My doctor thought it was probably because I was getting into stuff I shouldn't have been. I was…drinking a lot with Owen and … um…he would do some stuff…drugs…and he talked me into doing it, too."

"Oh, geez," I said as I slumped back in my chair. "Does Spencer know what a bastard his friend is?"

"No," Tori said. "Only Collin knows. I asked him not to say anything to anyone." She turned her watery eyes on me and tried to smile. "I was very embarrassed and very ashamed."

"Look, Tori," I said as gently as I could. "I'm sorry for what happened to you, I really am. But I won't let that happen to Morgan."

"How are you going to stop her?" Collin asked. "She won't talk to any of us."

"I don't know," I said as I bit my lip. "Good question."

"He likes you," Tori threw out casually. "I've seen the way he looks at you."

"Hm," I said as a thought popped in my head.

"What?" Collin asked warily.

"Just thinking," I said with a shrug.

"Uh uh," he said, shaking his head.

I scowled. "You don't even know what I'm thinking."

"Yes I do and you're not going to do it, Bailey," he said, his jaw set firmly. "I won't let you."

I snorted out a laugh. "Collin, who the hell are you to tell me what I can and can't do? Besides, you have no clue what I'm thinking about."

"You're thinking that if you can get him to …sleep with you, that he'll leave Morgan alone."

Oh, that hurt. Did he really think that lowly of me? "Yeah, nice thought there," I said as I stood. "Sorry, Collin, but I don't sleep with everyone."

I waved at Tori and fled through the living room to the front door. I nearly made it, too, but he was quick and grabbed my arm, swinging me around to face him.

"I didn't mean it that way and you know it," he growled. "Not in the least."

"I know," I sighed. "And if you're worried that I would try something like that, then save your breath. I'd never sleep with filth like that."

"What are you planning?" he asked as he loosened his hold.

"Not sure exactly but I do intend on getting him away from Morgan."

"I wish you wouldn't do this," he pleaded. "I don't want him touching you."

"And I don't want him touching Morgan," I said. "Look, I can handle him – Morgan can't."

"Bailey, don't go back there, please," he said. He tugged me closer and captured my eyes with his. I swallowed.

"I'm not," I said as my hands rested on his chest. "I'm tired. I'm going home to bed."

I pushed to my toes and pressed a quick kiss to his lips. But he wouldn't let it end there. He wound an arm around my waist and planted a hand on the small of my back. His tongue traced my lips and I opened my mouth. He quickly took advantage as I tangled my hand in his hair, wanting nothing more but to drag him back to his bedroom. The only thing stopping me was that I remembered a ragged, pale Tori sitting at the kitchen table. As I slowly parted my lips from his, I realized that if he did indeed want Tori, he was going about things the wrong way.

"Good night, Collin," I whispered as I tore my body away. "I'll talk to you later."

"Think about it, Bailey," he said as he watched me walk out the door. "Please."

"Sure," I said even though I knew I was not changing my mind. I wasn't going to let that scum do to Morgan what he'd done to Tori.

***

I didn't sleep much that night at all. I tossed and turned as I tried to figure out how I could lure Owen away from Morgan or vice versa. I didn't want to totally destroy my friendship with Morgan but I didn't want her ending up like Tori, either. It was a sacrifice I was going to have to make.

I also pondered that kiss. There was no way in hell he'd kiss me like that if he was in love with Tori – not with her being in the next room. But could he really be interested in me? I was hardly his type. Oh, the attraction was there – no doubt about that. But was there anything more?

I stopped those thoughts immediately. I didn't want to hope.

I got up Saturday morning and took Otis for a long walk, hoping to clear my head so perhaps inspiration would strike. We ended up at the dog park somehow and I reluctantly unleashed Otis and rested on a bench.

It wouldn't be hard to show up at Owen's club and flirt with him. And it wouldn't take much to convince him that he'd be better off with me. But then what? How would I keep him away from Morgan? I would not sleep with him – not a chance it hell that would happen. But I'd have to convince him somehow that I might if he left Morgan alone.

Unless…

What if I let Morgan think I slept with him? Let her see me going to that infamous room above the club with him. Or let her see me coming out of the room. I'd have to arrange it somehow. I just needed to think and figure it all out.

"Hello, Bailey," a familiar voice called.

I started and jerked my head in the direction of the voice. My stomach clenched. "Hey, Craig. How are you?"

"Heartbroken," he said with a fake pout. "You never called."

"Yeah, well, I told you not to hold your breath."

He laughed and sat next to me, crossing his leg over his knee. He tapped on his shoe and watched the dogs frolic in the enclosure. "I must not have made much of an impression on you."

"What can I say – I've had a lot on my mind lately."

"Sorry to hear that," he said, his brows furrowed. "I take your bad week has extended to include this week?"

"Something like that," I said, not at all wanting to get into any of it with this man. "But I'm not one to dwell," I said with a false smile.

"Great," he smiled. "How about if I take you to dinner tonight?"

"Thanks but no thanks," I said. "I think I have plans."

"Oh?" he asked as a brow rose above the rim of his eyeglasses. "Hope they're good plans."

I contemplated his words as the first phase of my plan began to form in the back of my mind. I needed to get out of there and get home. I had a lot to do.

"Yeah, they're good ones," I said as I stood and whistled for Otis. "I think I'm headed for a club tonight. The Tail Feather Club. And I really need to get going. I'm sure I'll see you here again." I was thinking out loud as more ideas popped inside my head.

"Have fun tonight. And I hope things get better," he said.

***

I ignored my cell phone as I stood in front of the mirror. I'd decided on a tight, black skirt and silver halter that left my back bare. I dried my hair and brushed it until it flowed like a dark, velvet curtain over my shoulders.

I applied enough makeup to make my eyes look dark and mysterious and my lips full. I stepped into stiletto pumps, sprayed my favorite scent on my neck and grinned. Yeah, I'd catch his attention for sure.

I crammed some cash and my ID into my purse and just as I was reaching for my cell, it rang. I groaned as Collin's name came up but answered it anyway.

"What?" I barked.

"What are you doing tonight?" he asked, desperately working to keep the curiosity out of his voice.

"Going out. Why? What are you doing?" I asked casually.

"Nothing. Where are you going?"

Ah, the Spanish Inquisition. He was digging to see if I was going to work on Owen tonight. Well, I'd been expecting it. "I'm going out with a friend I met at the dog park."

"Oh," was his disappointed reply. "I see. Well, have fun and give me a call." He hung up before I could respond and it wrenched my heart. I didn't want him getting the wrong idea but I definitely didn't want him getting the right idea and then try to stop me.

My heart deflated and I wondered if I'd just shoved him away. I couldn't dwell on it, though. I was on a mission and I would not fail.

Chapter Sixteen

I swished my hips as I walked into the club like I owned it and slipped onto a stool at the bar. I smiled seductively as Scooter appeared before me. He rested his elbows on the bar and waited for my order, no flicker of recognition in his eyes.

"Hi Scooter. Bailey, remember?" I said as a smirk made its way on my face.

"Bailey?" he asked, his brow crunched in concentration. "Bailey who?"

I rolled my eyes and asked for a beer. He shuffled away slowly to fill my order and when he returned, he cocked his head briefly until his eyes grew wide.

"Bailey! I remember you!" he grinned as he slid the beer in front of me. "How are you?"

"Great," I said as I lifted the bottle to my lips. "Is Owen around anywhere?"

His jaw clenched as his eyes tightened. "Yeah, why? Bailey tell me you don't want to mess around with him."

"Hey, a girl gets a little lonely sometimes," I said coyly.

He grunted. "Then hook up with one of the guys on the dance floor. Or better yet – what about the guy who picked you up last time? He looked like he was really into you."

"I don't want to talk about that," I said as I turned my head and scanned the club. It didn't take me long to locate Owen and I was relieved to see Morgan nowhere near him. Hopefully she was home and had no plans to show up later. I wasn't ready for her to see me with Owen yet.

"Seriously, Bailey," Scooter said as he eyed Owen warily. "You seem like a nice girl..."

"I'm not a nice girl," I said hastily. "And there's more to this than you know. Please, Scooter, don't give me any slack, okay?"

"What are you up to?" he asked, his eyes leery.

I was tempted to spill my plan to him – it wouldn't hurt to have a little help. But I was on my own on this one – the fewer who knew the better. It was bad enough that Collin had an idea.

"I'm fine, honestly."

I finished my beer rather quickly and ordered another even though I needed to keep my head. Scooter handed me a bottle and waved off my money when I pulled it out of my purse. I thanked him with a smile and watched Owen from the corner of my eye. Sure enough, he spotted me and eventually made his way over to me.

"Well, look who it is," he said with a nasty sneer on his face. "You tell me I'm not good enough to be with your friend yet you find it acceptable to come to my club."

"What can I say?" I smirked. "I have double standards."

He chortled and gestured to Scooter to refill his glass. "So, are you slumming again?"

"Yes, I guess I am," I said as I swiveled on my stool to face him. I lowered my lids seductively but kept the flirting at that. He knew I couldn't stand him and if I came on too strongly, he'd figure out what I was up to. "I'm bored."

"Really?" he said as he lifted a brow. He accepted a glass from Scooter and sipped it, eyes still on me. "Maybe we can fix that."

His eyes traveled slowly up and down my body and I had to fight a fit of nausea. Still, it boded well in my favor to have him appreciate me the way he was. But I couldn't act out of character. I snorted and raked over his body in abhorrence. "Not likely."

He laughed and cupped my cheek. "You are a spitfire, all right. Spencer was a fool to let you go."

I rolled my eyes. "Spencer didn't let me go – we're still friends."

He lifted a lazy brow. "With benefits?"

"Is that what you and Morgan are?"

His lips curled suggestively. "Jealous?"

"Of what?" I asked.

He laughed again. "Ah, sweet little Morgan isn't just a roll in the hay – she's more of a challenge. Sure, she'll take time but I'm betting the reward will be wonderful."

"You're wasting your time, but hey – it's your life," I said nonchalantly. I lifted a shoulder as if I didn't care but he saw right through me.

"You don't like it a bit, do you?" he said as he leered in my face. He was very handsome but the looks were wasted on him. He was a snake – worse – he was a flea infested rat and I had to clench my teeth to keep from shuddering in disgust.

"Frankly, I just don't give a damn anymore. Morgan's a big girl and perfectly capable of controlling her own life. If she wants to throw it away on you then more power to her." I drained my beer and slid the bottle toward Scooter. He caught it deftly and winked at me as he tossed the bottle in the bin and fetched a fresh one from the cooler. "But to be fair," I continued in an aloof tone. "I think you can do better. I have feeling you have a voracious sexual appetite and I don't think she can satisfy it."

He chuckled and clinked his glass to my bottle. "So true, so true." He finished his drink and slammed his glass on the bar. "I think that's where you and I are very much alike. And I also think you and I would burn the sheets and start a fire."

I lifted a brow and looked pointedly at the crotch of his jeans. "I'm not quite sure you have much to work with."

He laughed heartily and pounded on the bar. "Oh, yes, you are something else, Bailey. Very, very interesting indeed."

"What can I say?" I asked as I lifted the bottle to my lips. "But you do present a challenge."

His mouth opened in astonishment. "I do?"

I nodded, a smirk making its way across my face. "Yep."

"How so?" he asked, perplexed.

I set my beer carefully on the bar and took his hand. "Let's dance and maybe I'll tell you."

I led him toward the dance floor, making sure to swing my hips just enough to capture his attention. I muscled my way through the crowd then turned and pressed my body close to his. Satisfaction washed over his handsome features as his hands gripped my hips. I tossed my arms loosely over his shoulders and began to grind.

He wasn't a bad dancer and kept up easily with me – I was a novice at best. We got through a few songs before he tugged me back to the bar and ordered Scooter to freshen our drinks.

"You intrigue me, Bailey," he said as he wiped the sweat off his brow with a napkin. "Very much."

"Hm, too bad," I said as I took a long drink. The beer went down a little too easily – refreshing my throat.

"Why is it too bad?" he asked.

"Because, I don't mess around with other people's men," I said. "Contrary to what people think."

"So much for those double standards," he quipped.

"I guess," I said.

"I thought you didn't much care who you slept with," he said. "As long as it was good."

My heart plunged into a bucket of ice water but I managed to keep control of the mask on my face.

"Think what you will." I finished my beer and stood. I grabbed Owen's lapel and yanked his face to mine. I pressed a deep, lingering kiss on his lips then grinned. "Thanks for tonight. Maybe I'll see you again. Soon."

"Maybe," he said with a lazy drawl. He'd recovered from the kiss and wrapped an arm around my waist to escort me to the door.

I paused, my hand on the glass, and turned to him, brandishing my sexiest smile. "Why don't you give me a call sometime?" I suggested in a throaty voice. I pecked his cheek and pushed open the door.

"I will," he called as my heels crunched the gravel. I smiled my satisfaction as I got into my car and started the engine.

It wasn't until I reached the highway that repulsion hit me. I fought for control over my rolling stomach as I maneuvered my car through traffic. The few beers I'd had didn't help any at all. Self-disgust smacked me in the face and shame jabbed at my heart.

I knew the truth – knew who and what I really was – so why did it bother me what a piece of filth like Owen thought? Besides, that's the reputation I'd worked hard to maintain. It kept people from thinking I cared about things.

A couple tears leaked from my eyes and pissed me off. I swiped at them and groaned, clearing my throat of the self-pitying misery that threatened to explode.

I yanked on the steering wheel to change lanes and cut off another car in the process. The driver honked angrily at me but I ignored him as I exited the highway and found myself wandering the dark streets near Collin's place.

Once I had my emotions under control, I parked in front of his house and ambled slowly to his front door. I knocked once and frowned when he didn't answer. His SUV was in the drive but that didn't mean he was home. He could have gone somewhere with Tori or someone.

My heart plunged again until the door opened and Collin stood in the threshold. "Bailey?"

"Hey," I said as I attempted a smile. "Can I come in or are you busy?"

He stepped back and allowed me to enter. I sank to the sofa and pinched the bridge of my nose. "Thanks."

He sat gingerly next to me and laced his fingers together. "You look pretty hot," he said with a smirk. "What's up?"

"I'm not a whore, Collin," I whispered.

He placed a causal hand on my shoulder. "I know that - we've had this conversation, remember? What's the matter?"

I leaned into him and he held me to his chest, his hands rubbing my back. I took several long, deep breaths to keep from crying. When I was once again under control, I drew back to smile. "I got my reputation in high school but I assure you that I didn't earn it."

He cupped my cheek, his thumb stroking my skin. "I don't think you're a whore, Bailey. I never have. I swear."

"I dated this guy my junior year – his name was Ben. He was a sweet kid and I really liked him. I didn't love him and I don't think he loved me – we weren't at that point in our relationship." I reached for Collin's hand and he twined our fingers together. "Well, this guy, Clay Redburn, transferred to our school. He was pretty hot and all the girls were lusting after him. I wasn't – not really – but I did think he was cute. Anyway, Veronica and I were friends then and she was crazy for Clay. I was happy with Ben and thought it would be cool if she had the same sort of thing with Clay. I talked her into just confronting him – told her to ask him out."

I paused and leaned back into the couch. Collin kept hold of my hand and gave it an encouraging squeeze. "What happened?"

"Well, she found him near a classroom one morning and approached him. I was standing a little way off with a group of our friends so we could see what happened. When she asked him out, he laughed at her and said she wasn't his type. He said he preferred girls like…like me."

Collin's eyes widened and I gave him a grim smile. "So, she got pissed?"

"Yep. She was humiliated and wouldn't speak to me or anyone else for the rest of the day. The next week, she told me we no longer had anything in common and she didn't want to be my friend anymore. I was hurt but I figured she'd get over it. I was still seeing Ben and I definitely didn't want anything to do with Clay. But Veronica wouldn't believe it."

"What did she do?" Collin asked.

"She started spreading rumors about me – telling people that I slept around a lot and that the only reason why Clay liked me was that I had sex with him in the boys' locker room." I snorted. "Collin, I was a virgin then. I hadn't had sex with Ben, my boyfriend, let alone anyone else. But people always want to believe the worst and they started looking at me differently. It didn't help that Clay – whose popularity increased with the rumors – started going along with them. Pretty soon, Ben became fed up with all the talk and didn't believe me when I tried to defend myself."

"Damn," Collin murmured. "Bailey, I'm …"

"Save it," I said, holding up my free hand. "It happened and that's that."

"What did you do?" he asked breathlessly.

I shrugged. "School ended and I tried to avoid everyone that summer but when school started again, so did the rumors. But instead of defending myself, I just let them all say what they wanted. I acted like I didn't care and even encouraged some of the rumors. People steered clear of me – most of them were intimidated. It worked for me."

"Geez," Collin said as he pulled me back in his arms. "That really sucks. You didn't deserve that."

"Collin," I muttered in his chest. "Do you want to know the truth? The absolute truth of how many men I've been with?"

He tensed but didn't release me. He kissed the top of his head. "Only if you want to tell me."

"Well, you were number four," I said as I edged back and rubbed my tired eyes. "I dated two different guys my senior year and I really liked them. They were the only ones I'd slept with back then. Spencer was the third."

I smiled feebly at him. He cupped my cheeks with both hands and bent to kiss me softly. My eyes fluttered shut as I lifted arms and wrapped them around his neck. He deepened the kiss and a low moan escaped my lips. My pulse throbbed in my veins as I scooted closer. He dropped his hands from my face and collected me in his arms.

I dragged my lips near his ear. "I want you, Collin."

He stood and took my hands. "Are you sure?"

I snorted and drew a smile on his face. "Yes."

He led me to his bedroom and closed the door. His confidence seemed to ebb as we faced each other. I took the initiative and heaved his shirt over his head. That buoyed him to remove my top and help me out of my skirt.

He lowered me to the bed and kicked off his jeans. His lips met mine and a thrill swept through my body.

His kisses remained sweet and nearly stole my breath. He kissed his way to my jaw and throat, drawing goose bumps on my skin. I gasped and clutched his shoulders, arching my back. He continued to kiss my entire face until our lips once again met. My entire body was nothing but molten lava yet he seemed perfectly content to kiss me and seemed in no hurry to move things along.

My desire only increased at his tenderness as my heart beat happily in my chest. I twined my fingers in his hair, delighting in his soft tresses.

He finally removed my undergarments but carried on with his slow, thorough explorations. I squirmed in anticipation, anxious for him.

He eased back to look into my face and my heart stopped briefly as my lungs heaved. The look in his eyes wasn't one I could identify but it restarted my heart and made it pump a little quicker. I reached up and pushed the bangs off his forehead. He kissed me again and at last, he entered me with such tenderness I had a sudden urge to cry.

I expected fervent passion but wasn't disappointed with his easy, unhurried motions. It was as if he wanted me to see some other side of him and I loved it. I loved everything about him and his gentle lovemaking only endeared him to me more.

He did pick up the pace as we both neared our climax and when we were both gasping for breath, he dropped beside me and gathered me in his arms.

I toyed with the sprinkling of hair on his chest as I recovered, my heart overflowing with so many emotions. I wanted to confess so many things to him – especially how much I loved him – but I didn't want to ruin the moment.

He kissed the top of my head. "Will you stay here tonight?"

"Yes," I said, still quite breathless.

"What about Otis?" he asked.

"I left him with my neighbor earlier," I explained. "I wasn't sure what I was going to do tonight."

He squeezed my shoulder and kissed my forehead. I pressed my ear to his chest, reveling in how his heartbeat seemed as erratic as mine. It gave me quite the thrill to know that I had that affect on him.

"You went to see Owen tonight, didn't you?" he asked in a quiet voice.

"Yeah," I admitted. "He's such a puke."

"I know," Collin said. "Did he try anything with you?"

"No," I snorted. "But I gave him something to think about besides Morgan."

He sighed heavily and his breath tousled my hair. I knew he was going to object and try to persuade me from going ahead with my plan. I didn't want that – especially not after the extraordinary way he'd made love to me. I didn't want anything to mess up the night.

"Collin, please," I begged. "I don't want to talk about it tonight. I just want to lay here with you."

He ran his hand up and down my arm a few times and I lifted my face to his. He kissed me, allowing his lips to linger on mine and jolting my heart. When he pulled away, he smiled at me. My heart flipped.

"Okay," he said. He kissed me again. "We won't talk about it tonight."

"You're agreeing to this far too easily," I said warily.

He chuckled and kissed me again. He shifted to his side and traced my face with his finger. "Only because I just want to lay here with you, too." He bent to press his lips to mine. "But we will talk about it tomorrow."

I rolled my eyes but couldn't suppress a grin. At that moment, I could care less about anything or anyone. Screw Disneyland – I was in the happiest place on earth; cuddled up next to Collin in his bed.

"I'm sure we will," I said. I wriggled closer and he fell to his back, pulling me partially on top of his chest. "But until then, I'd like to get a little sleep. Haven't had much lately."

"We can't have that," he teased. He situated me comfortably and kissed me once more. "Get some sleep, Bailey," he murmured in my hair. "And you can make me breakfast in the morning."

"Not likely," I snorted as I closed my eyes. I drifted off with a queer smile on my face.

Chapter Seventeen

I woke slowly as the events of the previous evening rolled through my mind. I smiled as I stretched and reached for Collin. My smile slipped as the spot next to me was empty. I sat up, taking the sheet with me, and searched the room.

"Damn!" came an oath from the kitchen. I chuckled and fumbled around the floor until I located an article of clothing. It was Collin's shirt. I slipped it over my head. I tossed the sheets back and padded into the kitchen.

Collin was standing before the stove, only in his jeans, one hand on a pan handle and his pinky finger in his mouth. "Son of a bitch," he muttered.

I crept behind him and slithered my arms around his waist, admiring the bunched muscles in his bare back. "Aw, did you burn yourself?"

He turned off the fire and twisted in my arms, broad smile on his face. Grabbing my face, he pressed a hard kiss to my lips. "Yes, I did, making your breakfast."

I lifted his hand and sucked on his finger. His eyes narrowed and he tugged me closer. "Your breakfast will get cold," he said in a husky voice.

I laughed and dropped his hand. "I thought I was supposed to cook?"

He shrugged, his cheeks coloring slightly. "You said you haven't been sleeping well so I thought I'd let you sleep in and surprise you with breakfast."

My heart tingled and a goofy smile engulfed my face. "Thanks."

He kissed me again. "Any time. Now sit."

I did as he dished up the eggs and bacon. He set a plate before me then proceeded to fill two glasses with orange juice. He joined me and we ate pretty much in silence, though we both kept throwing surreptitious glances at each other.

When we finished, we cleaned up the kitchen together and it was very hard to keep my hands off of him. My heart was a jittery mess already and the knowing looks only intensified it. Once the dishwasher was loaded, he leaned against it, pulling me into his arms.

"So, what are you going to do today?" he asked.

An evil grin spread across my lips. "You?"

He laughed, his eyes sparkling. "Well, I won't object but I wondered if you had any other plans."

"Not really," I said as I stepped into him. My heart was thumping and I was slightly worried he'd hear it. I rested my forearms on his shoulders. "Want to hang out?"

"Yeah," he said as his eyes lingered on my lips. "I'll take you by your place so you can change. Maybe we can take the dogs to the dog park or something."

I snorted. "Yeah then maybe you can meet my new buddy." I laughed when I thought of Craig.

"What new buddy?"

I quickly explained to him about my last few visits to the dog park and laughed harder at the interest in Collin's eyes. He kissed me, massaging my lips softly. I sighed and leaned into him for support. When he pulled back, he winked.

"Let's go meet this friend of yours."

* * *

I didn't know exactly how to define my relationship with Collin. It was quite obvious that things had changed – possibly improved – but I didn't know what it meant. And I was in no hurry to find out, either. I was happy with things the way they were.

We walked, hand-in-hand, to the dog park, Otis and Milo trotting joyfully. It didn't take long to reach the park and once we released the hounds, we sat close together on the bench.

But Collin didn't relax – his eyes scoured the park. I laughed and rested a hand on his thigh.

"He might not show up and even if he does, what are you going to do?"

He draped an arm around my shoulders and whispered in my ear. "I'll just show him that he's wasting his time trying to pick you up."

Snorting, I suppressed a shudder. He chortled and kissed my cheek.

We watched the dogs play for awhile but Craig never showed up. It didn't break my heart any because I really could care less. I was with Collin and that was all that mattered.

Yeah, I was definitely a lovesick girl. I giggled.

"What?" he asked, raising a brow.

"Nothing," I said as I scooted closer.

"Hey, what do you say if we go out tonight?" Collin asked shyly. "You know, like to dinner or something?"

My heart flipped. "Sure. That'd be great."

His smile did weird things to my insides and I could do nothing more but kiss him. We rounded up the dogs shortly after and he dropped me off at home, taking Otis with him.

"I'll pick you up in a couple hours," he said as he kissed me in the doorway. "And I'll take Otis to my place, you know, in case you want to spend the night again." His flushed cheeks tickled me.

"Okay,"

* * *

I skipped the shower and opted instead for a luxurious bath with my favorite scented bubbles. When I finished, I dried my hair and let it hang down my back. Collin hadn't mentioned where we'd be dining so I wasn't quite sure what to wear. I decided to keep it casual and if he showed up all dressy, I'd change.

I was a wreck when the doorbell rang and hurried on shaky legs to answer it. I ripped the door open and nearly lost my breath. He grinned, his eyes never leaving my face. He was dressed in nice jeans and a green button up shirt that brought out the flecks in his eyes.

"You clean up nice," I said as I openly appraised him.

Grabbing my waist, he yanked me flush with his body. His lips hovered over mine. "And you look as beautiful as ever." He kissed me and all coherent thought flew from my head. When he pulled back I was still flustered and a flicker of triumph flashed in his eyes.

"Are you ready?" he asked.

"Sure," I said as I grabbed my bag and locked the door. "Where are we going?"

He took my hand as we walked to the elevator. "No place real fancy," he said with a slight blush. "I didn't think you'd like that."

"Not particularly," I muttered.

He smiled and gave my hand a squeeze. "I was thinking we'd hit that new steakhouse downtown. Is that okay?"

"Perfect," I said with a nervous smile.

When we arrived at the steakhouse, we were seated immediately. We placed our order, hardly glancing at the menu, too busy studying each other. Once the waitress disappeared, my nerves returned. I couldn't understand it – it was Collin. We'd hung out plenty of times – not to mention other things. But sitting across the table from him in a restaurant was unnerving. And I was dying to know what all this meant. Were we dating now?

"So, um," he stammered, concentrating on his silverware. "I was thinking that I should probably talk to Spencer."

My eyes widened at his suggestion. Maybe I was about to get my answer. "Really?"

Taking my reaction as horror, he reached across the table and grabbed my hand. "I wasn't going to tell him about …you know," he said as color flooded his cheeks again. It was far too cute. "I just thought…well…that I'd tell him I wanted to…date you." He spoke the last part so quietly that I had to strain to hear him.

My heart jumped and skipped all over the place. "Okay," I said, unsure what to say.

"*Is* it okay with you?" he asked, his eyes finding mine.

My self-confidence grew at his uncertainty. I obviously wasn't alone in this. "It's more than okay," I said as I laced my fingers with his.

His smile lit up his eyes. "Well, I know you didn't want anything serious with Spencer – not that I'm asking you to get serious with me."

"Collin," I said as I gave his hand a little squeeze. "What I felt for Spencer is totally different than this." I gestured between the two of us.

He flashed a half smile. "That's comforting to know."

"So what are you going to say to him?" I asked. I was relieved that he wanted to take things further but I was also concerned about

Spencer's feelings. He was too great of a guy to get hurt. Besides, I'd already hurt one friend – I didn't want to make it two.

"No idea," he shrugged. "But I have a plan that I hope will soften the blow." A knowing smirk covered his face.

"Care to share?" I asked, my curiosity aroused.

"Not yet," he winked. "I'm not sure if it will work."

I bent over the table and lowered my voice. "You're not going to hire a ... professional, are you?"

"Professional?" he asked, his brow furrowed.

"You know," I said, trying to keep the amusement out of my voice. "A prostitute?"

He snorted his laughter and picked up my hand to press it to his lips. "No, not at all."

"That's a relief," I said as I sat back in my chair. The waitress appeared with our food and our conversation turned casual as we ate. I couldn't remember the last time I'd enjoyed myself so much on a date and I had to chalk it up to the love I felt for him. Maybe there was hope for me yet.

When we finished our meal and the dishes were cleared, Collin paid the check and led me back to his car. I wasn't eager for the evening to be finished even though I knew where I'd be when the date ended.

"So, what would you like to do now?" Collin asked as he started the engine. "Do you want to catch a movie or something?"

Even though sitting close to Collin in the dark was appealing, that wasn't exactly what I wanted at the moment. Of course we didn't have many options since it was a Sunday evening.

"You probably won't believe this is coming from my mouth," I smirked. "But how about if we take a walk around the park?"

A slow smile spread across his lips. "Aw, Bailey does have a romantic streak in her." I blushed furiously as he leaned closer to me. "You're a closet romantic, aren't you?"

I lifted a brow though the heat in my cheeks ruined the effect. "Would you like me to punch you?"

He chuckled. "Not really. I'm sure you pack a punch."

"And I'm pretty sure you could take me," I teased as he parked the car.

We both got out and joined hands as we made our way through the park. The night was warm and we weren't the only couple enjoying the evening. It really was quite romantic and it surprised me how much I liked it.

"So, back to Spencer," he said as we approached the duck pond. The dim lamps cast long shadows on the path and I imagined it would be rather creepy in inclement October weather.

"What about him?" I asked, instantly on guard.

"Well, if you want to continue this," he said, lifting our linked hands to gesture between us, "then I need to speak to him as soon as possible."

"Collin," I said, taking the plunge. I wouldn't plunge all the way and admit my deepest feelings, but if he was willing to go out on a limb for us, then I'd need to be honest. "I like you, a lot. I do want to see you again and I'd prefer not to have to hide."

Stopping, he turned to face me, taking my other hand. "I don't want to hide, either. I watched my brother go through hell last year and I don't want to see the same thing happen to us." He leaned in to kiss me quickly.

"Any idea what you're going to say?" I asked.

"Not really," he sighed. He dropped one hand and tugged me forward, continuing our walk. "I guess just be as honest as possible. I don't want to tell him too much but I don't want to outright lie to him."

I tossed it around in my head a little bit, considering what I could do to make it easier on both of them. "Do you want me to talk to him?"

"Nah, I think it's best if I do," he said. "He is my cousin and my best friend."

"If you insist," I said.

He laughed and yanked on my hand, causing me to stumble into his side. He wrapped his arms around me and planted a long kiss on my lips. It took me a second to figure out what was going on before I grabbed his shoulders and returned his kiss.

"Ready to go?" he whispered as his lips left mine and traveled up to my ear. He trailed his lips along my jaw and down my neck. I shivered and twined my arms tightly around his neck.

"Yes," I hissed. "Let's go."

We barely made it into the house, let alone the bedroom, before I was whipping the shirt off his body. He grinned and helped me out of my clothes just as eagerly. Every inch of my skin was on fire and every time he touched me, that fire burned out of control. I just couldn't get enough of him.

His kisses turned fervent as we fell to the bed and I kissed him back just as hungrily. I held on to him tightly as I writhed underneath him and when we finished, we both struggled to find our breath.

"Damn, Bailey," he said, his chest heaving. "I don't know how the hell I manage to keep up with you."

Chuckling, I rolled to my side. I swiped at the sweat on his brow and kissed him. "You do a fantastic job, trust me."

He laughed and pressed his hand in the small of my back, forcing me closer. His eyes searched mine as the smile slipped from his lips. My breath hitched as he eased me into another kiss – this one slower and much more thorough. My heart swelled as my emotions escalated and the desire to express myself increased.

His other hand tangled in my hair as he shifted me to my back and lingered over me. His fingers floated gracefully from my neck and shoulder and down my arm. I moaned softly and ran my hands through his hair before dropping them to his back. His muscles bunched under my touch and I tingled inside at how I affected him as much as he did me.

He leisurely explored my body as if he'd never done so before and I squirmed in delight. His kisses were deliberate and tender as if he read my mind and knew exactly how I felt.

I fell asleep that night tucked securely in his arms with his warm breath and soft snores caressing my cheek and my hair.

***

His alarm clock woke me up before the sun even peeked its head. Groaning, he reached over me to hit the snooze button.

"You have to work, don't you?" I mumbled as I snuggled into his chest.

"Yes," he said with another groan. He pressed a sleepy kiss in my hair. "Sucks, huh?"

"Mm hm," I answered.

He chuckled, kissed me again and scrambled out of the bed. "I have to hop in the shower and if you want, I'll take you for breakfast before I drop you off at home."

I sat up and yawned, admiring his naked body. "I have a better idea. How about if I help you shower then you can drop me off at home and you can grab some breakfast on the way to work?"

He planted his hands on either side of my body and kissed me. "I love how you think."

Frigid water forced us out of the shower, luckily, or else Collin would have been even later to work. I took care of the dogs while he rushed around locating his work clothes. By the time we made it to his car, he had barely enough time to get to the body shop.

He kissed me quickly in front of my building while a squirming Otis tried to lick his cheek. "I'll call you when I get home."

I jumped out of the car and hurried up to the condo. I changed my clothes and checked my voice messages as Otis attacked his favorite squeak toy. My heart sang happily as I dialed Irelyn's number. The lovesick girl was emerging and I couldn't stand it any longer – I had to share my joy with a friend.

"What's up?" Irelyn asked, a yawn in her voice.

"Well, just thought you'd like to know where I spent my weekend," I said as I studied my nails.

"Oh?" she asked and I could visualize her raising a brow. "Where?"

I repressed a giggle – I didn't want to sound too school-girly. "With Collin."

"Seriously?" she asked incredulously. "Wow. Luke was wondering why Collin didn't call him all weekend."

"That would be me," I said, beaming.

"So, are you guys dating now? Officially, or whatever?"

"I guess," I said. "He took me to dinner last night. He said he's going to talk to Spencer."

"Ouch, I'd hate to be a fly on the wall for that conversation," she said.

"I know," I said. "Hey, I offered to do the talking but he said he thought it should be him. I just hope Spencer doesn't turn out to be the violent type. I'd hate it if he ripped Collin's balls off."

"Oh, geez, Bailey," Irelyn snickered. "That's real nice."

I laughed. "Just being honest, babe. So, any luck with Morgan?"

"No," she said, disheartened. "Not at all. She won't answer my calls. And I heard she's been actually dating Owen. I don't like that at all."

"Me, either," I said as I bit my lip. "I'm working on that."

"What are you up to?" she asked.

"I'll tell you when I get a better grip on it," I said. "And I'm going to let you go so you can go join the other working stiffs. Call me later."

"Sure," she said.

I hung up and carefully set the phone down. I leaned against the wall, my mind mulling the Owen situation. It was quite obvious that I hadn't made that big of an impression on him if he was still seeing Morgan and hadn't called. I'd have to step it up a notch.

But, things were going so great with Collin - did I dare take a chance on messing that up for Morgan's sake?

I pictured Tori's pained face when she'd confessed her horrid relationship with Owen. I didn't want to see Morgan looking the same way. I didn't know Tori as well as I knew Morgan but I had a feeling that Morgan was stronger. I couldn't see her succumbing to Owen's lifestyle but she was upset and very vulnerable.

"Damn it!" I shouted, startling Otis. He scampered beneath the coffee table and peered up at me cautiously, his brown eyes frightened. I sighed and squatted, tapping my thigh. He sidled up to me and I scratched his ears until the quivering stopped.

"Sorry, buddy," I cooed. His tail thumped the floor. "What the hell am I going to do?"

He yipped as if offering a solution but it wasn't the answer I was looking for. I considered speaking to Collin about it but I knew he'd be totally against my original plan and as I had no clue what else to do, it looked like I was on my own.

And it totally sucked.

Chapter Eighteen

The next week was a rollercoaster ride through hell. On the one hand, things with Collin were rolling along smoothly. He called me every night when he got home from work and we saw each other twice during the week. He even said that he'd spoken to Spencer but he wouldn't disclose what was said – all he would tell me is that Spencer took it well.

I had my doubts but I didn't push it. They had their regular gig at Rusty's Friday and I'd just have to wait and see how things played out.

Collin called me Friday just as I was about to walk out the door and warned me to keep things cool in front of Spencer. That immediately put me on guard but I sucked it up and agreed. I wasn't exactly anxious to flaunt my new relationship – or whatever it was- under Spencer's nose.

I got there as the boys were setting up their equipment and found Irelyn at our regular table. I dropped into a chair next to her, my eyes on Spencer.

"Has Spencer said anything?" I whispered.

"About what?" Irelyn asked as she turned her head toward me. "Oh, Collin must have talked to him."

"Yeah, he said he did but he didn't exactly elaborate on the details," I said in a bitter tone. I motioned for Marissa to bring us some drinks.

I caught Spencer glance at our table but when I looked at him, he quickly averted his eyes. My stomach plunged to my feet and my blood iced. I desperately wanted to talk to him and try to smooth things over but I hadn't had the best of luck lately so things weren't exactly looking good for me.

The guys didn't join us for a pre-gig drink and when I raised a brow at Collin, he gave me a swift head shake. My stomach fell even further and I couldn't get comfortable or relax. I did, however, take it easy on the alcohol, although it was tempting to just get sloshed.

The guys were nearing the end of their last set when Tori joined us, adding to the awkward tension cloud lingering over my head. She smiled feebly at me before turning her attention to the stage. I couldn't look at her.

When they finished, they settled around the table and absent was the usual raucous chatter that always thrived on their adrenaline. Only Lucas seemed at ease and the urge to punch him was damn near irrepressible.

"Hey, Bailey," Spencer said as he stood. His hands clutched the back of his chair and his knuckles turned white. "I'm going to step outside for some air – care to join me?"

I fought to keep my eyes on Spencer's and not let them dart to Collin. I slid my chair away from the table with a tight smile. "Sure."

He held the door open for me and placed a hand on my back. He steered me to the metal steps that led to his apartment. He sat on the third one and patted the spot next to him. I settled on the cool metal and took a deep breath.

"All right, Spence, spill," I ordered.

"Why didn't you just tell me, Bailey?" he asked, his voice pitiful.

"Tell you what? About Collin?" I asked but didn't wait for an answer. "Spencer, there was nothing to tell. I was totally honest with you when I broke things off. There was no one else – I just didn't have the feelings for you – not romantic feelings."

"But Collin said that he wanted to date you – that you wanted to date him," he said.

"That's the truth," I said as I craned my head to look at him. "But at the time, I had no idea that he liked me in that way."

"Did you like him – that way?" he asked, his eyes earnest.

I swallowed. "Yeah, I did – but I didn't think he felt the same way. I never thought he would."

Spencer narrowed his eyes. "Why?"

"Geez, Spence," I said as I dropped my head. "I never thought you'd feel anything real for me, either. I'm just not that girl, you know?"

"Oh, bull," he said as he grabbed my chin. "That's bull shit, Bailey. Maybe if you'd stop putting yourself down for a few minutes you'll see that other people really care about you."

I could only nod. I knew he had a point but for the past few years, I'd relied heavily on my reputation – it was easier than letting my guard down. But since Irelyn and Morgan stormed into my life – followed closely by Spencer, Collin, and Lucas – I'd lowered the walls a bit. It was nice having real friends and people who accepted you no matter what.

And now I was hurting them all. First Morgan and now Spencer.

I sighed heavily, expelling all the negative air that I could. "Spencer, I didn't do you right. I didn't do Morgan right. Hell, I probably won't do Collin right."

"Stop," he said, laying a hand on my arm. "You're different around Collin – I've noticed. Maybe you tried to hide it but I could see. I could see before Irelyn and Morgan could. Hell, I probably saw it before you."

"What are you talking about?" I asked as I lifted my head.

He ran his hands through his hair. "The tension – the chemistry. You two must have been blind and stupid not to notice it or else I was paying more attention."

I shrugged. "Maybe we ignored it because we didn't want to hurt you."

He laughed a hollow sort of laugh. "Maybe. But listen, I love both of you and I'd hate for us to not talk. I don't want us to end up like…you know…Morgan."

I cringed a little and he wrapped an arm around my shoulders. "I sort of saw it coming and I've been trying to prepare myself. Yeah, it bugs me a little bit but I'll get over it."

I bobbed my head up and down. "Thanks, Spence."

He kissed my cheek. "Will you tell me one thing?"

"Sure," I said, my heart lightening.

"Did you...did you sleep with him...you know, while we were together?"

It was like a sharp smack in the face and my breath left me in a gush. "No, Spencer. Damn. How could you think that about Collin? Do you think he'd do that to you?" I asked, the pitch of my voice rising. "I mean, I know I deserve that because – well, I do sort of have that reputation..."

"Hell, Bailey, I didn't mean..." Spencer started.

"Well, well, well," Owen drawled as he approached us, his arm wound tightly around Morgan's waist. "Lover's spat?"

"Bug off," I spit, my eyes shooting darts at him. The little weasel had forgotten our conversation from the previous weekend and dared to show up again with Morgan. I'd make him pay.

"What are you doing here?" Spencer asked in an icy tone. I was mildly surprised – Spencer usually spoke warmly to his friend.

"Thought we'd hang out, didn't we darling?" he said as he kissed Morgan's cheek, making my skin crawl.

"Yes," she whispered, her eyes skipping all over the place.

"Well, if you'll excuse us," I said with venom in my voice, "we're having a private conversation. Move along."

Owen shot me a wink and urged Morgan inside the bar.

Spencer watched them closely until the door closed behind them. "Collin let me in on the situation with Tori. Man, I knew Owen could be a dick but I didn't know he could be that bad. I hate to see Morgan with him."

"Tell me," I said as my body began to tremble. "I can't stand it. And I won't. I'm going to get her away from him anyway I can."

"Yeah, so I hear," Spencer said as he twisted slowly to face me again. "And you need to stay away from him, too."

"I can take care of myself," I iterated firmly. "Morgan, on the other hand..."

"Morgan has made a choice," Spencer said as he gripped my arm.

"Morgan is trying to get back at us," I said.

"Do you honestly think she's that spiteful?"

I leaned back on the step behind me. "I'm beginning to think so." I hoisted my body off the steps and clumped to the ground. My blood began to race as anger stirred inside my stomach. "And I am going to get him away from her. No matter what it takes."

***

"Absolutely not," Irelyn said as we sat around Collin's table later that night. She turned her eyes on Lucas, begging him to agree.

"Irelyn's right," Collin said. He leaned back in his chair, full bottle of beer in his hand. "The only thing we can do is keep trying to talk to Morgan."

"That's what you guys think," I said as I stood and moved to stand near the counter. "But I can handle him. He wants me. I just – didn't keep up with him. I let too much time pass."

"No, Bailey," Spencer said. "Listen to us. He's trouble."

I laughed. "You thought he was a great guy until a few days ago."

"Well I was wrong," he muttered as he shot a quick look at Tori's pinched, pale face. He took her hand on top of the table.

"But Tori's not," I said as I narrowed my eyes at her.

"Leave her out of it," Collin warned, finally looking at me.

I raised a brow, not at all happy he was defending her. I understood, but didn't like his sharp tone. "I'm not attacking her – just pointing out that she is the one who really knows him."

"Yes," she said, quietly. "And I don't think it's a good idea for anyone to get mixed up with him."

"But it's a good idea for Morgan?" I asked, my anger climbing toward hysteria.

"Not at all," Tori said. "And I don't know why he's with her - Owen has a thing for you – I can tell."

"Exactly," I said, throwing my hands in the air. "And Owen wants me. It won't take much to get him upstairs."

Collin nearly knocked his chair over as he leapt to his feet. He took my shoulders gently and ducked to meet my eyes. "You cannot force Morgan to do anything she doesn't want to do and getting yourself involved with Owen is only going to make her want him more."

"Not if you guys get her to the club tomorrow night," I said desperately. "I can make him think I want him and she'll see me go upstairs with him. That's all it will take."

"And what happens when he gets you upstairs, huh?" Collin asked, shaking me slightly. "What then?"

I gritted my teeth. "I can handle him."

"If anyone can, she can," Tori added. "I mean, Owen thinks she's..."

I rolled my eyes. "He thinks I'm a whore – you can say it. I know what people think."

"I didn't..." Tori stumbled. "I just meant..."

"Don't worry about it," I said as I held up a hand.

"No," Collin said, dropping his hands and shaking his head. "No, way. There's no way in hell I'll allow this."

I blinked rapidly as my mouth opened. I was momentarily shocked stupid. "You...you'll not allow it? What the hell?"

"You know what I mean," he said, his eyes unwavering.

"No," I said as I recovered and crossed my arms over my chest. "I'm afraid I don't."

"Okay, cool down you two," Irelyn ordered as she rose and stepped between us.

"Forget that, Irelyn," I said as I stormed out of the room. "If he can run off for a week with Tori because of Owen then I sure as hell can make Morgan think I'm screwing him."

"Bailey," Spencer called as he chased after me. He snagged my arm. "Think about it. Think about what you're planning," he said as he lowered his voice. "Not only will you be hurting Morgan but you'll be hurting Collin, too."

I snorted. "How? He knows the truth. I don't want Owen – I can't stand him. Collin knows he's the only one I want."

"Does he?" Spencer asked.

"Bailey," Collin said as he stepped into the room. "Don't do this."

"I have to," I said quietly. "I'm the one who caused this and I'm the one who needs to fix it."

"No you don't," he said. "It's not up to you to fix everything."

"You didn't cause this," Spencer added. "I'm the one who cried on her shoulder – I made her think you hurt me worse than you actually had."

I couldn't face him. I couldn't look him honestly in the eye. He had no clue what really set Morgan off and I wouldn't tell him. I wouldn't push him away from Collin.

"I'm doing this with or without your help," I said. "I'll get Morgan to that club somehow."

"Bailey, if you do," Collin said, his eyes dark and angry. "I swear…"

"What, you're threatening me now?" I asked.

He stepped back, his jaw set and his arms across his chest. "Take it how you will."

I stared at him, looking for the bluff. I couldn't find it. But it wasn't going to stop me. He'd come to his senses – he had to. He was the one who'd taken Tori by the hand and helped her through her nightmare. He should be the first to understand why it was so important to get Morgan away from Owen before it was too late.

I stepped toward Collin and rested a hand on his chest. "Collin, I have to do this. I caused it and I need to fix it." I stood on my toes and pecked his lips. "I'm sorry."

I fled before anyone could stop me.

***

I spent the entire night wracking my brain to figure out a way to get Morgan to the club the following evening and when the sun came up Saturday morning, I still hadn't come up with anything.

My cell rang and I glanced at the ID. It was Collin this time. I ignored it like I had all the other calls from him, Irelyn, and Spencer that had disturbed my poor phone all night. Once I was sure his call went to voice mail, I opened my phone and toyed with the phonebook, looking for Morgan's number and wondering if she'd answer if I called.

I stopped when I came to a number I'd never called and an idea suddenly sprang to mind. A queer smile crossed my lips as I contemplated calling him. I wondered if he'd be willing to help – or at least have lunch.

***

"I have to say that I am surprised you called," Craig said as he settled in the booth across from me. "And I'm even more curious about this plan."

I smiled warmly at him, a little surprised that he'd agreed to meet me after I'd poured out the whole ridiculous story to him on the phone. "Well, it's probably a long shot but my luck's bound to change, huh?"

"Do you actually think your friend Morgan will go out with me?" he asked dubiously. "I mean, if she's already supposedly seeing this Owen guy?"

"It's worth a shot," I shrugged as the waitress took our order. I waited for her to leave before continuing. "Like I said, I don't think she's really into him – I think she's using him to piss us off."

"Sounds like it's working," Craig smirked.

"Like a charm," I muttered as I dropped my eyes to the table.

"I told you on the phone that I'd try," Craig said softly. "I've been in that bookstore countless times so I know exactly who you're talking about." He leaned back and scrunched up his face in concentration. "Maybe a different approach would be better."

My head jerked up immediately as my brows crammed together. "What do you mean?"

"Well," he started as his face cleared. "She might not go for the idea of accompanying me to a club since we don't know each other. But," he leaned over the table. "Do you think she'd be hip to meeting with my book club?"

My brows dipped further as I snorted. "I don't think I'll manage to get Owen to a book club and even if I did, I doubt seriously that Morgan would believe that I'm going to screw him in the library."

He laughed richly and it was a nice sound. Wouldn't it be just peachy if Craig and Morgan actually fell for each other? I hurriedly shoved that thought to the side. I couldn't play Cupid right now – I needed to play the part of the horrible, back-stabbing friend.

"I'm not suggesting you drag Owen to my book club," he said as he sipped his soft drink.

"Do you actually have a book club?"

His smile widened, revealing his dimples. How cute. Too bad I was already in love with Collin even though I was about to possibly throw it all away. "Not really but I do have a group of friends from the university that would more than likely be happy to pose as a book club."

"Okay," I said slowly. "That's great. But how is that going to help get Morgan to Owen's club?"

"Well," he drawled as he rested his arm on the back of the chair. His grin was mischievous and I was beginning to suspect he had a devious mind. "That will be my in, you see? I'll tell her that I've seen her at the book store on several occasions and ask her if she'd like to meet my book club. I'll have her join us somewhere – I haven't figured out a place yet – and we'll sit around and talk about books for awhile. Then, I'll have one of my friends suggest we go out for a drink and we'll somehow get Morgan to the Tail Feather Club." He lifted his hands as if to say 'Duh!'

"That could work," I said in awe. "It would work brilliantly as long as you don't tell her what club you're going to."

"That's simple," he smirked. "We'll all ride together and drive past and I'll have one of the girls say she always wanted to go there and we'll just pull in and park. I'll charm Morgan into going if she makes a fuss."

I appraised him carefully. He was more of Morgan's type – studious, handsome, charming. If anyone could do this, he could. I wasn't one hundred percent comfortable with this plan but it was the best I had.

He pulled a cell phone from his pocket. "Let me call my sister," he said as he pressed buttons. "I'll have her help. She's only a year older than me and she likes to hang out with my friends. She'll help me think of a place for our faux book club."

I nodded. The waitress brought our food while he was on the phone. He made two more phone calls while I pushed my fries around on my plate. When he finished, he smiled.

"Okay, all set. My sister and her boyfriend are in on it as well as my friend, Cal, and his girlfriend." He picked up his cheeseburger and bit off a huge chunk.

"Where is this meeting of the minds going to take place?" I asked.

He held up a finger as he chewed furiously. "At Cuppa's. It's a coffee shop not too far from the Tail Feather."

"Brilliant," I said admirably.

"Thanks," he blushed. "But my sister came up with the place." He shoved a bunch of fries in his mouth and tilted his head. "I'll call you as we leave the coffee shop and let you know we're on our way. Now, what's your plan?"

"What do you mean?" I asked.

"I'm more than willing to help you get a nice girl away from a perverted asshole but I'm not too crazy about you being all alone with him in some room upstairs."

I was touched – honestly. "Don't worry about me – I've handled worse."

"What about your boyfriend," he asked, his eyes boring into mine. "What does he say about all this?"

I shrugged. "He hates it."

"Is he going to be around to protect you?"

I laughed as I narrowed my eyes at him. "I don't need some white knight coming to my rescue and saving the day – I'm hardly a damsel in distress. I will be fine."

He nodded slowly. "That's all fine and good, Bailey, but don't think that me and my friends won't be watching this idiot closely and don't think that we'll stand by and do nothing if we think you're in trouble."

I cracked a grin. "That's nice to know. Now, finish your food – I need to get home and prepare."

He nodded again but didn't smile back as he picked up the remains of his cheeseburger and ate it in one gulp.

After I left the diner and drove home, all the things that could possibly go wrong with this plan rolled through my head. I shivered but did not change my mind. I would do this for Morgan even if she hated me for the rest of her life.

I owed it to her.

Chapter Nineteen

I was a total nervous wreck when I parked my car in front of the Tail Feather Club. I had to take long, deep breaths before I could even open the car door. I gathered my bearings, adjusted my top, and swept my hair over my shoulders as I stepped onto the gravel and made my way to the entrance.

I dressed for the part, too. I wore a black leather mini, black stockings, and black heels. To add a little spice, I chose a blood red halter that didn't leave much to the imagination. Yeah, I looked pretty trashy but Owen wouldn't be able to resist.

Scooter recognized me immediately and placed a beer in front of me before I could ask. I smiled at him but he shook his head, anger clouding his face.

"Bailey, I don't know why you bother with him," he said. "He has a different girl on his arm every night."

"More reason to do this," I said. "Maybe my best friend will see what a slime ball he is and leave him alone."

"Oh, no, not another one," Scooter groaned, arousing my curiosity. "He didn't get her pregnant, too, did he?"

"No," I said slowly. "Does he have a knocked up girlfriend somewhere?"

He lifted a shoulder. "I don't know what he's got and where he's got it. I don't even try to keep track. But I know a few months ago some girl was always in here crying and calling and I thought I overheard her say she was pregnant."

I wondered briefly if that girl was Tori. I shuddered as I imagined Morgan in that position.

"Scooter, please, let me handle this, okay? I'm not naïve and I'm certainly not totally stupid. I intend to make sure my friend stays away from him."

"Don't take things too far, Bailey," Scooter warned. "He may seem harmless but he has a quick temper that is getting more and more out of control."

"So do I," I grinned. I lifted the bottle to my lips and scanned the room. Owen was occupying his usual spot at the corner of the bar and hadn't noticed me yet. I wouldn't approach him – I'd wait for him to approach me.

Sure enough, just as I was finishing my beer, he sauntered over to me. He placed a tentative hand on my shoulder and brushed my hair back so he could lean over and whisper in my ear.

"Somebody's looking like they want to get laid tonight," he said.

I knocked his hand away and turned to face him fully. "Well, if that were true, then I could find far better than you," I snorted. "There's a homeless guy out back digging in your dumpster."

Chuckling, he lightly touched the small of my back. "You weren't saying that last weekend."

"Things change," I said as I motioned to Scooter for another drink. He hurriedly fetched a fresh bottle, opened it, and set it before me. "Owen's paying for this one, Scooter, thanks," I said with a smile. "In fact, he said I'm drinking on the house all night so keep them coming."

Scooter winked and rushed off to help his other customers.

Owen grinned and pressed into me, his lips close to my ear. "What's with the cold shoulder tonight? Are you angry because I was with your friend last night?"

I straightened the collar of his silk shirt and unbuttoned one of the buttons. "Let's just say that I don't like to be played with, okay? If you prefer Morgan over me then that's your choice. But I'm not playing against her."

"Oh," he said, eyes brightening. He really was a handsome man. "So, if I ditch Morgan I can have Bailey. Interesting."

"Who knows," I said as I slid my nail from his throat down his chest. "Guess *we* never will."

"Why is that?" he asked as he wrapped an arm around my waist.

"Because who would ever dump sweet little Morgan for the likes of me," I said coyly.

He kissed me softly – surprising me. "Only a man of taste."

It wouldn't take much at all to get him upstairs now but unfortunately, it was way too early. I glanced at the clock over his shoulder and figured that, if all was going well, Craig was just now getting Morgan out of the coffee shop. He hadn't called yet so I was going to have to stall some more.

"And what happens if this man of taste decides he'd rather have me but shows up at another bar next weekend with Morgan?"

He yanked me closer so that our bodies were flush. "Then that man of taste should be strung up by the balls."

"Interesting concept," I said with an alluring smile to hide the pleasure I found in the image of Owen actually being strung up that way. "Let's dance."

"Dance?" he asked, his brow furrowed in confusion.

I kissed his cheek and dragged my lips to his ear. "It turns me on – gets me all hot."

Owen took my hand and nearly pulled me out of my shoes in his effort to get me to the dance floor. The music was loud and the reverberating beat rattled my teeth but I quickly found a groove and danced as provocatively as possible. When my phone finally vibrated in my hip pocket, I breathed a silent sigh of relief. I waited until it went to voice mail then pulled it out and flipped it open. I held up a finger to Owen and slipped down the hall near the bathrooms. Craig had told me that in order to avoid suspicion from Morgan, when they were on the way he would call my phone, let it go to voice mail, and just hang up without a word. If things weren't going right, he'd leave me a detailed message.

He didn't leave a message. They were on the way.

I found Owen again, standing near the bar, draining a glass of some kind of liquor. I grabbed his hand and tugged him toward the floor.

"Come on, darling," he wheedled when I wrapped my arms around his neck. "Aren't you tired of dancing yet?"

I smashed my breasts into his chest and yanked his head down so I could capture his lips. His hands tightened on my hips as he returned the kiss and a wave of nausea rolled through my stomach.

"Very nice," he said as he pulled back, a little breathless. "Very nice."

"It gets better," I said as I rubbed my body over his. "Just wait."

"Don't know how much longer I can wait," he said as he kissed his way up my neck. I shifted him so I could watch the door and before long, Craig entered with a small group. Including Morgan.

It was show time.

Now I just had to get her to notice us without him noticing her. Craig had promised to help in that department, too, though I worried he'd be a bit too obvious.

The staircase to the upper level rooms was located next to the hall to the bathrooms. The bar ran perpendicular to it so I had a tiny window of opportunity that I could get him to the stairs without him seeing Morgan. I had a feeling that once I got him halfway up the stairs that if he saw her, he wouldn't much care - as long as he thought he was going to score. Knowing him and his big ego, he'd probably figure that he could just charm his way back into her good graces. And I prayed Morgan wasn't that stupid.

I wrapped a leg around his thigh and he gasped. I grinned at him as he ran a hand over the smooth stockings up toward my hip. I kissed him again. "I really want you, Owen," I muttered, my mouth so close to his.

Beaming, he dropped my leg. "Are you ready to go upstairs?"

"Yes," I said as I stood on my toes to kiss his neck. I glanced at Craig over Owen's shoulder and he nodded. I laced my fingers with Owen's and smiled seductively as I walked backwards toward the stairs. My eyes never left Owen's and I had to put all my trust in Craig, hoping like hell he would get Morgan to notice us. I couldn't take a chance at looking that way or she'd know it was all a ruse.

I shook my hair away from my face as I approached the stairs, giving Morgan a clear, unobstructed view of who I was. I wrapped Owen's arms around my waist and mounted the steps as he kissed my neck. I repressed a shudder and hoped fervently that Morgan was watching.

Once we reached the landing, Owen took charge and steered me into a room. He flipped a switch then adjusted the light to make it dimmer. He shut and locked the door and crossed his arms over his chest as I inspected the room. It was bare except for a bed and a nightstand with a digital clock. The blankets were black and the pillowcases silk. I rolled my eyes.

"Very romantic," I said dryly.

"It serves its purpose," he said as his eyes followed me. "Want me to call down for a bottle of champagne? A dozen roses? Or do you just want to get down to business?"

I plastered a seductive smile on my lips and lowered my lids. I sauntered toward him, watching as his face lit up in anticipation. He reached for me as I drew near and pulled me flush with his body.

"I've been waiting for this since the first time I laid eyes on you."

"Is that so?" I purred as I trailed my hands up his chest and connected them behind his head. "Do you know what I've wanted to do since the first time I met you?"

"What?" he asked in a throaty voice. He smirked knowingly and it only fueled my contempt.

I reared back and spit in his face.

He shoved me away with one hand while his other frantically wiped away my saliva. A low growl erupted from his throat and I took a cautious step back – all the while smiling triumphantly at him.

"You bitch," he said, his eyes narrowed. "You dick teasing bitch."

"Yeah, maybe so, but you need to keep your slimy hands off my friend," I said.

He inched toward me, dangerous glint in his eyes. "So, Bailey couldn't stand that Morgan had someone interested in her, huh?"

I snorted. "You weren't interested in her – you used her to piss us off, didn't you? You flaunted her in front of us knowing we'd be worried after what you did to Tori."

He barked out a mirthless laugh. "Yeah, whatever. Tori was nothing but a clingy, sniveling little girl. She thought from the get go that we'd be together forever."

I lifted a brow. "Isn't that what you told her to get her to sleep with you?"

"I don't need to lie to get women in my bed," he said.

I lifted a shoulder. "Oh, so you just use drugs and alcohol, huh?"

He pushed his sneering face into mine. "Whatever works, sweetheart."

"You disgust me," I said, not backing away. "You're nothing but filth."

"And you're nothing but trash," he said. "Pure trash. I was glad when you and Spencer split. He deserves far better than you."

"You were pretty anxious to get me in your bed," I said.

His eyes scanned my body. "I'm not picky. I don't care how trashy as long as it looks good. Hell, I can throw two condoms on to protect myself."

I ignored his jib – he was lashing out in an effort to save face. I did the best I could not to let his words penetrate.

"Do they make them that small, I wonder?" I said. Immature, but I couldn't resist.

"Want to see?" he asked as he stepped closer.

"Not particularly."

"Let's skip past the childish name calling, shall we, and get to what's really going on here," he said. "You got me up here, now what do you intend to do? Spit in my face again?"

"No," I chortled. "I'll leave you here to your own devices."

I attempted to move past him but he grabbed my arm and hauled me back. "I don't think so. Listen, bitch, you got me up here for a reason, tell me what it was. Unless you do want to go at it? Spencer's a great guy and all but I bet he's not much in the sack."

I smacked him as hard as I could and reveled when his head fell to the side with the blow. He recovered and grasped my shoulders, shoving me roughly into the wall. His face leered in mine and his eyes took on a crazy glint.

"Don't ever touch me again, you bitch," he said, saliva spraying in my face. He yanked me to his chest and slammed me back again. "Do you hear me?"

"Get off me you son of a bitch," I said as I planted my hands on his chest and heaved.

He laughed eerily and caught me way off guard. "I know your little secret, Bailey. Morgan told me."

I froze, my heart stopping in my chest. "What secret?"

"You want Collin now, huh? Already lured him in your bed, didn't you?"

He took advantage of my shock to prowl closer to me. "Get real, sweetheart – he'll sleep with you, sure, and maybe keep you around for awhile, but you're not the sort of girl he takes home to Mama. You don't have enough class. You're the type of girl a guy likes to have on the side – the one you don't take out in public but keep in the bedroom. You're the type that would embarrass a man." He grinned. "You're not the type of girl a man falls in love with – especially good guys like Collin Newton."

"And you're full of shit," I said, my heart ready to explode. I tried to remind myself that they were just words, nothing else. But they were the same words that had run around my head over and over. Maybe I was just kidding myself.

"What a worthless piece of trash you are, Bailey. You can't even finish what you start! You drag me up here and don't even follow through," he taunted. "You are so worthless, you can't even be a lousy whore."

"Go to hell," I said as I shook off his words and lifted my chin.

He grabbed my right arm and squeezed tight enough to draw tears to my eyes. "You put a lot of effort into getting me up here now you're going to follow through."

I narrowed my eyes and made a fist with my left hand. "No way in hell." I swung and connected weakly with his chin.

He laughed in my face and backhanded me, drawing even more tears but riling up my anger. I wrested my arm out of his grip and pushed him away from me.

"Don't ever think of hitting me again," I warned.

Chuckling, he seized me by the shoulders to swing me away from the door. "Why? You going to beat me up?"

"I can take you," I said in a nonchalant tone, although my insides were quivering. This is what Collin and Spencer and the others had tried to warn me about, but I wasn't going to back down. I wasn't going to let him think that just because I was female that he was in control of the situation.

His laughter bounced off the walls. "I should kick your skanky ass now and put you in your place. It would serve you right."

"Bring it, then," I hissed. "Like I said, I can take you."

He lunged forward and grabbed a fistful of hair, yanking down hard. I punched him with as much strength as I could muster with my right hand and was satisfied when warm blood dripped over my knuckles. He let me go immediately.

"Son of a bitch!" he shouted as his hands cupped his nose. "Shit!"

"Get out of my way," I said, my chest heaving. "I'm out of here."

He straightened, one hand still covering his nose, and blocked the doorway. "You're going to pay for that."

"Like hell," I said as I charged him and rammed my knee into his groin. He dropped to his knees and I shoved him aside. I disengaged the lock, gasping for air to chase away the sob climbing my throat, and ripped the door open.

I stepped into the hall and heard my name.

"Bailey!" It was Irelyn. I flew to her and buried my head in the crook of her neck as her comforting arms wrapped around me. "Are you okay? Did he hurt you?"

"Where the hell is he?" Collin asked as he tried to disengage me from Irelyn. She twisted her body away and tightened her hold. I lifted my eyes to Collin's.

"Get that no good filthy tramp out of my club!" Owen ordered as he leaned in the doorway, gripping the frame for support. "All of you get the hell out of here and don't come back. And keep your silly little friend, Morgan away from me too!"

Collin crossed the hall in two huge steps and fisted Owen's shirt. He shoved him into the wall, red hot anger contorting his handsome face. "What did you do to her?"

"I didn't do a damn thing to her," Owen said as he attempted to push Collin away. "Look what the bitch did to me!"

"Dude," Lucas said as he grabbed Collin's arm. "Come on. We got Bailey, let's just go."

Spencer took Collin's other arm and they managed to wrestle him off of Owen. Irelyn wrapped an arm around my shoulder and guided me down the stairs. I searched frantically for Morgan or Craig and didn't see either of them anywhere. I wondered where they'd gone until Irelyn pushed me out the door and toward the parking lot.

"She's supposed to be my friend!" I heard Morgan shout.

"That's why she did this," Tori's low voice answered.

I wiggled out of Irelyn's embrace and trotted toward Morgan. "Morg," I pleaded. "Please, listen."

"No," Morgan said, shaking her head. "I'm through with you. I'm through with all of you!"

"Morgan," Spencer said as he attempted to take her arm. She shook him off and stepped toward Craig and his group.

"If Owen was such a monster, why didn't any of you try to just tell me?" she asked, tears streaking down her cheeks

"We did," I claimed. "Holy hell, Morg, you wouldn't answer any of our calls!"

"Did you sleep with him, too?" Morgan asked, her eyes rimmed in red. "Did you?"

"No, of course not," Irelyn said, a hint of pride in her voice. "She kicked his ass. For you."

"Whatever," Morgan snorted, dropping her eyes to the ground. "I...I just want to go home." She spun on her heel and marched toward a minivan.

"Morg," I called but she just picked up the pace. "Damn."

"I'll make sure she gets home and I'll call you, okay?" Craig said softly. I nodded. "Are you all right?"

"Yeah, just fine," I said, my voice breaking. A stupid tear trickled down my cheek but I wiped it away quickly. Irelyn put her arm around my shoulders again. "Thanks, Craig."

"No problem. I'll see you around."

"Who is that?" Collin asked as he came up beside me.

"My dog park buddy," I said, shivering.

"Oh," he muttered. We watched as the van carrying Morgan pulled out of the parking lot and drove away into the dark. With a sigh, Collin stepped in front of me. His sad eyes searched my face desperately and my stomach clenched. I just knew he was going to carry through with his threat.

He pinched the bridge of his nose. "Spence," he said, helplessly as if in a world of pain. "Spence, man."

Spencer clapped him on the back and gave him a half-hearted grin. "Dude, it's cool, so long as you love her."

Collin gazed at his friend, an echo of a smile flitting across his lips. "I do, man, I swear."

My confused heart didn't know what to think as I watched the two of them. Spencer winked at me and left Collin's side to take Tori by the hand and lead her to his car.

"Take her home with you, Collin," Irelyn said as she kissed my cheek. "We'll go let Otis out tonight then you can go get him in the morning." She kissed Collin's cheek and dragged Lucas after Spencer.

"Bailey," Collin said as he stepped closer. He cupped my chin and wiped the pesky tears from my face. "Come here." He pulled me into an embrace and kissed my hair. "Don't ever do that to me again."

I wrapped my arms around his waist and let the tears flow just so I could get it out of my system – thinking my tear ducts were like a radiator and needed a good flushing once in awhile.

"Come on," I muttered. "Life would be rather boring then, wouldn't it?"

He edged me back to shake his head at me. "I'll take boring." He leaned in and kissed me tenderly. "Let's go back to my place, okay? And get some sleep."

I nodded and he wrapped his arm around my shoulders. I leaned into him. "I need to take my car, though. I'm not leaving it here. Owen will probably either tear it up or have it towed."

"I'll follow you," Collin said as he opened my car door. He lifted my chin and kissed me again. "Drive safe."

My heart teetered as I started my car and hopped on the highway. I rewound back to what Spencer had said before he'd left:

It's cool, so long as you love her.

And didn't Collin say he did? Did he mean me?

I stepped on the accelerator, suddenly anxious to get to Collin's to find out.

Chapter Twenty

Collin took me by the hand as soon as he let us into the house. He towed me directly to the sofa and sat me down.

"I'm going to let the dog out and get us something to drink," he said, his eyes solemn. "Then we'll talk."

I could only nod.

Closing my eyes, I rested my head on the back of the couch. I listened as he coaxed Milo out of his crate and out the back door. I heard him open the refrigerator followed by his soft footsteps returning to the living room. He plopped down beside me and only then did I open my eyes.

"Here," he said as he handed me a soda. He set his on the coffee table. "Talk to me, Bailey. Tell me what happened."

I sipped at my soda, stalling so I could get my thoughts together. I started to slowly describe the entire day, beginning with my idea to involve Craig, and picked up speed as I got to the part about the club. When I told him about the incident in the room upstairs, he cursed and rose quickly from the sofa.

"That's exactly why I didn't want you to go!" he said, spinning away from me. "He could have really hurt you."

"But he didn't," I objected. "And I managed to take perfect care of myself."

"Did you?" he said as he faced me again. He crossed the room and dropped to his knees before me, lifting a finger to gently trace my cheek. "Is that why you have a mark on your face?"

I jerked my head away from him. "That was nothing. I think he came off worse."

"No doubt about that," Collin said as he squeezed my hand. "But it could have turned out really bad."

"But it didn't, Collin," I said as I leapt to my feet, jerking my hand out of his grip. I stalked toward the kitchen but he followed. I scrubbed my hand over my face, wincing slightly as I brushed the tender spot on my cheek. "It didn't, okay? Now it's over with – can we please move past it?"

"Not yet," he said sternly, his voice directly behind me. "Not until you realize just how lucky you are and not until you realize how serious the situation could have been."

"Everything turned out fine, okay?" I said, frustrated. I turned to face him, angry that he wouldn't just drop it. "Why are you dwelling on what *could* have happened?"

"Because I was scared, Bailey," he said, glaring at me. "I was afraid that he was going to do something terrible to you. I didn't want to see you in worse shape than Tori."

"And I didn't want to see Morgan that way, either," I defended.

"Why do you care so much, huh?" he asked in disbelief, lifting his hands in the air and letting them fall helplessly to his sides. "After the way she's treated you and Irelyn? Why are you still so desperate to save her? You did nothing wrong to her. And so what if she's upset that we slept together – that's something she needs to get over on her own."

"I don't know," I sighed. "I wish I didn't care. She sort of reminds me of how I used to be a long time ago – only, maybe a little more naïve. I guess I didn't want to see her turn out to be like how I am now."

"Geez," he groaned. "Bailey, you're not bad. You're the one who likes to let people think that but I know better. I know what you're really like and so do those that are closest to you. Morgan knows what you're like deep down, too."

"Don't psychoanalyze me, Collin," I warned as I poked a finger in his chest. "I don't want it and I don't need it."

"I'm not," he said as he leaned on the doorframe. "Honest. I'm just trying to understand why you'd take such a chance." He blew a puff of air at his bangs. "Guess I sort of knew all along."

His last comment took me by surprise and I raised a curious brow. "What did you know?"

A tiny smile appeared in the corners of his mouth. "That super-overprotective Bailey would swoop down and rescue her friend, no matter the danger to herself."

"I didn't need to be rescued," I said, straightening my spine. "I told you I could handle him."

He reached out to chuck me under the chin, his smile proud. "I know. But I was still worried."

I lifted a shoulder and shuffled my feet, studying the remarkably clean floor. When did the man find time to clean? And why was his house always cleaner than mine? I sighed, dispelling the housekeeping thoughts from my head.

"He's all talk anyway."

I remembered his ugly words that had settled in the bottom of my heart. They would rot there awhile and prod me from time to time – just to remind me that they were there, but eventually I would forget about them. I'd get over it.

"What did he say to you that made you so upset?" Collin asked.

"Nothing," I said defensively, gritting my teeth. "Nothing at all. He's just full of crap."

"Did he say something about us?" Collin asked softly. "Tell me, Bailey."

I shook my head and expelled a long breath. I folded my arms over my chest and avoided his eyes. He was stirring up the tears again and I'd cried enough lately to bathe in them – I would shed no more.

"It doesn't matter what he said. He was only trying to make himself look good."

"Tell me what he said," Collin ordered, his voice still soft but firm. "Please."

I shrugged and let my hands fall to my sides. I bit my lip and repeated what I could remember. "He mostly called me a whore. He said I was trashy and it was a good thing Spencer and I split up because he deserved better."

I chanced a quick glance at Collin but his face was passive. I continued. "He said that he knew you and I had slept together – Morgan told him – and that…" I had to swallow to loosen the huge lump in my throat. "He said that I'd only embarrass you and that I wasn't the type of girl that you would date. He said you'd sleep with me but that was all." I raised a brow and faced him fully. "He said you could never love someone like me."

His eyes narrowed as his head bobbed up and down slowly. A faraway look drifted across his face and I wondered if he'd heard a word I'd said. He snapped back to reality and touched my arm. "Do you believe that?"

"I don't know," I said in a shrill voice. "I don't know what to believe."

"Damn it, Bailey!" he cursed, startling me. "What the hell? I've gone out of my way to show you. I've called you, come over, hung out with you. I pretended to be your boyfriend in front of that spiteful little bitch, and defended your honor. Last weekend, when you stayed with me, I did everything I could to show you how much I love you."

He clenched his jaw and a flicker of pain passed over his face. "Hell, I even gave you a puppy!" He raked his fingers through his hair. "I mean, damn, what more do I have to do to prove to you that I love you?"

"What?" I said, doing a double take. "Huh?"

"What else do I have to do?" he asked.

I cleared the fog out of my brain as my mind focused on what he'd just asked. "How about just telling me!"

"You never would have believed me," he said as he stepped closer, clutched my shoulders, and kissed me. "After that first night, I couldn't get you out of my head. I'd always been attracted to you but after that night, all I wanted was to be with you again – and not just in bed." He released my shoulders and paced. "At first I thought I was just feeling guilty, but the more time I spent with you, the more I realized that that wasn't it."

"So, you do love me?" I asked, still grappling with his words. "You love me?"

"Yes," he grinned as he stopped in front of me. He pecked my lips. "I told Spencer I did and I told him I didn't know if you felt the same but I thought you might." He smiled feebly. "I spilled the entire truth to him last night. He hung out over here after everyone else had left and we talked. I told him everything. I didn't want him hearing about any of it from someone else. I was worried he'd be pissed but he took it all calmly. He was a little put out by it but he told me he'd get over it."

I snaked my arms around his neck. "I love you, too, you know," I said quickly. "I realized it one day at the pool."

He furrowed his brow. "At the pool?"

"Don't ask," I said. "I, um, realized this before our first night. That's why I broke up with Spencer."

His eyes darted all over my face before he leaned in and captured my lips with his. I fell into him and he tightened his hold. My heartbeat tripled.

"Bailey," he said as he edged back. "I want to explain about Tori."

"What about her?" I asked, my heart back on the defensive.

"Well, you said something last night that got me thinking," he said as he slipped his arms off my waist and took my hand. He led me back to the sofa and we sat together. "I never had anything going on with her – I hope you know that. When I left with her that week, I took her to see her parents." He dropped his gaze to our entwined hands. "She drank a little too much one night and became depressed. She contemplated...taking her life but she called me instead."

I couldn't believe it. What was going through her mind? Owen wasn't worth all that. "Why?"

"She's embarrassed, Bailey. She's embarrassed about her entire relationship with Owen. She messed around with drugs and he convinced her to...this has to stay between us, okay?" I nodded emphatically. "He convinced her to do some...things she normally wouldn't. She didn't prostitute herself or anything but he got her to do some things that she's embarrassed about. She told me about it that night. Actually, she cried a torrent of tears and totally fell apart and sort of blabbed it all. So, I drove her to her parents' house out in the country the next morning and she begged me to stay. She wanted moral support. I couldn't just leave her."

"I understand," I whispered, sympathy flooding me. I was more convinced than ever that I'd done the right thing.

"I'm sorry if you thought it was something else," he said as he caught my eyes and smiled.

My heart flipped. "Don't apologize. I should apologize. I thought you were in love with her."

He chuckled. "No, not at all. Oh, I do care about her, but she's just a friend."

"I feel pretty stupid," I muttered and he dragged me into his lap, winding his arms around my middle.

"You feel pretty good to me," he said, trying to lighten the mood.

I managed a smile. "That was really cheesy."

"Yeah, I know," he shrugged as color flooded his cheeks.

I kissed him, putting all the love I could into it. My heart throbbed as he held me closer and deepened the kiss. His hands traveled up my sides and tangled in my hair. I shifted so that I was facing him and my legs were straddling his lap.

"Hang on, Bailey," he mumbled in my mouth.

"What's the matter?" I asked as I eased my face back to look at him.

He held my head in his hands as he caught his breath. "I don't want to get carried away until we talk a few things out."

"What's left to say?" I asked as I pressed my breasts into his chest. I knew his weakness.

He glanced down but reluctantly dragged his eyes back up and focused on my face with a tiny smirk flittering on his lips. "Nice try."

"Hey, a girl's gotta do what a girl's gotta do," I said.

He drew my face closer and kissed me again, softly. "I want to make sure everything is sorted, that's all."

"I love you, you love me – it's sorted." I faked a yawn and an exaggerated stretch. "Now I'm tired. Let's go to bed."

He chuckled but showed no signs of moving. "We will but first I want to know something."

"What?" I asked.

"What are we now?"

My heart stopped and I stared at him slack-jawed. "That's what you're worried about?"

"Well, I'm not worried," he said bashfully as he dropped his eyes. "Just curious."

I really loved him even more. I slid off his lap and snatched his hand. I urged him to his feet and led him toward the bedroom. He made me wait as he let in the dog and put him in his crate. He rejoined me with a smile and followed me into the bedroom. I pinned him against the door and stood on my toes to kiss him.

"I'm your girlfriend, Collin," I declared. "Your real one – not fake. I'm a little more serious about you than I ever was about Spencer." I grinned at him and he relaxed. "Okay, maybe a lot more serious but he doesn't need to know that yet."

"I do love you, Bailey," he said as he backed me up to the bed. He lifted my shirt over my head and even though I was pretty tired, I perked up immediately. I helped him out of his clothes and crawled on the bed. I fumbled for his hand and tugged him on top of me. His eager lips found mine as my hands thoroughly explored the complicated muscles in his back.

His kisses burned a trail down my chin and throat, working their way to my breasts. I grinned when a satisfied moan escaped his mouth.

"I'm a lucky man," he whispered. I didn't argue – just let him continue his ministrations. It didn't take him long to return to my lips, his need pressing firmly against my leg. He whispered sweet words in my ear but I barely heard them. I was on fire and I wanted him terribly.

"Collin," I groaned as I sank my nails into his shoulders. I arched into him, his body like a magnet for mine. I tasted the salty skin of his neck as I kissed and nipped out my frustrations. Finally, he put me out of my misery and slipped inside me, causing me to clamp down on his neck.

"Ow," he chuckled as he kissed me. "That's going to leave a mark."

"Sorry," I said, not the least bit perturbed. I was too busy matching his easy rhythm as I clung to his neck.

"No you're not," he laughed as he unlatched my hands and carefully pushed me flat on the mattress. He still moved slowly, bringing me pleasure like I'd never known, but he watched my face carefully; brushing the hair out of eyes or kissing the corner of my mouth. My heart pounded wildly and it was so liberating to finally be able to express verbally how I felt.

"I love you," I whispered as his pace picked up speed. He kissed me again, unable to talk, as passion overtook us both. Shortly after, he collapsed beside me in a gasping heap.

I waited for his breathing to even, as well as my own, before I cuddled up next to him. As I snuggled into him, I felt his chest vibrate with suppressed chuckles.

"What?" I asked.

He kissed the top of my head. "I can't believe you thought I was in love with Tori."

I yawned, for real, and nestled my head under his chin. "Yeah, well, what can I say? You're a hottie with a smoking body and I thought every woman wanted you."

He snorted. "Whatever." He chuckled again. "Honestly, you don't understand how ironic that is."

"Okay, I'll bite," I said sleepily.

"I was actually trying to get Tori and Spencer together," he said.

I lifted my head to try to locate his face in the nearly nonexistent light. "What?"

"They used to sort of have a thing for each other before we even met you and Irelyn and Morgan," he explained. "They never got together because they were both too shy to say anything. I don't know that they ever would have, actually. But Owen stepped in and Tori fell for him. Spencer didn't really care because some chick he met at a party started calling him and he took her out a few times. Then a couple weeks later, we met you guys."

"Seriously?" I asked. He nodded. "Hm."

"Yeah," he said.

"So, why were you trying to get them together?" I asked as I settled on his chest. I closed my eyes, lulled by the beat of his heart.

"I thought maybe if Spencer and Tori hooked up, then he wouldn't mind so much if you and I did," he said. I was willing to bet that his cheeks were blazing red.

I wanted to look at him – to gape actually – but I was sort of frozen. I couldn't believe he'd actually gone to that extreme. How blind I'd been. When I looked back now and honestly thought about it, the signs were there. He'd been so sweet and attentive and I'd taken it as either acting out of guilt or friendship.

"I think I've been a little blind, huh? Or stupid," I mumbled.

"Nah," he said as he squeezed me. "Bailey, all this is new to you. Hell, it's new to me, too." He pressed his lips to my hair. "I didn't know how you felt. I didn't know if you just wanted a casual relationship or if you wanted something more. It drove me crazy."

I snorted in his chest. How could he be so unsure of himself? He didn't have the reputation I had. The one I would now fight to get over. I didn't want it any longer. Oh, I wouldn't roll over and become some sunshiny sap – hell no. But I wouldn't be afraid to let him know how I felt.

I kissed him firmly. "You drive me crazy," I whispered and kissed him again. I rested my chin on his chest and watched a smile cross his lips.

"Not as crazy as you drive me," he said. "Now sleep. Tomorrow we start all over. And it will be better than before."

I laughed and nestled my head under his chin. "Collin, that was more cheese than I care to ever hear again."

"Not on your life," he chuckled. "It's only going to get worse."

I smiled in the dark and closed my eyes. I could take it.

Epilogue

Hoisting my bag further over my shoulder, I hurried across the campus, eager to get to my car. The October wind was merciless as it whipped my hair, causing it to pummel my face.

Just as the parking lot came into view, I heard someone shout my name. Uttering a groan, I stopped, pushing my hair behind me ears, and turned.

It was Morgan.

I waited for her to catch up to me and practiced what I'd say. I'd spotted her several times on campus, though we didn't have any classes together, but she'd never so much as indicated that she'd seen me. This was definitely a surprise.

"Hi," she said shyly.

"Hey," I said as I tugged my coat closed to fight the wind. "What's up?"

"Um, are the guys playing at Rusty's tomorrow night?" she asked, still too afraid to meet my eyes.

"Yeah, they are," I said, slightly amused. "You coming down?"

She looked at me, startled, her mouth partly open. "I'm not sure."

I lifted a nonchalant shoulder. "Suit yourself, but I think you'd enjoy it. They've been working on new music and changed up their set lists."

She nodded, her lips in a straight line. "Listen, Bailey, I, um, I guess I sort of over reacted. I know I tend to do that."

"Don't worry about it," I said, waving away her words before she could hit her stride. I didn't really care for the drawn-out, sappy, teary-eyed apology scenes. Say what you want and shut the hell up.

A ghost of a smile flitted across her lips. "I am worried about it," she said. "I know I was wrong but sometimes I don't think you and Irelyn understand what it's like being on the outside looking in."

I could only gape at her, momentarily stunned. "Morgan, when did we ever treat you that way?"

She bowed her head and readjusted the strap on her bag. "It wasn't really you two – it was me. You know what I'm like. I just get a little jealous and wish I could be more like you guys."

"You dumb ass," I said. Her head shot up. "We like you for who you are. Hell, we don't need another me or Irelyn in this little group. We need you to keep us moral. We go to hell without you."

A real smile appeared, along with a couple of tears, and I had an irresistible urge to hug her. I refrained, though, because all was not fine and dandy just yet. She had acted like a huge crybaby – among other things.

"Um, I guess I just wanted to say I'm sorry," she mumbled as she ran a finger under each eye to banish her tears. "I really am."

"I know," I said as I bobbed my head in agreement. "I am, too. I probably could have handled the whole situation better – especially the Owen thing…"

"No, thank you for that," she said firmly. She bit her lip. "Your friend Craig told me all about what Owen did to Tori. I didn't want to hear it at first but he was persistent."

"Are you dating Craig?" I asked, brow lifted. I'd only talked to Craig a few times after the whole Owen thing blew over and he hadn't mentioned Morgan.

"No," she smiled. "He's nice and all but we just talk from time to time."

"Oh," I said, wondering if she still wanted Spencer. Collin's attempts to pair him off with Tori never really worked -she was now dating a nice guy she'd met at the church she'd started attending. And Spencer fell head over heels for Jessica, a girl who worked with Irelyn at the diner. They were sort of cute, in a disgustingly obvious way.

"I might stop down at the bar tomorrow night," Morgan said. She stared uneasily at the leaves blowing across the sidewalk. "I don't know how well I'll be received."

"Morgan," I said gently. "Everyone misses you."

She frowned and nodded. "I have to get to work. Maybe I'll see you tomorrow."

"Okay," I said as I watched her rush off toward her car, shoulders hunched. I doubted seriously if she would show up at Rusty's but at least she was making an attempt. Irelyn would be thrilled.

When I got home, I entered the house and gratefully dropped my book bag on the floor. I was immediately assaulted by two overgrown pups jumping on my legs, eager for attention.

"Go away you mongrels," I said as I knelt to scratch each one behind the ears. "Go now."

I gave them each one more affectionate pat then stood and crept to the kitchen. I grinned as I spotted my prey standing with his back to me, hovering over a large sack of food on the table.

"I know you're behind me," he said. "Don't think you're being sneaky."

"Whatever," I said as I wrapped my arms around his waist. "You could pretend once in awhile."

He turned in my arms and kissed me, making my heart pound in my chest. "How was class?"

"Boring," I said as I ran my hands under his shirt. "But afterwards was sort of interesting."

Collin lifted a brow as he leaned in to kiss me again. "Interesting how?"

I relayed the entire Morgan scene to him as leaned against the table in total awe. He rested his hands on my hips and pulled me between his legs so he could wind his arms around me. "Do you think she'll be there tomorrow night?"

"I have no clue," I said. "I'm leaning towards the negative."

"Me, too," he agreed. He kissed me quickly. "I brought Mexican home – let's eat. The guys will be here soon to practice."

He described his day to me while we ate and I marveled, like I did every evening, how domestic I'd become. If I didn't watch out, I'd turn into Irelyn.

Collin had solved my roommate dilemma when he'd suggested I just give up the condo and move in with him. I was all for it, of course, because we always ended up together every night – either at his place or mine.

Daddy hadn't been entirely happy about the arrangements but he hadn't stopped my allowance. Instead, he decided that I should earn it. I had no qualms about it, really, since the pool closed for the winter and I'd lost my job. It hadn't been much to speak of but it was something to do while all my friends worked.

But what Daddy had in mind was a little more complicated than sitting in the sun and making sure teenagers didn't drown. He had set me up with an elaborate computer system and emailed me sales reports and other documents frequently. As I was trying to earn a Business degree, he decided a little hands-on experience couldn't hurt. Plus, he really wanted me to join him once I graduated.

Collin had cleared out Lucas's old room and set me up with an impressive office. Even Daddy had marveled over it when he and Steffi had come to visit. Now, I ended up working on reports a few nights a week while juggling coursework and my still developing relationship.

I glanced at Collin and my heart turned somersaults like it did every time I looked at him. It amazed me how much I loved him and how much he loved me. I remembered a time when I'd thought that I'd never feel this way yet here I was doubting I could ever live without him. Funny how things change.

After we ate and cleaned up the dishes, he trapped me against the counter, shoving my hair aside so he could kiss my neck. "We have about a half hour until everyone gets here."

I snorted. "What do you think we can actually do in thirty minutes?"

"Want me to draw you a picture?" he asked, his breath hot on my skin. I craned my neck to allow him better access. "How about a quickie?"

Laughing, I hopped up on the counter. I tugged him between my knees and wrapped my legs around his waist. "A quickie is never enough for me, Collin," I said as I kissed him. "You'll have to wait until later." He captured my lips again. "Besides, you know…"

"Oh, geez," Spencer groaned as he breezed into the kitchen, Jessica in tow. "Is that all you guys do?"

Collin's cheeks reddened as he edged back. He lifted me off the counter then took my hand. "We're like rabbits, man."

"Too much info, bro," Spencer grinned, shooting me a wink. "So, guess who called me today?"

I snorted a laugh - it looked as though Morgan was making the rounds. "Um, Morgan?"

Spencer's brow dipped as he frowned. "How'd you know?"

"She talked to me earlier after classes. So, what did she have to say?" I asked.

"Just that she was sorry," he said. "She asked how everyone was doing and stuff like that. She asked me about you and Collin and how I was handling it."

I snorted again and squeezed Collin's hand. "And? How are you handling it?"

"Bailey, Bailey, Bailey," he said as he disengaged himself from Jessica and wrapped an arm around my shoulders. "Some days are better than others." He wiped a fake tear from his eye. "But I get by."

I shoved him away in laughter. "What a loser."

"Bailey, are you in here?" Irelyn called from the front door. I rolled my eyes.

"No," I shouted.

She rushed into the room, her eyes bright. "Morgan called me."

"Join the club," I said.

Her face fell slightly. "She called you, too?"

I quickly explained my conversation near the parking lot. Irelyn nodded as she bit her lip. "Yeah, she pretty much said the same to me. So, do you think she'll be at Rusty's tomorrow night?"

"I doubt it," I said. "But it's a start."

Collin kissed my cheek and gave my hip a squeeze. "Where's Luke? Outside?" Irelyn nodded. "Great. Come on, Spence, let's get to work."

***

Later that night, after everyone left, Collin and I snuggled in bed together. He kissed the top of my head before he reached over me and set his alarm clock.

"You really don't think Morgan will be at Rusty's tomorrow?" he asked.

"Probably not."

"Well, she's called everyone – maybe she thinks she's made amends."

"I don't know," I said as I nestled my head under his chin. "I guess we'll just wait and see."

He tightened his arms around me as I closed my eyes. Maybe Morgan would surprise us and show up - but things wouldn't be like they were before – not right away and perhaps not ever. But I couldn't help but to hope they were on their way. I did miss Morgan – especially since the pieces of my life were finally falling into place. I liked the job my father had given me; my friendships with Irelyn, Lucas and Spencer were stronger than ever; and my love for Collin was deep. If Morgan would only come back to us, it would make things that much better.

I squeezed my eyes tighter, a little angry at how sentimental I was becoming. Being in love was turning me into a softie. I sighed and lifted my head to look at Collin's dozing face in the pale light. I smiled and kissed his cheek.

As I placed my head on his chest I banished my thoughts. Who really cared if I was going soft – Collin was well worth it. And I'd finally broken that vicious circle.

Coming Soon from JL Paul:
On the Outside Looking In

Other titles by JL Paul:
All the Wrong Reasons
Out at Home
Finding Home
Shift
Rough Waters
Playing the Game
Cardiac Arrest

Made in the USA
Columbia, SC
02 June 2019